Leo Loves Aries

**Cheeky, cheerful Leo has met the perfect Aries match . . .
for his sister.**

When his sister challenges Theo Wallace to find her a date for a
spring wedding, Theo realizes that all his "friends" were in fact his
ex-girlfriend's friends.

Not willing to admit his pathetic social state, he decides not only to
find his sister the perfect date, but to find himself the perfect friend.

Theo's ex economics tutor and newest roommate Mr. Jamie Cooper
seems to be a possible and convenient match. Real convenient. Like
written in the stars, convenient.

All he has to do is make sure this Jamie is good enough. Could really
be The One for her, and the friend for him.

Watch out, Leo, the stars have a surprise in store...

LEO LOVES ARIES

Signs of Love #1

ANYTA SUNDAY

First published in 2016 by Anyta Sunday,
Contact at Bürogemeinschaft ATP24, Am Treptower Park 24, 12435 Berlin,
Germany

An Anyta Sunday publication
http://www.anytasunday.com

Second edition

Copyright 2023 Anyta Sunday

ISBN 978-3-947909-60-5

Cover Design: Natasha Snow
Leo and Aries Art Design: Maria Gandolfo (Renflowergrapx)

Content Editor: Teresa Crawford
Line Editor: HJS Editing
Proof Editor: Wolfgang Eulenberg

For my very special Leo.
I love you.

"Stop trying to clean up the past, Theo. Focus on sweeping a path for the future."

Leone to Theo at New Year's Eve.

Chapter One

Theo Wallace stood in front of the mailbox, pinching a gold-edged card, his throat constricting with a rush of betrayal. Rain drummed over the card, making the ink of Samantha's name weep.

A year ago last January, he and Sam were making snow angels right here in front of his two-story Victorian rental. His sister Leone and her boyfriend Derek had joined them. They had laughed so hard he'd felt it in his gut for the rest of the day.

Out of nowhere, Sam slammed him with the truth. She would prefer to spend her life with someone else. Someone easier to live with. *Derek.*

Theo swallowed and closed his eyes on the memory, focusing on the rain slithering down the gaps of his jacket hood rather than the emptiness he felt. A right sad sack he was. Fuck.

He moved to the trashcan at the curb, lifted the freezing, wet lid, and then slammed it down again.

The card still lay clutched in his hand.

He couldn't bring himself to toss that damn embossed card away. Because...because... it was addressed to him *and* Leone.

Yeah. That was it.

He rolled his shoulders and tucked the card with the other two minor annoyances that had arrived with the mail. He splashed up the white stone path to the front door and let himself in.

"Leone?" he called over earsplitting indie electropop.

He toed off his shoes and slid them into the shoe rack, making sure to tuck the laces away. "You're gonna want to hear this." He hung his wet jacket.

"I'm in the living room."

Theo rounded into the main room of their house. The previous tenants had knocked down a few walls, making a great room and open plan kitchen.

He found his sister in a pair of yoga pants and tank top, using one of the heavy wooden pillars that studded the space to stretch out her calves. She picked up her phone from the base of the pillar and spoke. The music pumping from the sound system faded.

Cola-brown hair swung with her ponytail as she turned in his direction and sniffed. "You smell like rain, bro."

"I'm drenched. You didn't hear it pounding out there?"

"Thought it got a bit darker," she said. "But I wasn't sure."

Dragging her hand over their navy-blue couch, she moved toward the kitchen.

It didn't look like she had to count every step. Didn't look like she had difficulty pulling a black mug from the white cabinets and filling it with water.

Didn't look like she was legally blind.

Water guzzled, Leone plunked herself onto the armchair. "What am I gonna want to hear?"

Theo pulled out the mail from under his arm and set it on the coffee table. He flung himself onto the couch, tipped his head against the arm, and pinched his nose. "It came."

"It came?" Confusion edged Leone's voice, and then she breathed in sharply. "It came." Taut silence followed, then, "When is it?"

"It's the square card on the end closest to you. I was tempted to throw it out."

But he obviously had masochist tendencies, because some part of him wanted to suffer its contents.

Leone asked, "Are you doing the honors? Or do you want me to stick it under my magnifier?"

Theo rolled onto his side and plucked the offending card from the table.

Scrawled in large, now bleeding cursive at the top of a soft gold-and-cream card were the stomach-clenching words:

SAVE THE DATE.
SAMANTHA ROYCE & DEREK JOHNSON.

"Middle of May." His voice cracked and his throat felt like he had swallowed fire.

Leone made a choking sound. Her light-green eyes filmed over with tears.

Theo tossed the card onto the coffee table and slid onto the armchair next to her. Her head cradled against his shoulder as he stroked a stray lock behind her ear. "Fuck 'em, right?"

"Not anymore," she said.

Theo let out a raw laugh. "I guess you're right."

Derek had been Leone's boyfriend for three years and Samantha —Sam, Sammy—had been Theo's girlfriend for two.

A week after the snow angels, they'd discovered the two had fallen out of love with them and in love with each other.

He thought he'd gotten over the pain.

Seeing them together last Halloween, a twinkly rock bedazzling her ring finger, was hard enough.

Now this invitation…

His stomach knotted.

"I wish I could hate them," Leone said.

"Me too."

But Theo couldn't. Sammy and Derek hadn't snuck around or cheated on them. Bit by bit over all the weeknights, weekends, and holidays Theo and Leone had them over, they'd become close. While Theo had focused on other things—programming, marathon training, rewriting papers—and Leone on her thesis proposal, Sam and Derek had fallen in love.

They'd both cried when they confessed they had feelings for each other.

Over and over they apologized.

Leone had been sitting on the armchair and Theo had been stretched out on the couch flipping yoghurt raisins into his mouth like he didn't care. But he did.

He hadn't touched a yoghurt-covered raisin since.

Nor had he found another girlfriend.

Flings, yes—he liked sex—but there had been no one he trusted enough to call his girlfriend. No one he thought would care for his flaws.

His sister hadn't re-entered the dating pool, either.

"What do you say about ordering in tonight?" Theo suggested. "We could get that sun-died tomato and chicken calzone you like, crank up some sappy music, and bitch until morning?"

Leone chuckled. "Sun-*dried*, Theo."

He knew that. Had known since the tender age of *last fucking year.* He'd bought a jar and laughed at the misspelled label.

"Whatever." He kissed her forehead, climbed back onto the couch, and picked up the envelope from their mom. "The sun dried all those tomatoes dead. Sun-died made a lot of fucking sense."

Leone snickered. "Are you reading the rest of the mail?"

"Yep. Kick back and get ready to scoff. Mom sent us our yearly horoscope." Horoscope, singular, because he and Leone were twins.

Theo unfolded the page their mom had torn from her favorite astrology magazine and read it aloud. "It's a new year, Leo. Resolve to make big changes in your life and use your pride and stubbornness to see them through."

Theo knew horoscopes were made-up crap meant to make you feel like life had a bigger purpose. Nevertheless, his neck prickled.

Easy to see how the horoscope might apply to him. Him and Leone both.

He cleared his throat and continued reading. "A new person will enter your life early in the year; look past any moments of frustration they might bring and laugh, Leo—this could be the start of a thriving friendship."

"A roommate, perhaps?" Leone said, tucking a leg under her. "Our first interview is Monday morning before classes, by the way."

"Before classes? I'm a hot mess in the mornings."

"Ain't that true," Leone said. "Stop giving me that face."

"How do you know what face I'm giving you?"

"I wasn't blind the first fifteen years. I *know* you." She grinned and waved a hand. "Go on, go on."

"If you feel overwhelmed during the early spring, take a deep breath and let someone close to you be the rock you lean on. Friendships may evolve in later spring, and you may receive news that will shock you—but fret not, this could be the news you need to hear! The heart and the head may not be in sync the first half of this year, Leo, and there's potential to overlook the obvious. Listen hard to your inner voice and if confused, talk it through with a loved one. Fear not rejection and heartbreak, Leo. Hold your head up high, be your glowing, fiery self, and the right people will gravitate to you; maybe even a soul mate among them."

At Leone's request, he reread the last paragraph.

She hummed thoughtfully, then leaned forward to the coffee table and felt for the save-the date card.

Theo frowned as his sister carefully made her way to the fridge and stuck the card to it. "What are you doing?"

"I think, this time, our horoscope might be right."

A hollow laugh. "There was no warning for how screwed up our love lives turned out last year. Don't get your hopes up." *Tsk.* "Soul mate!"

"That's not the part I care about." She rolled her shoulders and lifted her chin. "We need to fear not rejection and heartbreak. We need to move on."

The edge of the horoscope crinkled in Theo's grip. "Go to their wedding? Dance and laugh and not care that they left us?"

"That's right," Leone said. "We'll take our own dates. It'll be great."

Theo looked from the save-the-date card to the bottle of Zinfandel on top of the fridge. "I need a drink."

"LET'S MOVE PAST THIS," THEO SAID.

At the bottom of the Zinfandel bottle—and after two calzones and five mopey love songs— Theo fished for his phone to change the music.

Leone laughed. "Let's."

But when he skipped the slow song, Leone used her phone to turn the music off. "Let's move past *them*."

"Isn't that what we are doing?" he said.

"No, but we will. We are going to find each other dates for the wedding."

"Why don't we find our own dates?"

Leone chuckled darkly. "Because we suck. Otherwise we wouldn't be here, brother and sister, drowning our sorrows on a Friday night."

She had a point.

Theo grabbed his laptop and logged onto Facebook.

Leone hiccupped, legs hanging over one arm of her armchair, shoulders resting on the other. "Who do you know that might be a match for me?"

Theo had hundreds of "friends," people he'd met once or twice in passing. He made friends easily. Keeping them seemed to be the hard part.

He scrolled through the list of guys he knew-knew and winced when the total number came to three. Alex, Ben, and Kyle.

That was sobering.

"So? Anyone?"

Theo bit his lip. "I'm still looking."

He went back to Ben's wall and stared at the photos of the two couples. All smiles and flushed cheeks, Ben and Kyle flanked Sammy and Derek in front of snow-capped trees. The post revealed that they had gone for a weekend trip to Lake Erie.

Theo eyed the empty wine bottle on the coffee table, then remembered the freezer in the kitchen might hold some vodka.

"What do you want in a guy anyway?" Theo asked.

Ben's pictures drew him back.

To think, just a year ago, Theo would have been the one in this photo gazing at Sam.

"Honesty? Understanding," Leone said. "I want someone who

doesn't make me *feel* blind. I want fun and I want to be swept off my feet."

The worst thing about breaking up was realizing his friends were in fact her friends.

"Strength, too," Leone continued. "Physical and mental."

Theo hummed his nod. "Strength, honesty, understanding. Got it."

He and Ben used to shoot the shit all the time. Hang out at bars. Take turns kicking ass at gaming.

"Also compassion. And blind loyalty." Leone laughed. "See what I did there?"

"You word-playing mastermind, you."

She felt for a cushion and whipped it in his direction. Theo batted it away.

"There are too many guys here to choose from," he lied. "I'll need time to narrow it down."

"We have until May."

He hopped to Alex's profile, the guy in his marketing course who Theo was doing web work for. The first picture to pop out at him was taken five minutes ago. Alex was dancing at a club with his girlfriend.

So. Yeah.

No match there, either.

The thought of telling Leone he had no matches made heat claw up his neck.

Things in the friends department fucking sucked but that was going to change. Not because his horoscope said it would, but because he was going to make it change.

Finding Leone the perfect date just turned personal.

"Where did all the snakes go? They swiped my peanut butter."

Theo sleep talking on the couch.

Chapter Two

Theo lounged at the back of his applied economics tutorial with an inner shake of his head.

This tutor was nothing like last semester's.

This tutor rambled through concepts in monotone, mumbling about seasonal business cycles and glaring when any one of the twenty students in the room dared to ask for clarification.

Theo scribbled notes, barely refraining from hitting his head against the pockmarked desk.

Usually, he might have interrupted the teacher and told him to slow it down a notch. But the day—hell, the whole week—had driven him to the point of submission.

And maybe he'd woken up too early only to be disappointed with their fifth roommate interview of the week. None of the candidates fit, and none of them were *friend* material. Three were ex-frat guys, and not the responsible kind. One was involved in a religious cult that heavily involved the use of a kitchen and incense. Leone had told the guy how many steps it was to the curbside and would he mind double-checking?

This morning, the girl who'd shown up had been pleasant. Her soft brown locks, wide eyes, and dimpled chin made her look sweet, funny, and fuckable—and maybe that was a point against her. He didn't want to simply fuck someone, and he wasn't sure getting involved with a roommate was a clever idea.

His head throbbed.

Adding this convoluted tutorial—in the only subject of his dual degree Theo never earned an A—made him want to curl up and laugh hysterically.

"What might the implications be?" their tutor asked.

The implications of taking this tutorial course would be a B- and major headache at best.

Someone in the room drawled out an answer, leading the tutor to nod stiffly and ask, "And what might be done about it?"

Theo leaned back in his chair and hooked his hands behind his head, grinning wryly.

What might be done?

He might visit the economics department and schedule different tutoring sessions into his schedule. Hopefully run by his last semester's tutor.

Here I come, Mr. Jamie Cooper.

A CUTE GIRL WITH LONG LASHES AND A QUIRKY GRIN STOOD AT THE staff coffee machine. "Jamie's in a meeting with his master's advisor."

Stirring sugar into her coffee, she showed him to the staff contact board. Theo dug around for a pen from his satchel and jotted down Jamie's email address.

"Or, you know," she said, cheeks flushing. "If you give me your number I can tell you when he's available?"

With her golden wavy bangs and flushed freckled cheeks, she was pretty. Theo considered flashing her a grin, grazing her elbow while asking to hand over her phone, and winking as he walked backward to the elevators.

She was pretty all right.

But she looked too much like Sam.

He couldn't show up to the wedding with Sam's doppelganger. They'd think he wasn't over her.

Theo gently turned Ms. Pretty down and left. Leone sure had her work cut out for her.

When he arrived home that evening, he endured another mediocre interview, then left Leone to host this month's book club and stowed himself in his room.

Like all the furniture in the house, his room was arranged in stark contrast to make it easier for Leone to navigate. His walls were white, his desk and bookshelf stained black, his chest of drawers and double bed a dark wood on light floorboards.

Even in the privacy of his room, he carefully and habitually arranged his belongings. Textbooks on the third shelf, stationery to the left of the desk, dirty clothes in a bursting hamper in the corner of the room.

He wasn't a naturally tidy person, so every day he fought the urge to toss his clothes on the floor and leave his bed a rumpled mess.

He wanted his sister to feel welcome.

Theo grabbed his laptop, plopped on the bed, and leaned against the headboard. The dark crimson linens were soft and snuggly, but judging by the splotch of dried ketchup he spotted, they were ready for a wash.

Theo opened his laptop and began drafting an email to Jamie, his former tutor.

Introducing himself was harder than he thought.

He could have said he was the guy in Jamie's tutorials who had made Jamie's jaw twitch in frustration. But that wouldn't help much.

He could have said he was the guy who put his feet on the table and took in the discussions with his eyes closed. But again, that didn't make a strong case for swapping to Mr. Jamie Cooper's tutorials.

Theo flashed back to a moment last semester when Jamie had, without stopping his animated discussion of tax revenue and deadweight loss, calmly walked up to him, gripped his feet and plonked them off the table. The guy had looked right at him when he did it, lifting one eyebrow, daring Theo to piss him off again.

Theo had waited all of five minutes before propping his feet up again.

The firm look Jamie leveled him with made Theo grin. He'd kept his feet propped up the rest of the session. But the next time he came into the class, Jamie had shoved the tables to the sides of the room, and the dozen students sat on chairs in a semi-circle around him.

Staring at the blank *Compose New Message* box, Theo smirked. Mr. Jamie Cooper sure liked things to go his way.

He started typing, avoiding any introduction that might remind Jamie of who he was. His name would show up, but Jamie had never addressed his students by name anyway.

To: Jamie Cooper

From: Theo Wallace

Subject: Keen to Earn A's

I completed your microeconomics tutorial class last semester. I was wondering when you run honors level applied-economic tutorials? How do I sign up? How many other Econ411 students have asked to swap to your tutorials? Seriously, Dylan (Gobbed?) can really put a class to sleep.

Theo hit *Send* and checked his inbox to find an email from Mom.

To: Theo Wallace, Leone Wallace

From: Crystal Wallace

Subject: Eat more vegetables!

Just want to remind my Leos to be health conscious this week during the new moon. Sleep in and eat well. No takeout! Leone, how is your history thesis coming along? Theo, I miss your smooth, cheeky voice—just like your dad's. Give me a call sometime soon. Love you!

He sent off a reply telling her he ate pizza tonight, and didn't that count as a vegetable?

A new email popped into his inbox. Theo glanced at the green symbol next to Jamie Cooper's name indicating he was online.

He read the email with a growing grin.

To: Theo Wallace

From: Jamie Cooper

Subject: Keen to Earn A's

You are the first Econ411 student to contact me, and the last one I expected to. I suggest sticking it out with Dylan (Gothe?) this semester. Perhaps his tutorials pick up. You were not thrilled with our first tutoring session, and now you're emailing me to get into one of my classes. I'm flattered, really. Unfortunately (more for you than me), I do not run applied-economics tutorials. Give Dylan another go. And might I suggest a little less shut-eye and a little more participation in class to earn that A?

Theo hit *Reply*, torn between amusement at the guy's directness and frustration that he'd have to suffer more of Dylan what's-his-name's tutorials. He did care about his grades. He was a straight-A student and wanted to keep it that way. Even with a good tutor, he'd barely scraped an A- in microeconomics. He couldn't mar his record when he was this close to wrapping up his degree.

To: Jamie Cooper

From: Theo Wallace

Subject: Keen to Earn A's

I'd forgotten about that first class you ran. Let's call a spade a spade—it was dismal. What changed? After that

anomaly, your tutorials were more thought-out, interest-ing, and approachable. Stop lifting that brow, I *was* paying attention. I just take things in better with my eyes closed.

Now tell me: Why don't you run applied-economics tutorials? Don't you need to maximize your earnings to minimize the need for financial aid? You are an econ-omist, after all.

He hit *Send* and then stared at his screen for a reply.

Five minutes later, he shook himself out of it and fired up a text editor and a browser to continue the design work he was doing for a romance author. He'd worked for a few years designing websites for authors, artists, and entrepreneurs. He was good enough to earn his way through his undergraduate. Well, almost.

Theo glared at the tray on his desk where he kept all the finance crap he had to deal with. He'd qualified for a small loan with a 5-year interest plan. All he had to do was sign some papers and it was as good as done.

He was loath to do it though. He crunched the numbers, hoping he could devise a way to finish his last semester without plunging into debt.

Probably less takeout would help.

A familiar *ding* had Theo clicking back to his inbox. Jamie had messaged him via chat.

Jamie: Gotobed.

Theo instantly replied.

Theo: If I didn't so badly want you to tutor me, I might call you out on that shit.

Jamie: It wouldn't be the first time. But, Gotobed. As in Dylan Gotobed, your tutor this semester.

Theo: Gotobed! Riiiight. How can I get you to explain all I

need to ace applied econ? Also, I'm not going to lie, I'm surprised you remembered me.

It took a minute before Jamie replied. Theo assumed the guy had written something and deleted it, because it looked like he'd been typing for a while yet all that showed up with the next *ding* was:

Jamie: You're not easy to forget.

Theo: Stop making me blush...

Jamie: Stop making me snort. Who wouldn't remember the guy who (on my first ever tutorial), leans back in his chair, folds his arms against his chest, and yells out "KISS."

Theo: When you put it like that...

Jamie: For a few startled moments, I had no idea you meant Keep It Simple, Stupid. I looked around the class wondering with whom you could be so ineptly flirting.

Theo laughed. A few moments later, a knock sounded at his door. Leone's voice leaked into the room.

"What's so funny, bro?"

"That'd be *who* is so funny," he replied.

"Who, then?"

She opened the door, walked to the end of his bed, and looked in his general direction. "Who's making you laugh?"

"Jamie Cooper."

Leone felt the bed and sat down. Her smile was bright and curious. "New friend?"

"Tutor."

"It's nice to hear you laugh again. Been a long time."

Theo cleared his throat, unsure how to respond. "How was your book club?"

"The girls want to read a book that isn't available on audio and

I'm not a fan of text to speech so I'll skip the next one. I found a date for you, though. She's whip-smart and she finds you "attractive as hell." Said something about your intense green eyes and dimples? I don't know. The point is, she's worth a shot. She's away for a couple of weeks, so said date will have to wait until she gets back."

"Who is this precious?"

"Liz. Elizabeth Perkins."

"She wasn't the one I drenched in beer last month, right?" He'd tripped over someone's feet and drenched a cute, red-haired damsel hugging her knees on their couch. Her shirt could be saved; not so much her book.

"It made an impression."

Another *ding* sounded and Theo barely refrained from glancing at the screen.

"Shall I set it up then?" Leone asked.

He hesitated, pressured by the same inner resistance he'd felt when Ms. Pretty had hit on him. But Leone had said he didn't smile often. If he was down in the dumps, he had to change something. "I trust you, sis," he murmured and gave in to the pull of the chat.

Jamie: As to how you can ace applied econ... I have some books I could lend you. They even come with notes in the margin.

"How about you keep chatting with Jamie and we talk again over breakfast?" Leone said.

Theo looked up at his sister making her way out of his room. "We don't have another interview tomorrow, do we?"

"No, thank God."

"Hey, Leone?"

"Yeah?"

"I'll read you next month's book."

Leone rounded out of sight with a murmur. "You're going to sweep some girl off her feet, someday."

Theo couldn't imagine it would be any time soon.

He focused on his chat with Jamie. It wasn't his first choice, but the books would have to do.

Theo: Meet you at the econ staff coffee machine around 10 am tomorrow?

Jamie: No can do. I'm meeting up with some post-grads looking for a roommate.

Wait, what? Jamie Cooper needed a room?

Theo straightened, opened a new tab, and checked his daily horoscope. Had the stars aligned and—rather conveniently—pushed their next roommate toward them?

Things not going your way, Leo? Addressing the situation head-on is your only option. But be nice, leave the growls behind, and opt for pleases and thank yous instead.

Finding a roommate hadn't been going his way. Maybe he should ask Jamie if he wanted to come by and check out their place?

Maybe this astrology thing had something going for it after all.

He wriggled his fingers and then snickered as he typed again.

Theo: It's destiny.

Jamie: What is?

Theo: Us.

Jamie: Come again?

Theo: It's written in the stars.

Jamie: Is this another KISS moment? I am confused.

Theo: My sister and I have been searching for a roommate all week. Obviously, you have to cancel on the post-grads and check out our place.

Jamie: And live with you?

Theo: Why do I hear emphasis on 'you'? Am I that hard to be around?

Jamie: You said it.

Theo: Bastard.

Jamie: When should I come by?

Theo grinned.

Theo: Is tomorrow at 10 am going to be a problem now?

"Rabbits should attack you like they once did Napoleon."

Leone to Theo during a fight.

Chapter Three

After returning from a morning run, Theo shaved, showered, and darted into his room to dress.

One glance at his bedside clock had him frantically searching for a pair of boxer-briefs. Jamie would be ringing the doorbell any moment now.

Where was his damn underwear?

He eyed his laundry hamper suspiciously, then double-checked his drawers. "Well, fuck." All that was left was a pair of tighty whities.

He grumbled as he pulled them on, making a mental note to do the laundry.

The doorbell rang as the elastic snapped low on his hips.

"Can you grab that, Leone?"

"I'm in a precarious state of undress, Theo," she replied, words somewhat muffled.

He wasn't in the best state of dress, either. But they were both guys, and they'd seen more in a locker room. Ditching his search for clean jeans, he strode to the front door and swung it open.

A half-inch taller than Theo and firmly muscled, his former economics tutor stood on the porch step. He dressed as Theo remembered: boots, jeans, cashmere pullover with one sleeve bunched up behind his silver watch. He had cut his light brown hair shorter, but it complemented the brush of stubble over his strong jaw and made his gray eyes his most prominent feature.

Theo noted the suppressed amusement in Jamie's stare and leaned against the cool doorjamb, crossing an ankle. "Well, well, well. Mr. Jamie Cooper."

Jamie quirked an eyebrow, then drummed his fingers over two textbooks he held. "Is this how you greet all your prospective roommates?"

"You'd be the first."

"Lucky me."

Theo grinned at the dry response, grabbed a handful of his pullover and hauled Jamie inside. "Laundry day was, well, *any* day before today. Shoes in the rack, middle shelf next to mine, laces tucked in." Theo heard Leone moving in the next room. "Then come meet the most amazing woman you'll ever have the pleasure of meeting."

Leone must have overheard him, because she scoffed. "You're meant to *lower* expectations, stupid."

Jamie put his shoes away and knocked out a deep, warm, comfortable laugh. Yeah, Jamie would fit right in here.

Theo beckoned him across the living-dining room, where Leone stood in the kitchen pouring water into a kettle. She was dressed in a frayed crochet sweater layered over a black singlet and clean jeans. Clean jeans like he needed to shimmy into. "Give me two secs to put some clothes on."

Leone shifted her body in his vague direction. "Clothes on? Good God, do I want to know?"

Jamie laughed and walked over to Leone as Theo dashed into his room. The brown slacks he wore yesterday would suffice. At least his Capital Cities' "Safe and Sound" shirt was clean, and maybe it'd make Mr. Jamie Cooper smirk.

The buzz of conversation hummed in the background, punctuated by Leone's easy laugh. He smiled smugly. Thanks to his finagling, they had a bona fide candidate for the room upstairs. Hopefully the torturous interviews could now end. Of course, he'd have to make sure Leone felt good about having Jamie in her space.

Leone's oddly high-pitched giggle told Theo he was probably in luck.

Theo joined the two in the kitchen just as the kettle was hissing.

Jamie ran a quick eye over Theo's T-shirt. He leaned against the kitchen island and folded his arms, leveling a gray stare at him.

"The same shirt you wore the first day we met," he said. "Are you trying to scare me off?"

"Scare you off? And here I was aiming for sentimental."

Jamie looked at Leone. "Your brother used my tutoring sessions as his personal bedroom."

Theo hopped up on the bench opposite Jamie and sat on his hands. "I told you, I take things in better with my eyes shut."

"It wasn't just the cavalier way you stretched your limbs over table tops. You tossed your coat over the back of my chair, your scarf over your classmate's desk. One time you even took your boots off."

This was true. "In all fairness, I was soaked that day. Who wouldn't take their boots off and use the classroom heaters to dry their socks?"

"Just about *anyone* else." Jamie shook his head, but a trace of humor sparkled in his eyes.

Leone pivoted toward Jamie. "Sounds just like my lazy Leo brother. Protective, stubborn, driven—and the more he can do from the couch, the better."

"Hey!" Theo said, hauling in a battle-ready breath, but it seemed like too much effort to defend himself, so he let his breath deflate and shrugged. "Yeah, that's about right."

Jamie gave him a sideways glance. "I admit, I came here expecting any questions starting with 'where is the' to be answered with 'on the floor.'"

Theo narrowed his eyes and growled at him.

"If it weren't for me," Leone said, smiling bigger than he had seen her smile in months. "I imagine you'd be right. But Theo would do anything for those he loves, no matter what it costs him. Including standing three hours on a freezing platform waiting for my delayed train to arrive. Do you want tea?"

"Sure," Jamie said, staring at him strangely. Almost…softly.

"What do you fancy?" Leone asked, hauling down three mugs. "Black or fruity?"

"Fruity," Jamie said, glancing back at her. "Definitely fruity."

"You take after my brother's own heart." Leone opened the drawer next to Theo, grazing the side of his leg, and pulled out two berry-apple teabags and an English Breakfast.

"That's…good to know."

After Leone handed them their tea, she leaned back on the counter next to Theo and cradled her mug. "I vote yes," she said. "This is our next roomie."

Theo smiled again. "You sure?" he asked. "You haven't asked many questions."

Jamie stared at them over the rim of his tea. "Ask away."

Instead of addressing Jamie, Leone spoke again to Theo. "Is this the guy you were messaging last night?"

"Uh huh."

"Then I don't need to ask anything else. He'll do just fine."

"Already sure of me?" Jamie said.

Leone gave a small shrug and moved a step closer to Jamie. "Tell me. What do you look like? My vision is like instant photoshopping. I can see your outline and the colors of your clothes, but all the flaws are blurred."

"What flaws? I'm tall, sandy-haired and handsome."

Theo snorted. "Add modest to the list too. He has that in spades."

"How would you describe him, then?" Leone asked.

Jamie raised an inquisitive brow. "Yeah, how would you describe me, Theo?"

Theo swept an assessing look over the guy. He couldn't deny that Jamie was tall or sandy-haired, and kept himself in shape, dressed just fine. He had an understated strength to him that might be appealing to some. Also his confidence was attractive. To Leone too, it seemed. And—

Wait.

Was Leone attracted to Jamie?

He glanced at his grinning sister and back at Jamie, who was still waiting for Theo to talk him up. Maybe there was a spark between the two?

How…opportune.

Jamie seemed like a decent guy. Smart, kind, charming. Maybe he would be a good match for Leone.

He sucked in a breath and cocked his head as he swept the length of Jamie once more. Leone was right; he would do —say— anything for those he loves. "He has a pair of startling gray eyes and an ass that would make your book club swoon." Theo jumped off the bench. "Right then. When do you want to move in?"

For a long second Jamie gazed at him, the humor in his eyes replaced by something else that brought Theo to the brink of shivering.

Jamie abruptly turned to the textbooks he'd placed on the kitchen island behind him. He passed them to Theo. "Maybe I could see the space first?"

Leone almost choked on a gulp of tea. "Jesus. We didn't even show him around! Talk about presumptuous."

Theo tucked the textbooks under one arm and curled a finger for Jamie to follow him. "Trust me, Leone. He wants what this place has to offer."

Jamie harrumphed and followed Theo up the stairs and across the carpeted balcony that overlooked the living-dining area.

One door led to a bedroom with an en suite bathroom.

He told Jamie everything he could about their place: the ample sun his room got, their once-a-week trip to the supermarket if and when they cooked, and the location of the bus stops and parking spot, both close and far away.

"You'd even have your own shower," he said. "Was I right?"

"About wanting what this place has to offer?" Jamie leaned against the doorjamb to his future bedroom and looked at him. "I reckon you were."

Theo stood in the doorway and mirrored Jamie, resting against the doorframe. "Any questions?"

"Your sister is blind."

Theo stiffened. Was this going to be a problem after all? "She has had severely reduced vision since we were fifteen. Her lack of sight barely makes a difference. She does everything she wants, no excuses. She fights for what she needs and wants and—"

Jamie pushed off the jamb. "That wasn't a criticism. Your sister seems clever and capable."

"She is," he said, hands still balled at his sides. "I admire the hell out of her."

Jamie clasped him on the shoulder and squeezed, his thumb brushing over the neckline of his T-shirt and skating against his skin. "I like her."

Theo noted Jamie's sincerity and relaxed under his grip. "Then we'll get along just fine."

"Be frank about how you feel. Or, better yet, perfect your passive-aggressiveness."

Jamie to a procrastinating, glaring Theo.

Chapter Four

They didn't get along just fine.

Jamie was infuriating.

He made them eat vegetables. Actual vegetables.

He had moved in two days ago, and he'd not only taken over in the kitchen but he had the nerve to tell Theo to stop lounging on the couch and crack open his applied-econ book if he wanted that A.

Worse, Leone agreed with him.

Theo muttered under his breath, grabbed a couch cushion, and slipped it under his head. "I thought you living here would make econ a walk in the park. Like living with CliffNotes."

Jamie walked up to him on the couch and planted a fat textbook on his chest, knocking the breath from him. "Read that, and I'll quiz you."

Theo narrowed his eyes at him, but Jamie's expression remained unflinching. "Leone?" he called, still holding his gaze. "What dinners do you want this week? I'm going to make a run to the supermarket."

"I call shotgun," Theo said, trying to push the book away, but Jamie planted a firm hand on it, keeping it right where it was. "What? We are out of pizza and peanut butter."

"No more living off prepackaged dinners. You need proper nutrition. Both of you."

How hard would it be to slip in a pizza when Jamie wasn't looking? "Let's get on to that right now, then."

Jamie's lips twitched. "Read a chapter first, then you can come."

Theo opened the damn book. "It would help if I could read your atrocious handwriting."

"You have to have the last word, don't you?"

Theo looked up at him and smiled. "Who, me?"

Jamie stalked off to the kitchen, opened cupboards, and scribbled down a shopping list. Theo read the insipid introduction and half of the first chapter. Jamie's presence made it difficult to concentrate. He felt his gaze on him half the time checking to make sure he hadn't drifted off.

He wanted to drift off too, but pride. So.

Thankfully Jamie's phone rang and the guy answered it with a jovial, "Sean! How are you doing?" He pulled the phone from his ear and spared Theo a look. "You keep reading." He resumed his call, voice trailing off up the stairs as Jamie retreated to his bedroom.

Theo waited until Jamie's door shut to leap off the couch and lure Leone from her history thesis into the kitchen. "Yeah, okay," she said. "We can call Mom."

Leone felt for the landline phone they kept at the corner of the kitchen island and began dialing, and Theo picked up the notepaper and pen Jamie left on the kitchen bench.

"Jesus, his handwriting is a mess."

"So long as we can slip some chocolate on the list, I don't care. And he's right, you know. We don't eat well."

"I always make sure to get the *vegetarian* microwavable lasagna."

Leone pressed speaker and the kitchen filled with ringing. Their mom picked up and got right to it.

"Loved ones could confront me with news that may start a massive change for the family. I'm not to assume what that news is and am to take it in stride. Apparently, I have the propensity to butt in where it would be better to let things take their natural course. But now my Leo loves have called and it's all I can do not to harangue you for this news."

"Hey, Mom," he and Leone said together.

"Yes, yes, hello, of course. Hugs and kisses, too. The news?"

A hearty laugh came from upstairs only slightly muffled through Jamie's door. Who was this Sean person he was talking to? "News? There's no news."

"Theo, I love you, but you're oblivious half the time. Leone, you're usually more astute. Can you think of anything that might change the family dynamics?"

"Yes. Theo has been laughing more recently."

Theo's cheeks warmed. "So has Leone."

"We've decided to move on from Sam and Derek once and for all," Leone said.

At hearing Sam's name, Theo was struck with a small pang.

"Matters of the heart," Mom said, "yes, this could be the news. Lovely. Maybe it means you'll both soon meet someone new? In fact…oh never mind, I should mind my business. Maybe a little push in the right direction? Listen up, loves. Let's talk about Leo compatibility."

She was fooling herself if she thought he'd date based on a star sign.

"Samantha and Derek weren't good matches for you," she said. "Especially Samantha, Theo. Virgos are the absolute least compatible match for a Leo. No sexual chemistry whatsoever."

"There was *plenty* of sexual chemistry, thank you very much."

"That wasn't chemistry, darling. That was fucking."

"Mom!"

"Real chemistry makes sex fun *and* emotional."

"How do you know it wasn't emotional?" It wasn't, because sex never was, but still.

"Did either of you ever make love—"

"Two-minutes in and I'm already wishing this call was over."

"See, you haven't."

If Theo hadn't lived with this type of mothering his whole life, he'd be wishing for the ground to open and swallow him. As it was, this was just a Saturday.

"'Making love is a Hollywood invention. It's right next to Maglor and Middle Earth in a Tolkien dictionary."

"All I'm saying, Theo, is if you think a Virgo is good, you'll be blown away if you meet an Aries. Or Sagittarius."

Leone, who had been giggling throughout the not-so-enlightening back and forth, laughed harder. "Tell me more about Aries and Sagittarius."

Theo shook his head and added "chunky" to "peanut butter" on Jamie's list as his mom detailed the trust, communication, and sexual intimacy in a Sagittarius-Leo pairing.

He doodled a Leo and an Aries on the bottom of the paper as their mom dove into their most compatible matches.

"Aries and Leo are so passionate together—and the intimacy. The *intimacy*. There is a tendency to get jealous and possessive but it's compensated with absolute loyalty these two have for each other. Really, you couldn't find a better match. Aries feeds your need for attention while remaining steadfast in their own character. Both of you need to prove how amazing you are, and while doing so, Aries energizes Leo. And Leo in turn cherishes Aries. Despite the battle for dominance, the relationship flows with warmth, passion, and playfulness."

"Theo," Leone said, waggling her brows. "Make sure to find me an Aries."

He snorted. "You don't believe this, do you?"

"Don't be too dismissive," Mom said. "You might miss out."

As he finished the horns on the Aries, he heard the upstairs floorboards squeak. Leone must have heard it too, because she palmed her head and said, "Oh, yeah. We have a new roommate. He used to be Theo's econ tutor."

Speaking of econ… Theo glanced over at the textbook he had plunked on the coffee table. Maybe he should hurry back to his spot and pretend like he'd been studying the whole time, if only to keep Jamie from issuing another exasperating comment.

"His name's Jamie," Leone added.

Theo clicked speakerphone off and snapped the phone to his ear. "So maybe, and I mean this with all my love, maybe next time you call you can make sure you're speaking to us before diving into the secrets of the universe? Love you. Bye."

He placed the phone into Leone's hand and ushered her back

into her room. Grabbing his textbook, he jumped back on the couch as Jamie descended the stairs.

Jamie walked passed him into the kitchen with the barest glance. "Would be easier to absorb the principles of efficiency and equity in relation to tradeoffs with the book turned the right way around."

Dammit.

Theo peered at him over the top of the book. "You underestimate my talents, Jamie. I happen to be proficient at reading upside down. Also backwards, as a matter of fact."

"And yet my handwriting eludes you."

Point, Mr. Jamie Cooper.

Theo flashed his dimples at him.

Jamie scooped up the shopping list and grabbed his keys from the rack. Theo responded to the jingling like the last bell before summer break. He jumped off the couch, snagged his windbreaker, and stuffed his feet into his shoes.

Jamie knocked on Leone's door and offered her to join them. She came out with a bounce in her step, slipped into her jacket, and they stepped out into the frosty air to Jamie's teal Honda parked at the curb.

They clambered inside, Jamie giving Leone time to familiarize herself with his car and settle comfortably in the backseat. Jamie started the engine and cranked up the heat.

"Jesus it's clean in here," Theo said, glancing around the spotless leather interior.

"Just the way I like it."

Leone chuckled. "Don't let Theo eat in the car, then. There'll be crumbs in places in the upholstery you didn't even know about."

Jamie leaned an elbow on the middle armrest and glanced at him. "That so?"

Theo pressed his finger to the condensation on the front window and started writing. "I like my cars with personality."

"That means he cherishes the smell of stale crackers."

"Leone!"

She laughed. "Hey, I like it. All I have to do is feel the grains and I know I'm home."

Theo finished writing the windshield quote: *And yet my writing eludes you.*

Jamie read it, looking torn between irritation that fingerprints would stain the glass and mild amusement.

"I said that."

"Five points to Team Cooper." Theo scribbled Jamie's name under the quote.

Jamie smiled a half inch then dropped it and shook his head. "Belts on, Leos."

Jamie had overheard their mom's call, then. Theo palmed his head.

Buckled in and ready to go, Jamie eased away from the curb and drove down the road toward the supermarket. While he chatted with Leone about social and gender history during the nineteenth century, Theo cracked open the glove compartment and peered inside.

Car registration and documents. Two bottles of water and five Hershey's Bars past their use-by date.

"Anything incriminating?" Jamie asked in a low voice as they waited at a red light.

Theo gave him a quizzical look. "What's with all the expired chocolate?"

"In case I get stuck in traffic driving out of state, of course."

Of course. Jamie sure liked having his shit together.

"I'd better replace those, though. What's with the smile?" Jamie shifted into drive.

Theo felt his dimples deepen. "You're so organized. No wonder I drove you up the wall."

A few seconds passed before Jamie responded. "That's cute."

"What is?"

"Your use of past tense."

Theo punched Jamie in the arm. "Why did we choose this guy as a roommate?"

"Because he's smart and considerate, he cooks, he separates out the white laundry and he has a car and ..." His sister continued all the way to the supermarket parking lot.

Theo pivoted in his seat and stared at her. Was he witnessing the start of a beautiful friendship? Jamie was about the same age and shared the same determination Leone did, and Leone admired the guy's incessant need to keep things in order.

And, frustrations aside, Jamie was…

Well, he would be the insufferable brother-in-law that always wound him up the wrong way; and Theo would give it back just as good. He liked getting a rise out of him even if Jamie's gray stare made him a little nervous.

It was nothing he couldn't handle. Nothing at all.

He shifted in his seat and stared out the front window. Out of the corner of his eye, he saw Jamie grinning.

"Leone, thank you," Jamie said. "You're close to being my favorite girl ever."

"Stop feeding his ego." Theo climbed out of the car. "His head is big enough."

They made it inside, Theo offering Leone his shoulder to hold. Jamie pushed the grocery cart and eyed them as Theo swiftly navigated past the fruits and veggies aiming for the frozen section.

Theo didn't take three steps past the fresh produce before Jamie gripped his other shoulder and gently guided him to a stop. "Let's try that again." He looked at Leone. "May I lead you today?"

She shifted her hand from him to Jamie. "He made straight for the pizza, didn't he?"

Theo huffed. Jamie told him to handle the cart as he steered Leone back toward the broccoli and cauliflower.

If the guy wasn't so good to his sister, he'd think about throttling him with the green onions that had landed in their cart.

Painstakingly, they made it through the healthy sections filling up their cart with eggplant, garlic, carrots, and too many green items to name. It wasn't enough to get rice and pasta, so Jamie tossed in lentils, couscous, and quinoa—whatever the hell that was.

Turned out one frozen pizza was okay in the end, because, *moderation* or whatever.

But the final straw came in the peanut butter aisle.

Theo always ate chunky peanut butter.

Apparently, Jamie always ate smooth.

Theo stood next to Jamie hugging an extra-chunky peanut butter jar against him.

Leone made the final decision. "Shopping with you two is like listening to daytime soaps," she said. "The drama. I don't mind either type but I'm partial to smooth. Sorry, Theo."

His mouth dropped open. "We are not of the same blood. Smooth?"

Jamie's barely refrained smugness twitched at his lips. Clearly he found the situation amusing.

In went the smooth peanut butter, and away his traitorous sister and Jamie went.

Of course, they could have bought both, but smooth versus chunky felt like a game—and Theo had never been into cooperatives games. He liked a clear winner. He liked to *be* the winner.

Overseeing the cart made it easy to win. The smooth peanut butter fell out and the chunky fell in. Oops.

They made it through checkout and halfway back to the car when Leone's phone rang. Jamie stopped at a safe space on a pedestrian island and let her answer.

"Derek?" Her voice sounded breathless, and Theo froze with the cart. He knew the way her stomach must be filling with butterflies. Every time Sam's ringtone sounded, he'd hoped there was a chance Derek and her hadn't worked out and she was calling to beg for another chance.

Jamie swung his gaze from Theo to Leone, a curious brow rising, then beckoned Theo over to swap jobs.

Theo moved to his sister's side and Jamie pushed the cart to his car and opened the trunk.

Leone squeezed his hand and let out a familiar bitter laugh. "Your birthday…party at your new place…can bring a date."

For a moment Theo thought she'd hang up on Derek, but she straightened her shoulders and held up her chin. "I'll be there."

He wasn't surprised when his phone went off moments later.

"Hey, Theodore," Sam said when he answered with a grunt. He hated that he could tell she was smiling. "Maybe you already know why I'm calling?"

"Let's see. Your car got a flat and you need me to hoof it to the burbs to change it for you? You need someone to give your philosophy paper a good edit? You need me to help you choose a gift for your boyfriend—fiancé's—birthday?" Theo shut his eyes, breathed in, and released the pain. He had had enough of this. "I gotta stop doing things for you, Sam," he said softly. "You've moved on and I am too."

"You're right," she said quietly. "I'm sorry. If you want to come to the party to hang out, well, you're welcome. I hope you show up. You're a good guy, Theodore. I like you in my life."

Theo swallowed, staring dumbly toward Jamie shutting his trunk. Jamie looked up then, their gazes clashed, and Jamie hesitated before retreating to the driver's side.

Theo hung up and, in taut silence, led Leone to the passenger side of Jamie's car. She could sit up front this time.

Jamie said nothing as they piled into the car, but he glanced at him through the rearview mirror once, twice, three times before they left the parking lot.

Finally, Jamie spoke. "Who was on the phone?"

Theo pulled out a small smile. "My ex."

Jamie nodded grimly. "One of *those*."

Something about the sad way he said it made Theo believe he understood. "Anyway," Theo said, playfully tugging Leone's hair through the gap in the headrest. "What are we making for dinner?"

"We?" Leone scoffed.

"Okay. What are *you* making, Mr. Jamie Cooper?"

"We," Jamie said, pegging him with a look through the rearview mirror, "are learning how to make lasagna. The non-microwave variety."

When they parked outside their home, Jamie fished out the shopping list and reached it back to Theo.

"What's this for?" Theo asked, climbing out of the car and following Jamie to the trunk.

Jamie grabbed six bags and lifted them effortlessly. "You drew a little something at the bottom."

The Leo and the Aries. "I'm sure you can guess why, eavesdropper."

"A subconscious need to find some real chemistry perhaps?"

"I know chemistry, Jamie." Theo waggled his brows. "It's hot."

Leone, waiting at the side of the car, snickered, and Theo grabbed the remaining bags, turned on his heel, and offered her his shoulder.

"I still wouldn't mind finding an Aries," Leone whispered.

Theo hadn't thought her soft words had traveled. They must have, though, because once Leone disappeared into the kitchen and Theo was toeing off his shoes, Jamie slid past, pinning him with a twinkling gaze. "Did you know I'm an Aries?"

"I wonder how much fly poop the average person eats in their lives?"

Leone to Theo eating an unwashed apple.

Chapter Five

Derek had seemed perfect for Leone yet she still ended up heartbroken. This was why Theo couldn't tell his sister the perfect man might be right in front of her nose.

He first had to be sure Jamie was The One.

That meant spending time with him. A lot of time with him.

The hardship.

Seriously. Theo had to wake up at seven in the morning to score a ride with Jamie to campus, and he did this four times a week.

Two of those times, Leone also took up Jamie's offer to drive them into town, which gave Theo a chance to subtly observe their interaction. Genuine. Kind. Cheeky.

Theo liked Jamie's style of cheekiness. It was the only highlight of getting up at sparrow's fart. That, and writing daily quotes on the fridge or fogged windows or once on a handy towel. The last quote had been Theo's favorite: *A fear of headless mannequins is damn rational.* A Jamie quote, after Theo caught him shuddering as they passed a storefront window.

On Thursdays, Theo didn't have classes until the afternoon and bussed to campus. But today Jamie had suggested they meet up after his applied econ class for a coffee at Starbucks. Theo intended to hound the man for help deciphering the convolutedness that was Dylan Gotobed.

"I've given him a chance. More than one. And it's not working."

They were sitting at an outside table with their latte-filled paper cups in a shaft of soft sunlight. Jamie soaked in the warmth resting his head against the café wall, eyes closed as he hummed in response to Theo's complaint.

Theo sketched another Aries on Gotobed's assignment sheet. He'd been drawing the ram lately, like it had crawled under his skin and taken control of various limbs. And, yeah, there was nothing PG about that.

Thank you, stupid compatibility charts.

He finished the ram with a flourish at the horns. "He's just not *you*."

Jamie peeked at him out of the corner of his eye. His stare lingered for a few skin-tingling seconds but it didn't come with the offer of unlimited assistance Theo had been aiming for.

He had a feeling Jamie was holding out on offering because he *liked* torturing him.

As if to prove Theo's theory, Jamie swept his gaze to the assignment sheet and smirked. Then the bastard went back to breathing in the sunshine.

Only, Theo couldn't call him a bastard since Jamie had bought them both coffee. Unexpected and…nice. He had a feeling that it was Jamie's style to make sure others got everything they needed. Possibly explaining the salad sandwiches Jamie had been packing for them each day. A toying, opinionated, cocky, caring bastard—and Theo liked it.

He even liked this teasing game Jamie was playing with him.

Because games were fun.

And Theo loved to win.

He picked up his latte and sipped, staring at Jamie's hard jaw and sharp nose and how the light pulled the copper and golds from his brown hair. There he sat, confident, comfortable, relaxed, and with Theo in the palm of his hand.

Before Mr. Jamie Cooper knew it, he'd be offering Theo help with a sweet side of smile.

"You're staring at me," Jamie murmured without opening his eyes.

"I'm wondering about your take on double standards."

Jamie's eyebrow quirked up. "I feel like this is trap, but I'll take the bait. Not a fan."

Theo took another sip of his coffee, mainly to hide an obnoxious grin. "So it's not okay for me to indulge in a little shut-eye during our interactions, but it's okay for you?"

Jamie opened his eyes and slowly twisted on his chair until they were facing each other. The way his gray eyes pinned Theo had him hurriedly taking a nervous sip of … air. He'd finished his latte then. Right. Well, Jamie didn't know that.

Theo continued to sip.

"I didn't realize I was participating in class." He leaned toward him over his coffee. "But let me assure you, Mr. Theo Wallace, I'm taking everything in."

Jamie stared at his mouth as if he were expecting Theo to throw back a retort. But Theo only choked on a gulp of coffee flavored air.

Theo coolly leaned an elbow against the back of his chair, hand gripping his paper cup, grinning as he said, "And how is Theodore Wallace 101?"

Jamie did a sweeping assessment of him, taking in the pullover he'd shoved over his polo shirt without caring to pull out the collar. Or maybe he was taking in the excessive times Theo was swallowing. "I might be interested in the advanced classes. If they're on offer."

Theo laughed. "Let's see you ace 101 first."

"Quiz me any time, I'll be ready."

"Oh yeah?"

Jamie tapped his temple. "I take notes."

Theo took another sip of air. He needed to get his game back on track. "How did the meeting with your master's advisor go?"

Jamie was working hard on his master's thesis: "Keynes in the Record Store: On the use of game theory to adjust for uncertainty and irrationality in customer behavior."

"Meeting went well," Jamie said. "I'm on target to wrap it up by the end of summer."

Theo didn't doubt it. Not a day passed without Jamie sitting studiously at his bedroom desk pounding away at the computer, the fruit teas Theo made always cold before Jamie paused to drink them.

Just last weekend, Theo had snuck into the upstairs room while Jamie was hard at work. He curled up into the olive-green armchair with a beast of an econ book and stared at Jamie's crammed bookshelves and neatly-made king-size bed, waiting to see how long it would take Jamie to realize he was in the room.

The answer? Forty minutes.

And when he did, Jamie spat out his gulp of cold tea. The glare Theo received as Jamie tugged off his soiled jeans had been priceless.

Theo shook himself out of the memory as Jamie sank back into his chair and continued, "I've been asked to give a lecture on Keynesian economics next week to undergrads."

"Really? Awesome opportunity." Students would mop up his wisdom and then greedily hassle him after class to teach them more.

Get in line.

"You can sit in if you like. If you promise there'll be no KISSing."

"That'd take away half the fun," Theo said. "But I'd love to sit in."

Jamie nodded. "Good. I think you could use the instruction."

Theo threw his pen at him, which Jamie lazily caught. Was he skilled at everything?

Snatching back his pen, Theo dived into the endgame. He picked up Jamie's latte and wrote on the cup. Jamie picked it up and read it silently.

He peered at Theo over the lid and shook his head. "No one said that," he said.

"Said what?" Theo asked innocently.

"What's written here."

"And what's that?"

Jamie's lips twitched, and Theo knew he'd won.

"How can I help you with econ, Theo?" Jamie read aloud.

Theo planted his assignment in front of Jamie. "Thought you'd never ask."

Jamie smirked and watched as Theo smugly lifted his paper cup to his mouth. Just before the lid touched his lips, Jamie reached out and pried the cup away.

For a startled second, Theo froze.

Jamie calmly stood. "I'll go over the assignment with you, Theo. But first, let me buy you another drink."

SATURDAY MORNING STARTED WITH THEO'S USUAL RUN. HE MADE A habit of running seven miles most days of the week. He loved the sting of the cold February air at the back of his throat, the way his skin prickled with exertion.

Theo came to an abrupt halt between a dilapidated bus stop and a boarded-up villa. Sam, jogging toward him, slowed to a stop. She wore tight leggings and a thin hoodie. Bright purple headphones clamped over the top of her blonde hair, which she'd cut short. A stray curl was matted to her cheek just above the freckle he used to worship with his tongue.

"Theodore," she said, shoving back her headphones. Daylight glinted off the rock on her finger and brought him crashing back to reality.

He shoved his hands into the pockets of his shorts and feigned nonchalance. "Hey, Sam."

"Funny we should bump into each other. I was just thinking about you."

A month ago those words would have swelled his chest with hope. Now there was a mere flutter behind his ribs. Maybe he'd found closure in their last conversation.

It hurt seeing the woman he thought he'd always wake up with.

But he'd gotten used to waking up alone. And recently, mornings had been easier. Possibly because of Jamie's strict schedule.

There was no time for nostalgia.

"I was wondering if you'd decided about the party next week-end?" she said.

"Oh, right." He wiped the sweat off his forehead with the back of his forearm. He'd forgotten about the party, which indicated he'd reached a healthy fucking milestone. Would the party ruin his progress? Probably. But if Leone insisted on showing up, he couldn't let her suffer alone. Leone knew how to navigate foreign surroundings, and she wasn't shy to ask for a helping hand. It was all the emotional shit that came with this party that might be too much for her.

And he didn't trust Derek, Sam, or any of their friends to take care of his sister.

"I guess I'll come," he said.

Sam's face lit up with a smile and for a second Theo thought she'd throw her arms around his neck and pull him into a hug. Just in case, he rocked back on his heels. He wasn't strong enough for hugs. Yet, anyway.

They ended the moment with an awkward wave and Theo hoofed the rest of his run. He just wanted to get home. Shower. Forget about her.

He mostly managed.

He slipped up in the shower as he scrubbed himself down. Then slipped up some more as he tugged on his dick. But thankfully the memory of her sucking him morphed into a scene from the book he was reading.

Theo was the furthest from prude there was. In fact, he was a bit of an exhibitionist. But that was *not* the easiest book to read aloud. To his sister.

Theo wanted to be a fly on the wall for that book club meeting.

When Theo was done, he toweled off and hunted through his drawers for clean clothes. Finding nothing, he sauntered out of his room with the towel wrapped around his waist, wet hair dripping down his back, hoping to find clean clothes lying on the drying racks in the laundry-designated corner of the living room.

In the kitchen, Leone and Jamie were baking. Jamie was measuring a cup of flour over the black bowl that Leone was kneading dough in. He glanced up, and their gazes clashed.

"Just need some grundies," Theo said approaching the damp clothes on the racks.

Leone opened her mouth—probably to tell Jamie it was enough flour—when the phone rang.

"That'll be Mom," Theo and Leone said at the same time.

Jamie dropped the bag of flour and snapped forward to pick up the call. He held the phone to his ear for a good twenty seconds before he managed to squeeze in a word.

It was Mom, then.

"Mrs. Wallace, nice to talk to you."

Theo could imagine the momentary shocked silence his mother would have hearing Jamie's deep, amused voice rumbling down the line. And then she'd compose herself and begin a barrage of questions.

"Okay then, Crystal it is. Your Leos are . . . managing." Jamie pressed a button on the phone and set it down on the counter. "Leone's fine. It's your other one you have to worry about."

"Is that so?" His mom's voice flittered through the room, polite and curious.

"He seems to have a problem with laundry day." Jamie looked over at Theo fondling the third pair of wet boxers. He was giving up hope any of them would be dry. "It's not the first time he's running round looking for underwear."

Leone scoffed and Mom laughed too.

Theo flipped them all off, which broadened Jamie's smile.

"That might be why the stars are telling him to get organized," Mom said. "Can he hear me?"

"He sure can."

"Theo, love, turn yesterday's pair inside out."

"Jesus, Mom."

"What's the problem? You used to do that all the time as a teen."

A wave of warmth washed over Theo's chest, neck and cheeks. "I was thirteen, and it was one time."

"Have I embarrassed you, love? I was warned I might get flak for that today. Hold your head up proudly, there are far worse stories I could have told. Like the time when…"

Theo knew Jamie relished witnessing him getting taken down a peg—or three hundred—by his mom.

Which was why it surprised Theo when Jamie, looking like it was the hardest thing he'd ever had to do, switched the phone off loudspeaker and passed it to Leone.

Leone pressed the phone to her ear and leaned back against the oven while she told mom about her week, and Jamie busied himself rolling out dough onto a tray.

Theo stood dumbly for a few moments, trying to make sense of the soft tendril of gratitude in his belly. He wouldn't have minded if Jamie had ribbed him senselessly for the stupid stunts he'd pulled as a kid. He'd be embarrassed, sure, but not so mortified that he couldn't see the humor in it.

A part of him had wanted Jamie to tease him about his worst moments—it made payback that much sweeter—but it unnerved him how much more he liked it that Jamie hadn't teased him.

"Scones ready in ten minutes," Jamie said as he gently nudged Leone to the side and slipped the tray into the oven.

Theo came back to his senses and slunk to his room, where he slipped on a pair of jeans, T-shirt, and a warm gray hoodie.

He returned to the living room and helped set the table. Leone offered the phone to him and Theo spoke a few minutes to his mom before the delicious scent of melted cheese had him ending the call and joining the other two for breakfast.

His first bite of warm, buttery goodness elicited a moan from him.

"They are that good," Leone agreed.

"Fuck yeah," Theo said. "Makes me want to bow down to salivary glands."

Jamie paused, a scone hovering an inch from his parted lips. He set it down on his plate. "Shouldn't you want to bow down to Leone and me for baking?"

Theo pretended to think about that for a moment, then shook his head, his dimples coming out to play. "It doesn't matter how great of a cook you are, without saliva I wouldn't be able to taste this yumminess."

"Granted," Jamie said, leaning forward, gearing up for a heated debate. How did every second meal end up like this? "But without us there is no yummy."

"You just want me bowing down before you."

Jamie eyed him, and said dryly, "I wouldn't mind you on your knees, singing my praises."

"Never going to happen," Theo said. "No matter how much yumminess you bring to my life."

Leone frowned, tilting her head.

"Who's coming shopping?" Jamie asked after they had cleared the dishes. Neither had won this round. "Leone?"

Leone, standing next to Jamie at the sink, tightened her ponytail. "I could use the free time to do some yoga. You guys go without me."

Jamie took this with a nod and pressed a hand on Leone's shoulder, like he'd gotten into a habit of doing when he wanted to address her. "Is there anything you'd like us to get you?"

"Something with cocoa, milk, and sugar in it."

"As you wish," Jamie said.

Theo glanced up from the dishwasher, not believing his ears. Jamie had just as-you-wished her. He'd quoted William Goldman's *The Princess Bride*—her favorite book. It was one of her childhood wishes to one day be as-you-wished. She must be melting inside. Theo was almost melting on her behalf.

As though he had no idea of the effect of his words, Jamie rounded on Theo. "You about ready then?"

Theo shook off the moment and plucked Jamie's keys off their hook and jingled them.

Jamie, tailing him, reached around Theo's side and hit the back of his hand. The keys leaped into the air and Jamie snagged them, his large fist swallowing all the metal.

Theo yanked open the front door and charged down the path. "You think you're so smooth."

"I don't just think it."

Large strides kept up with him, and Theo raised both brows when he caught Jamie furtively glancing at his ass.

"You found a pair of underwear, then?" Jamie responded, remotely unlocking the car.

Theo grinned as he made for the passenger side. "Nope."

Jamie stopped a few feet from the car and threw his head back, muttering to the sky.

Theo opened his door. "You coming or what?"

With a clouding expression that made Theo nervous, Jamie kicked his way to the driver's side. "I'm gonna come all right."

"Sometimes I just want to get plastered and see if I can tell the difference between raspberry and strawberry juice."

Theo to Jamie in the supermarket.

Chapter Six

Wednesday evening Theo found himself on the couch, feet propped on the coffee table as he coded alterations for Alex's website, pro bono work in return for spreading the word. Theo liked the guy and his skateboard sticker art, and the website was an easy set up.

The scent of cinnamon and apple hung in the air, and a warm, cozy quiet cocooned the living room. Leone had left a couple of hours ago for her monthly book club—taking the apple pie she and Jamie had made—and Jamie was mucking around on his laptop at the dining table.

Neither of them had spoken for an hour, but it seemed like their keyboards were conversing through bursts of alternating typing.

Theo saved the code with a snap of the keys but it didn't cause Jamie to stir.

Sinking back on the couch with his laptop, Theo looked over at Jamie framed by the window. The darkness outside provided a backdrop so that the glass panel mirrored him. Theo could even see Jamie's computer screen. He knew when Jamie was typing on a document, checking his email, and surfing Facebook. When Jamie scrolled through the posts on Theo's wall, Theo smiled and wondered what Jamie thought about the photo he'd put up of the three of them on campus; Theo and Jamie grinning at each other over Leone's head.

A familiar *ding* sounded and, too lazy to reach his phone abandoned on the kitchen bench, he checked the message via email. Leone's name flashed in a text box. She used speech-to-text and sometimes the words were messed up. Like they were now.

Leone: Hey, bro. Lizard is back if you want to go out with her sometime.

Theo wrote back, aware Liz and the other girls might hear the automated voice that read his message aloud.

Theo: Tell Lizard I'm free and only slightly intimidated by the prospect of her tongue down my throat.

Leone: Dork. You're sure about the date?

Theo trusted Leone's judgment. Besides, what harm was there in meeting Liz?

Theo: Only if her tongue is blue. Otherwise it will never work.

Jamie had crossed his arms and was scowling at the computer screen. He grumbled and shut his eyes as he rubbed the bridge of his nose. He slumped back in his seat, tired and vulnerable.

At that bizarrely mundane moment, Theo was sure. His sister deserved everything: love, care, humor, tenderness, affection, and playfulness.

Jamie would give it to her.

The realization slammed through his chest, and the quiet warmth around him dropped away and left him flailing.

He pressed his fingers on the keyboard to tell Leone that he'd found her Aries—and then lifted them again.

He couldn't make his fingers type the words.

Because…because it would be better to let things play out naturally.

It was only a matter of time before Leone saw the romance right under her nose.

The way he always complimented her attempts at cooking, or read chapters of her thesis and offered his feedback, or held her shoulder when he thought she might stumble, or laughed at the same time, or the way he never made her feel blind.

Genuine, heartwarming respect percolated between them.

They didn't need him ruining all that beauty by blurting it out to Leone. And via text, no less. No, he would hang back and enjoy the show. Possibly give a small nudge if they needed it.

No rush for that, though. His sister appreciated a good slow burn.

Theo opened a new chat box and typed.

Theo: Whatcha doing?

Ding! Theo watched in the window as Jamie checked his email. He stared at the chat box and then peeked at him over the top of his laptop.

The exhaustion that had blanketed Jamie moments ago lifted and his eyes crinkled with amusement.

It always impressed Theo how Jamie could smile without using his lips. Theo sure couldn't do that.

He was pretty fucking dependent on his dimples, to tell the truth.

Jamie: Preparing for my lecture tomorrow. Not sure I've nailed my examples.

There was something thrilling about communicating via chat when they sat less than ten feet from each other. The moment Jamie responded, it had become a game. Who would crack and speak first?

Theo: Maybe you're overthinking it? You've been staring at that document all night.

Jamie: Almost as long as you've been staring at me, then.

Theo swallowed an indignant reply. He glared at his laptop and typed instead.

Theo: Just plotting how to distract you. I seem to be doing a good job of it.

Jamie: You most certainly are.

Theo caught Jamie's gaze and grinned. Then he was all fingers over the keyboard again.

Theo: But seriously. You'll be fine tomorrow. I know it.

Jamie: You're still coming?

Theo: Dunno. Is KISSing off the table?

Jamie: You enjoy torturing me, don't you?

Theo: Yep.

Jamie: If you weren't my roommate, I might lose my patience and KISS you.

A deep laugh filled Theo right to his toes.

He could imagine Jamie giving it as good as he'd gotten it in front of a whole class of econ students. In fact, if Theo had been tutoring, he was sure Jamie would have done it already.

He wasn't sure what the roommate comment was about—had Jamie developed a sense of loyalty since living with them that would stop him making a fool of Theo? Even if it was for shits and giggles?

He remembered the way Jamie had stopped his mom from humiliating him. It had cost him, but he'd done it.

Maybe being roommates changed their dynamics?

Yeah. Theo wouldn't yell in one of Jamie's classes now, either. Probably not, anyway.

Jamie lifted one eyebrow at him, and Theo typed, deleted, and typed again and then hit *Enter* before he could change his mind.

Theo: I'm sorry, you know? I shouldn't have yelled in your first ever lesson like that. You're a good tutor, Mr. Jamie Cooper. The best. Why do you think I work so hard wooing you into helping me ace applied econ? And the truth? I was staring so hard at you tonight because I fucking admire your concentration. You'll rock the lecture tomorrow and I'll see that for myself. I wouldn't miss it.

Jamie read his response. His expression stayed neutral, but then he read the message again. This time he swallowed, the ball in his throat dipping and rising. He rubbed the six-o'clock shadow darkening his jaw, and his mouth parted, about to break first.

Something in Theo's belly twisted. "Maybe you should take the rest of the night off?" He cleared his croaky throat and patted the couch beside him. "You know, kick back, relax. Watch some reruns of *Community* with me?"

Jamie stared at him longer than usual, then clapped his laptop shut and stood. A wave of cinnamon warmth rushed over Theo as Jamie neared. Traces of flour and spices still dusted his T-shirt. He neither sat in the middle nor at the end of the couch, just comfortably between the two, and he reclined against the cushions.

"Distract me some more, then."

Theo opened a browser, turned on his favorite *Community* episode, and set his laptop on the coffee table in front of them.

Jamie laughed within the first five minutes, tucked his linked hands behind his head and nestled deeper into the couch.

Theo tried finding that level of comfort too, but he wasn't used to sharing the couch and it was strange trying to keep his limbs to himself. He propped his stripy-socked feet on the table, but having them to one side of the laptop sent his upper half sinking toward Jamie. He swiveled perpendicular to Jamie, resting against the arm of the couch.

It wasn't ten minutes before his feet were on Jamie's lap.

He'd gotten caught up in the episode and hadn't even realized. Until Jamie squeezed the bridge of his right foot.

"You have a thing with your feet, don't you," Jamie said, and it wasn't a question.

Theo laughed and wriggled his toes, heels slipping further up Jamie's hard, jean-covered thigh. Jamie doubled his grip on Theo's foot. Amusement flashed over Jamie's face and he shook his head as he set Theo's feet on the cushion next to him.

"You know in five minutes they're going to be back on you, right?"

"I'll tickle you senseless if they are."

Theo slipped his toes under the side of Jamie's thigh instead. Jamie side-eyed him.

"Are you busy Saturday night?" Theo asked.

"Yes, why?"

A small thread of disappointment came at that. "Leone and I are heading to a party. Just wondered if you wanted to come along."

"Sean is driving down for the weekend. We have plans, sorry."

"Sean?" Theo recognized the name. The dude called Jamie multiple times a week, and they sure were chummy.

"Friend from home," Jamie said. "He's thinking of moving to the city and we're looking for apartments."

Theo carded a hand through his hair and glanced everywhere but at Jamie. "Were you, um, thinking of moving out?" He folded his arms and stared right at him. "I'm not sure I want you to leave."

Jamie looked puzzled. "No. We're searching for an apartment for *him*."

Theo's shoulders dropped and he pushed his toes a little more under Jamie's thigh. "Thank fuck for that."

"You'd miss me then." Again, not a question.

"There's no way I'm letting my applied econ A just up and walk out of here."

"Is that what I am to you? Your A?"

"Maybe even my A+."

Jamie raised a brow. "The way you study?"

Theo flipped him off.

"If Sean finds a place," Jamie said, "I'll likely head back home for the extended March 9 weekend to help him pack. Minneapolis is not much farther than my place in Wisconsin. I can take you and Leone home if you like."

"You'd do that? It's another four-hour drive."

"Half a day. No sweat."

"Half a day there and then back. A whole day out of your way."

He shrugged. "Road trip."

"We could bus up from your town."

"Or you could smile, say thanks, and take up my offer."

Theo didn't smile; he was too touched by the gesture. "Thanks, Jamie." Then, wiping his palms on his thighs, he broke his hold of Jamie's gray gaze. "Leone and I will have a blast cranking up the music and cracking into your emergency Hershey's supply. If you want, I can take a turn at the wheel."

"We'll see," Jamie said.

They went back to watching another *Community* episode and then two and three.

In the middle of the fifth, Theo brazenly lifted his feet onto Jamie's warm lap again. He couldn't help it. He loved to tease, to test, to stretch the limits. He didn't think Jamie meant it when he said he'd tickle him senseless.

No harm, then.

His heels had rested three seconds on Jamie's thighs when Jamie wordlessly captured his foot and peeled off one of his socks. Theo knee-jerked and gasped in surprise.

A smirk lit up Jamie's face as he ran the tip of his finger along the inner arch of Theo's foot and across the mounds of his toes until he reached the sensitive outer arch.

Theo instinctively tried to wriggle out of Jamie's grip, but Jamie's fingertips devilishly danced down to the front of his heel until, Jesus, Theo couldn't take it anymore. He threw back his head and let the pent-up screech burst out of him.

"Stop. I promise, I'll never do it again. Just stop."

Truthfully though? He'd totally do it again.

"You'd totally do it again," Jamie said, and let go of his foot.

They grinned at each other, and Jamie opened his mouth to say something. Theo held his breath, waiting for whatever teasing words might come out, but the front door banged and Leone came inside with a curse.

Theo and Jamie were at Leone's side in seconds.

"You okay?" Theo asked, taking her jacket and hanging it for her.

"Taxi driver was a douche. Thought he'd have fun by racing here, and when I told him to slow down, he said I can't be blind if I knew how fast he was going. I told him to pull over and let me out. I ended up in the middle of some godforsaken street with no clue where I was."

Theo wanted to pull her into a hug, but Jamie had his hand on her shoulder. He let Jamie have that one.

"Why didn't you call?" Jamie said. "We would have picked you up."

Leone shrugged out of Jamie's hold and, feeling her way around Theo, passed him into the living room.

"It made me feel so fucking dependent," she said, heading for the kitchen. For a cup of tea, no doubt. "I used my phone to tell me where I was and ordered another taxi."

Jamie moved to his laptop. "Did you get the driver's name? I'm making a complaint."

Leone told him she'd be fine and not to bother, but Theo leveled him with a look that told Jamie he'd better get that driver's ass fired.

Jamie spent the next hour giving more than one person an earful until he got the douche driver on the phone. Firm and unrelenting without being rude, Jamie insisted on him apologizing.

The fucker hung up after a few angry words and no apology.

Jamie ended the call, grimly satisfied. They hadn't expected any apologies, but the call had been recorded and now the taxi company would have to deal with him.

Leone, hands curled around a cup of tea in the armchair with Theo, rested her head against his shoulder. "I see why mom wants us to end up with an Aries," she murmured, and then louder, to Jamie. "Thank you. You might be my favorite person ever after my bro."

"You might be mine, too."

Theo rolled his eyes before peeling himself away from Leone and heading toward bed, bidding them a good night.

But he couldn't help feeling a little empty as he left the two of them to it.

∾

THEO WAS ON HIS BEST BEHAVIOR.

He was sitting upright at the back of the Roosevelt Atrium—feet on the floor, shoes on—with his attention focused on Jamie at the front of the room.

This was Jamie's element.

He always had examples at hand when he talked numbers, projections, and theories but his knowledge of Keynesian economics was not what made this lecture good. Nor was it the way he kept his facts concise and illustrations detailed.

It was his *confidence*.

The way he coolly paced, tapping the projector remote against his thigh, his voice cleanly cutting through the air. Passion radiated out of him and the students listened.

The crowd of three hundred swelled with a laugh as an enthusiastic Jamie held up his hands after praising Keynes and assured the room that he wouldn't bury money in the ground just to pay people to dig it back up. Theo liked how Jamie glowed. Liked it even more when Jamie's gaze sought him out and they shared a small smile.

Jamie's gaze dipped to the "Safe and Sound" T-shirt that Theo had put on under his hoodie this morning. For this moment.

This one moment when Jamie was, for a split second, thrown off his game. His eyes flickered to Theo's and his expression changed. Theo had been expecting a raised brow. Or an eye roll. Or even a carefully schooled face that Theo would spend all day wondering about.

But Jamie's expression wasn't any of those things.

It was softly amused.

For the rest of the lecture Theo could not concentrate. At least not on Keynesian economics. He'd never felt this before. This high, this ghost of a tickle in his right foot, this soaring-through-the-wind feeling.

Now he knew what real friendship felt like.

"…to other facets of life," Jamie said.

And then Jamie put him on the spot.

Theo snapped back to his senses and the economics at hand.

"Can you adapt the multiplier effect to another area of life, Safe and Sound?" Jamie asked.

Theo wasn't sure if Jamie were testing to see whether he'd paid attention, or whether he felt more comfortable targeting Theo because he trusted he'd give a half-okay answer. Either way this was why Theo had read a detailed summary of Keynesian economics in bed last night.

Theo leaned back in his seat and crossed his arms. He flashed his dimples at Jamie before answering. "Love."

The extra inch Jamie shot upright showed his surprise and interest. "Love? Elaborate."

"The more a person initially invests into a relationship, despite being unsure of the demand, the more they can get out of a relationship."

"You mean despite not knowing if the feelings are reciprocated?"

"The more time and emotional dollars you invest into a relationship, the more you inspire trust that encourages the other person to spend more of their own emotional dollars. In a positive outcome, this spending will lead to more emotional wealth. Or, translated, love."

Jamie stood there blinking at him. If Theo didn't know better, he'd say the man had been rendered speechless.

"Any other questions?" Theo asked, just *daring* him.

"No," Jamie said quietly. Then he cleared his voice. "Thank you, Safe and Sound, for your rather hopeful adaption of the multiplier theory."

Hopeful adaption of the multiplier theory. Theo would have to remember to use that line as a quote of the day.

"Good," Jamie said, surveying the rest of the theatre. "Any questions about this material?"

Jamie diligently clarified the students' questions and scored another collective laugh. When the lecture ended and people poured out of the atrium, a handful of devoted students engaged him in further discussion.

Theo moved to the front row and waited for Jamie to finish. Now that the lecture was over, he didn't have a problem with resting his elbows back on the seat, hooking an ankle over his knee, and closing his eyes.

A student thanked Jamie for the lesson and asked if he'd be teaching more classes. Jamie's voice dripped with satisfaction as he said he hoped his advisor would arrange a few optional lectures.

The first Theo had heard of it, but he would be there.

The last of the student voices disappeared and the atrium quieted.

They were alone.

Footsteps padded over the carpet and the air stirred over his arm and face as Jamie took the seat beside him.

Theo cracked open an eye. Jamie sat with his elbows on his knees staring at his note-and-laptop-stuffed satchel. "Do you really believe a Keynesian love approach could work?"

Theo considered it. Rarely was economics so cut and dry that it could accurately predict financial outcomes. Why would it be different for emotional outcomes? If he were honest, hadn't he tried this route with Sam? He'd listened to her, shared his own stories and thoughts and fantasies and future goals, and helped her out whenever she'd needed it. But it hadn't been reciprocated to the same degree. He'd ended up emotionally bankrupt and unable to find anyone who would loan him some emotional dollars other than his sister.

But he was starting to feel like maybe, possibly, Jamie was lending him some too.

"I don't know," he said finally.

Jamie leaned back with the eyebrow raise Theo had expected earlier. "Maybe we need to test it and find out."

Theo liked Jamie's driven, determined answer. Who knew, it might even become Jamie's doctorate research.

"In any case it was a good answer, Theo."

"Small confession. I have a tutor who drills all this econ nonsense into me."

"Sounds like this tutor has done his job well."

"I'll tell him how pleased you are with me. Maybe he'll give me a Saturday off studying as a reward."

Jamie looked at him amused, which didn't look promising for Theo. Still, worth a shot.

"Are you free?" Theo asked, standing up.

After a quick glance at his watch, Jamie nodded. "I have an hour or so."

Theo hitched a thumb toward the door. "Come then. It's my turn to buy you a coffee."

Or two.

"Stop being so melodramatic."

Jamie to Theo on a bi-daily basis.

Chapter Seven

So Derek's party happened.

Leone and Theo had bussed and then walked to Derek and Sam's new place, a large villa with a view over the Allegheny River.

Thanks to the chaos of forty-plus guests, they slipped inside the house without seeing the birthday boy or his fiancée. A friend of theirs ushered them through spacious rooms to the conservatory.

Fairy lights glittered from the glass ceiling and candles flickered on the tables. The gift under Theo's arm pinched as he stiffly guided Leone to a table.

She gripped his shoulder with enough force to crack a walnut. "Have you seen him?"

"Not yet," he responded as he helped her sit and moved the candles to one side.

And then he saw them.

Over a sea of faces Theo didn't recognize, Derek kissed Sam. Not a chaste kiss, either. A whole nine-yards kiss that included him squeezing her ass. Theo kept the drink-inducing sight to himself and told Leone the birthday boy looked bored.

"Thank you for lying," she said with the shake of her head. "I wish you were better at it."

Sam stood on a chair and tapped her cocktail glass. She looked good with her short haircut and tight sweater, and the boots she wore over her jeans added a good fuck-me inch.

She scanned the room and smiled when she saw him and Leone. Theo tensed.

Sam gave Derek a touching birthday speech, mushy but sufferable until she ended with a line that drained the tentative smile from his face. "Grab your coats, boys and girls, there are a few pontoons awaiting us at the river."

Sam hopped off the chair, grabbed a beaming Derek, and led him toward the surprise pontoons.

The generous gift she'd organized for Derek and their friends was a slap in the face. Sam had invited him here. Had double-checked he would come and hadn't cared to warn him. Or maybe—and this thought stung more—she hadn't *remembered*.

Leone swore under her breath. "I'm sorry, Theo."

Theo shrugged even though Leone wouldn't see it. He shuffled his seat forward to let a couple pass behind him. "It's okay." Why had they bothered coming? "Did you want to go?"

Thank fuck her answer was a defiant no.

Guests blew out the candles on their tables and left in a cloud of rambunctious laughter. Ben and Kyle, two of his Facebook friends, stayed behind too.

Blond and Blonder trundled over. Ben looked uncomfortable like he usually did passing him in commerce lectures, but Kyle took his hand and Ben visibly relaxed.

Ben coughed, his chest rattling. Probably why they decided to stay in.

"Room for us at your table?" Kyle asked.

Leone recognized his voice and bounced on her seat. "Fuck, Kyle. Ben. It's been too long. Sit down."

Leone felt for the gift they'd bought for Derek and ripped off the turquoise wrapping. "Someone get shot glasses," she said as she drew out a fifteen-year aged whiskey bottle from a tall box.

If Ben or Kyle wondered why she was opening their gift to Derek, they kept it to themselves. Likely, though, they were more surprised they had shown up at all.

Kyle found shot glasses and a bottle of apple juice for Ben, and Theo poured.

The first shot burned.

The second got them talking.

The third and fourth dissipated some of the awkwardness.

The fifth numbed the sting of Sam forgetting.

And the sixth had him retreating to Sam and Derek's kitchen, sitting on the marble bench, heels banging against the cupboards as he unlocked his phone…

Theo: Full disclosure, I'm drunk. Whatcha doing?

Jamie: Just had dinner with Sean. Eggplant parmesan. Another meal we could make at home. How drunk are you?

Theo: You're all about food, aren't you?

Jamie: Good food. How drunk?

Theo: How's Sean?

Jamie: Great to catch up. Have missed him around. About to play black-light badminton. Do I have to all-caps it?

Theo returned to Leone, Ben, and Kyle, a little sway in his step, and helped himself to another shot. He hoped it would rid him of the sudden and intense dislike he had of Sean. A guy he'd never even met. A guy he didn't want to meet, either.

He imagined him as a scrawny, beady-eyed, downright miserable, eggplant-eating, badminton-playing jerk.

His phone buzzed and he downed another shot.

Jamie: HOW DRUNK?

Theo hiccupped as he made his way to the back door, Leone and the guys giggling about old times. Wind breezed over him as he leaned dizzily against the doorframe. Before him, through the gaps in the trees, he watched the river light up with sailing pontoons.

He clenched his hands around his phone and focused on the screen as he wrote another message.

Theo: Almost everyone went pontooning.

Jamie: Where are you if the others are out pontooning?

Theo: In Sam and Derek's kick-ass house.

Jamie: Is it because of Leone?

Theo: Nope.

Jamie: Care to elaborate?

Theo: You don't want to know.

Jamie: I beg to differ.

Theo: Shouldn't you be playing badminton right now?

Jamie: Sean is driving us there. Tell me.

Theo's vision swam, dotted with fairy lights, and time played tricks on him, slowing as Ben rested his head on Kyle's shoulder and Kyle kissed his temple.

Theo fiddled with his phone and then shrugged to himself and went for it. The only person who knew other than his family was Sam. The trust he'd placed in their relationship by sharing it had not been as reciprocated as he'd imagined.

Considering that, he was nervous telling Jamie. What if he laughed? What if he rolled his eyes and told him to get over it? What if he told him it was his own fault for not learning how to swim?

And yet, despite all the usual concerns, he wanted Jamie to know.

He squinted at his screen and typed slowly.

Theo: Know how headless mannequins freak you out?

Jamie: What twisted person thought decapitated models were a good idea?

Theo: Large bodies of water are my headless mannequins.

Jamie: Unexpected. Is there a reason?

Theo hesitated, letting a wave of wooziness roll over him before replying. Then he held his breath. Being drunk made this that much easier.

Theo: Almost drowned as a kid.

Jamie: Should I call? Talk about this?

Theo let out his breath, relieved that Jamie took it seriously. But no need to call. He could handle it. He could.

Theo: It's not a big deal.

Jamie: Again, I beg to differ.

Theo: I guess I'm not a good swimmer? I don't like going out on deep bodies of water.
Want to know something stupid? Sometimes I hold my breath going over bridges. Like somehow that would keep me from falling off them into water.

Jamie: That's not stupid, Theo.

Theo: I like that your messages are all nicely punctuated, Mr. Jamie Cooper.

Jamie: It's not stupid.

Theo: Anyway… you should get back to badminton.

Jamie: Where is this party?

Theo: The other side of the city, with a smobering view of the river.

Jamie: Probably not "smobering" enough. Is Leone tipsy too?

Theo: You don't know this, because I haven't wanted to talk about it, but Sam and Derek are my and Leone's exes. They're getting married. To each other. Guess how drunk we are?

Even as he typed it, the room tilted on its axis, although it might have had something to do with the sudden explosion of nerves that rocketed through.

Jamie: I see.

Theo: You like to "see" things, did you know that?

Jamie: Get yourself and Leone some water.

Theo: As you wish, Mr. Jamie Cooper!

Jamie didn't reply and Theo closed the door and stumbled to the bathroom. After relieving himself and taking a moment at the sink where he cringed at blurting his fear to Jamie, he passed by the kitchen for a few bottles of water. Back at their table, he handed them out.

"Jamie said we have to hydrate."

"Is Jamie the one who—?" Ben yipped in pain.

Theo frowned as Kyle spoke up. "Who's Jamie?"

"Our roommate," Leone said, jumping up and down on her seat

with drunken exaggeration. "And he can piss Theo off better than anyone."

"You like him?"

"And then some."

Theo discarded his water and poured himself a celebratory shot for finding Leone's Aries.

"How'd you meet?"

Leone answered again, cheeks flushed. "Theo brought him into our lives, and I couldn't be happier."

That deserved another shot.

Theo leaned back in his chair and tipped his head up toward the fairy lights.

He listened as the three of them chatted about Jamie. Leone asked Ben a question and Theo stiffened. He thought about reaching for another shot but he was too assed to reach for the bottle.

"How did you know Kyle was the one for you?"

There. Proof that Leone was at least thinking about Jamie being the one for her.

Ben hummed and the sound of a kiss followed. "Lots of little clues added up over time to the most amazing feeling I've ever had."

"What types of clues?"

"Kyle was the first person I thought about when I woke up. He was there for me when I needed it, and he loves the quirks I find weird about myself. And, with him, I never just thought about the next day or next weekend. He was always there in my future."

Another kiss followed a low murmur, and then Kyle spoke. "Ben is the best part of my day, he always has been."

"Thanks, guys." Leone sighed. "You are both super cute in my imagination."

"In reality too, just so you know," Kyle said.

"What about you, Theo? Met anyone since Sam?"

There had been a couple of one-nighters but otherwise it was just him dancing the five-knuckle shuffle.

His words felt thick on his tongue, and he hoped they weren't slurred too much. "Leone set me up with a friend of hers. We're going out next week." Which reminded him he should think of a place to take her. His vision swam and he rubbed his forehead. *Sort it out tomorrow.*

Yeah. Tomorrow.

He was going to hurt tomorrow and Jamie was going to give him shit. But then, Jamie was always giving him shit. And, like… what the hell were they talking about again?

"You think this friend might be a good match for our Theo?" Ben asked.

Leone said, "She's great and I think he should try it but I don't know anymore."

Didn't know anymore? So what if Liz wasn't a perfect match? At this stage, it was good to test the waters and open himself up to the possibility of someone new. "Looking forward to hanging out with Lizard."

Leone snorted as she gulped a mouthful of water. Her nasty cough-laughing got Ben in stitches. His sister took it with a gracious flick of her middle finger.

That's when the doorbell rang.

Despite the fact his head—the whole damn room—was on a repeat spin cycle, Theo knew. Just *knew* who would be standing on the other side of the threshold. He looked at Leone, who had stopped laughing, color sweeping up her cheeks.

"Tell me you didn't!"

"What?" she said as she felt for Ben's hand and tapped him.

Ben laughed. "I'll get it."

Theo shook his head and quickly grabbed for his water bottle, toppling it over instead. "Shit."

"He called while you were out of the room," Leone said, still blushing. "Wanted to know the address to give us a ride home."

"We could. Have. Taxied," Theo said between large gulps of water.

He tried finishing the bottle before Jamie sauntered into the room, but only managed a quarter.

Jamie's voice came so close behind him it startled Theo halfway out of his chair. "There you are. Ready, then?"

Theo swiveled around.

Jamie stood clad in jeans, boots, and dress shirt, and next to him, elbow casually on Jamie's shoulder, was a Roman fucking God. Chiseled symmetrical face. Slightly curly blond hair. A body that intimately knew the workings of a gym. Shit. This was Sean?

He'd damn well better be a dumb jock.

"He's not dumb in the slightest," Jamie said.

Fuck. He'd said that aloud?

"Yes you did. And you can stop pointing."

Theo frowned and looked at the finger he was jabbing in Sean's direction.

"Why'd you come?" Theo said.

"Sounded like we needed to." Jamie reached over the table and picked up their almost empty whiskey bottle. "Looks like it, too."

Leone giggled. "Stop glowering, Theo."

"How do you know I'm glowering?"

"Because I know you. Your breath comes out a little growly when you glower. Jamie suggested picking us up because he didn't want me to have another bad taxi experience."

"I would have protected you," Theo said, following it up with a well-timed hiccup. He amended: "I would have tried, anyway."

Someone snickered, but when Theo looked around, he only saw Sean coolly introducing himself to Ben and Kyle with a nod of his damn perfect, not air-filled head.

Sean rubbed Jamie's arm and whispered in his ear. Theo did not get good vibes from this dude.

In fact, why did Jamie even bring him?

Jamie bent, eyes carefully scanning Theo's face. The low timbre of his voice skimmed Theo's ear. "Sean and I were going to play badminton. I asked him if he'd pick you two up instead. Like a good friend, he came."

"Am I saying *everything* out loud?"

Jamie's lips twitched. "Some things are written on your face. Or, in this case, written in the scowl you haven't stopped giving my friend."

Theo felt like he'd swallowed a lump of coal. He lifted the water bottle and drank.

"Are you ready, Leone?" Jamie asked, moving away from him to his sister's side.

"Yep." With a laugh she felt for Jamie's shoulder and hoisted herself to her feet. "You're awesome for picking us up. Ben? Kyle? Nice to chat with you guys again. Don't be strangers."

"Right back at you," Kyle said as Ben said, "You bet."

Sean looked at Jamie and Leone and of course offered to help. He had to be nice on top of everything. This time Theo was positive he didn't say it out loud because he'd made it a point to bite his lip.

Jamie paused on their way past and met Theo's gaze. "Can you walk?"

"Define walk."

"Do I have to carry you to the car?"

"I can walk."

Theo was on his feet as soon as he said it. Then wished he wasn't.

The floor lurched underneath him, and he was damn sure it was going to rise like a wave and smack him in the face.

But Jamie was watching him. So that. Couldn't. Happen.

Thankfully Leone was just as drunk. She handled alcohol a hell of a lot better than he did, but she got loud and harder to steer around.

Jamie slung one arm around her waist, hooked his other under her knees, and carried her down the dark, windy path to his car outside the gate.

Of course, it wasn't a surprise. They were falling for each other, and that's what romance looked like.

Another congratulatory shot tomorrow, then.

Sean looked over his shoulder at Theo and flashed him a grin. "You good, man?"

Theo was *totally* keeping his shit together. He was still on his feet!

"Don't open the car door for me," Theo growled. There had to be something not to like about him. Something Jamie hadn't yet noticed.

Sean hurried ahead of Jamie and opened the passenger door. He helped Jamie get a laughing Leone buckled into the front seat.

Theo managed to crawl into the backseat. Forget sitting upright; it was comfier this way with the cool leather sticking to his cheek.

Words were exchanged between Jamie and Leone, and Jamie

and Sean, but they were muffled. Jamie's car was not so spotless after all. A stray Hershey's wrapper lay tucked under a gym bag and cased rackets.

Air whooshed over him as the back door opened, and dammit, he didn't want to share the seat. Least of all with Jamie's friend. A friend who knew *real* things about Jamie. Secrets. Wishes. Hopes. They likely had shared jokes, code words, and a secret handshake.

And the way Sean felt comfortable practically cuddling Jamie in front of him! They were not merely friends. They were *best* friends.

A gurgle of disappointment made its way from his belly out of his mouth. The leather didn't disguise it at all.

Gentle hands helped him upright and a firm voice had him swinging his head. It wasn't Sean slipping into the backseat but Jamie. Jamie's lips pressed into a thin line and a small frown cut his brow. Jamie's top shirt buttons had come undone revealing a white singlet.

"Belt on, Theo."

Theo fumbled for it and drew it over his chest. Snapping it into the buckle proved tricky though. Could the world stop spinning for one second?

Jamie took the belt and clicked him in, then tugged the strap to make sure it was working right, knuckles grazing Theo's chest.

"We're good, you can drive," Jamie said to Sean.

The city blurred past him, making his stomach lurch. He still felt the awkward silence in the car that was only occasionally interrupted by Leone's startled snores when they turned corners.

"So…" he said, trying to break it. "Black-light badminton, huh?"

Jamie shot him a stare that told him to zip it. That he should suffer the silence for curbing their night short.

That wasn't fair at all. Nobody asked Jamie to rescue them.

"I wasn't going to let you wander home drunk," Jamie said. "If anything had happened to Leone, you'd be beside yourself tomorrow."

Theo leaned toward the armrest and console and stage-whispered to Sean. "Has he always been this way?"

"What way?" Sean asked, turning at a light.

"*Right.*" Theo fell back against his seat and watched Jamie shake his head at him.

Sean laughed. "Pretty much. Now I have a question for you… what did your sister mean when she said I smelled like Roger Petrelli? Who is Roger Petrelli? And more to the point, did he smell good?"

"Old man next door where we lived in Shadyside."

"I smell like some old dude? Jamie, tell me she was kidding."

"You can park up there behind your Audi."

"It's this damn aftershave, isn't it?"

The car stopped and Theo jumped out within seconds, gulping the frigid air like it would restart him. It didn't, but it gave him stamina to open the gate and the door for Jamie and Sean who each had an arm around Leone.

They helped her into her room, where Theo shooed them out. Jamie and his sister might be close to being an item, but she was clearly out of it. Theo would be the only one pulling off her boots and tucking her into bed.

It took him forever to finish the job, but he managed, all but crawling toward his own room after he was done.

Jamie walked toward him, haloed by the light from the kitchen, two glasses of water in hand. He passed one over and Theo took it, leaning against his bedroom door for support. The second water disappeared into Leone's room.

When Jamie came back out, Theo asked. "Where's Sean?"

"He left."

"Not crashing in your room, then?"

"Come again?"

Theo waved it off, feeling himself sink down the wall. He was going to pass out any second now. Crawling to bed on the cool, hard floorboards was a fine idea.

He set his glass at the skirting board and looked all the way up at Jamie. "You grab my blankets for me, and I'll sleep right here."

Jamie crouched and tucked a finger under Theo's chin. "How about I help you into bed?"

"I'm heavier than Leone."

"I'm sure I can manage."

"Bet you can't."

Jamie narrowed his eyes. "You don't want to bet me on this one. I'll win."

Theo snagged Jamie's shirt, pulling it down over the top of his arm. Then he prodded his muscle. Jesus, he'd been hiding *that* all semester? That was some serious toned-ness going on.

Jamie chuckled, then scooped Theo under the arms and heaved him to his feet. Theo sank against him, head slumping onto Jamie's shoulder. Jamie smelled warm, and like he'd been peeling oranges. Warm oranges.

"I ate fruit salad for dessert," Jamie said.

Theo snickered. Of course Jamie had been at the fruit bar while everyone else—Sean— was at the dessert bar. They'd been out to dinner, just the two of them.

He grumbled against Jamie's warm collar as Jamie successfully moved him into his room.

When Theo saw the bed, he let go and plonked face first into his blankets.

The bed dipped as Jamie climbed on the mattress and urged Theo onto his side. Theo sighed and mustered enough energy to toe off his shoes. "Gotta put them away."

He pushed up on his elbows about to swing off the bed, but Jamie pressed him back to the bed and picked up his shoes. "I'll put them on the rack."

Theo watched him leave the room and enter a few minutes later with a fresh glass of water, Tylenol, and a bucket. Jamie set them at the side of his bed.

Theo grabbed Jamie's arm before he could leave. "You're the most solid guy in the world. And not just here"—Theo squeezed the tight cords of Jamie's arm and hummed—"but in all the ways. I want to start a petition to put up your statue so everyone will know it."

A sudden burst of Jamie-laugh caught Theo's breath. "I cannot wait for the quote of the day tomorrow."

"What do you like about Sean?"

Jamie stopped laughing. He stared at Theo a long time before he answered, making Theo's neck prickle. "He's a decent guy."

The lump in Theo's throat rose again and he dropped his hand from Jamie's arm. "You guys are what? Best friends?"

Theo knew they were. Just wished Jamie would deny it.

"I've known him my whole life," Jamie said. "So, yes, he's one of my best friends. Funny and sweet, and a hell of a mean badminton player." Jamie's tongue clicked like he wanted to say more and then changed his mind. He gave Theo one last smile and said, "Sleep it off, Theo. We can chat more about it tomorrow if you like."

No, he would *not* like.

Jamie left the room and Theo scoffed loudly.

"Badminton! Anyone can play badminton."

"I thought you Aries were supposed to be an impatient, impulsive lot? Because I'm raring to see a throw down. Any of these people will do."

Theo to Jamie while waiting in the longest supermarket line ever.

Chapter Eight

Theo guessed—knew?—his drunken behavior was the reason he ended up at the local sports hall. With Jamie. To play badminton.

He might have once held a racket in high school gym, but it was a long time ago. He hadn't been great at any sport other than track. Still, it couldn't be that hard, right? He hoped not. He'd made a big deal about anyone being able to play it.

Good thing Leone hadn't come along. His huffing, puffing, and cussing would have thrown her into a fit of giggles.

Theo picked up the feathered birdie, pinched the tip, and swung the racket. The mesh met its target and the birdie flew—

—and wedged into the net.

"Anyone can play, huh?" Jamie rocked up to the net and popped the birdie free. It dropped and skidded to Theo's feet.

Theo ran a free hand through his hair and eyed his cocky econ tutor clothed in various shades of gray. Clothes worn, no doubt, to make his eyes more disarming.

It was a pity Leone would never feel the full impact of that stare.

"In all fairness, I'm hungover as hell."

Not that sobriety would have given him an edge.

"I am surprised you're able to move this much," Jamie conceded. "Quite the show last night."

Heat—unrelated to exertion—flooded his cheeks. He wished he

could forget last night. He'd been less than cool to Sean—in fact, he was surprised Jamie hadn't called him out on that shit this morning. Although bringing him here was punishment aplenty.

"So," Theo said, shifting his weight from foot to foot as he stared at the birdie before him. "I might have been out of line with your... friend." He couldn't bring himself to say "best" friend, but he raised his head and looked directly at Jamie. "Sorry about that."

Jamie studied his face, twirling the racket as if stuck on a thought. "Nothing to apologize for. You're allowed to feel the way you feel."

"I'm allowed to feel like a jealous dick?"

Surprise flickered over Jamie's face.

Jamie came forward, hooked his fingers into the net, and leaned toward him. "How about you can be a jealous dick, and I can find it secretly flattering?"

Apparently, Jamie's words were the cure to his hangover. Theo felt lighter, ready to give this birdie a piece of his mind. Theo swung his racket and the birdie flew over the net. Jamie met it with a hard and fast snap that sent it hurtling back to him.

But Theo was all deftness now.

He stepped to the side and let Jamie have that point along with all the others.

"Sean will be here in fifteen minutes," Jamie said, moving to the side of the court and slipping into a light sports jacket. He wasn't running after the birdie and sweating like Theo was. "You can choose who you want to team with. Also, maybe stop scowling whenever I say his name?"

"Thought I was allowed to feel like a jealous dick?" Theo said, smoothing his expression.

"You can feel it. Just don't show it to him, okay?"

Theo was about to retort when, for the second time since they arrived, his phone rang. He jogged off the court and dug into his sports bag, missing the call by one ring. Liz.

He listened to the voice message while watching Jamie swing his racket in a wide arc.

"Hi, Theo, Liz here. Wanted to know if we could change our date from

Wednesday to Friday? I have an emergency sociology group meeting. Let me know if that's doable. Take care."

Doable? No problem. He hadn't come up with a plan for their date anyway.

He walked back onto the court, scooping up the birdie on the way. "I have a date Friday night," he said as he served.

The birdie sailed over the net.

Jamie didn't go for it. He froze to the spot, racket in one hand and fingertips at its mesh.

Theo calmly walked to the net, Jamie watching him. "Did I score a point?"

With a slow blink, Jamie reanimated, though his voice sounded off. "You would have scored a point. If this were a game. Date Friday?"

"A friend of Leone's. I have no idea where to take her."

"Her?"

"Liz."

Jamie's face was blank; almost like he had no interest in Theo and his date. Which rather sucked, because shouldn't friends be cool to talk about this stuff?

"Where would you take a date?" Theo asked slyly, hoping Jamie's answer would both give him a good idea and trigger Jamie to think of himself and Leone on a date.

Jamie took a while processing Theo's question. He looked down at his racket and shrugged. "Somewhere fun."

"Badminton?"

"If you want her to run away and never look back."

Jamie picked up the birdie and served it to Theo. They continued to hit and miss—Jamie hitting, Theo missing—for a few tortuous minutes before Sean strode across the hall to meet them. Sean nicked his chin in hello at Theo, but strode onto the court for a hug with Jamie.

"Is he any good?" Sean asked.

"Well, he can't get A's in everything."

Theo hit the birdie and it flew towards its intended target. He'd been aiming for Jamie's head, but...

Jamie jumped and rubbed his butt cheek. He turned, cocking his eyebrow. No sign of a smile.

Theo slapped his racket and grinned. "Not so bad at this game after all."

Sean glanced between the two of them and pulled out his racket. "This should be fun. You can team with me, Theodory. Jamie, best of three sets?"

"Loser cooks dinner."

When Jamie said Sean was one hell of a mean badminton player, he was right. What Jamie failed to mention was that he was meaner.

Mr. Jamie Cooper dominated his side of the court the same way he did the lecture theater, with poise, confidence, and accuracy. He was all drive as if he had something to prove. Sweat made his sports gear cling to his torso as he rallied with Sean and came out on top every time.

After every win, he glanced at Theo. There was something gut hollowing about those looks. Maybe because the glitter was lost from his eyes. Or the fact, that despite his wins, he never showed a single second of elation. His face remained passive.

They played two sets before Theo bowed out and let the two long-time friends smash out what seemed like pent-up frustration.

From the sidelines, Theo admired the two play, intermittently scowling in Sean's direction.

Mostly, Theo dwelled on the "fun" that Jamie had said his date should be. He'd been tempted to take her out to a movie and dinner. But now, Jamie's casual words had drawn out the competitor in him. A movie and pizza wouldn't cut it.

Before he could organize it though, Sean and Theo had dinner duty.

The kitchen was Theo's least favorite place. When it turned out Sean was just as into cooking as Jamie was, Theo found his place: on the bench, heels bouncing on the bottom cupboards, passing over necessary utensils.

It gave Theo a perfect view of Jamie and Leone on the couch. Jamie was writing on a scrap of notepaper and talking to Leone, who was laughing lightly. Jamie hadn't even cracked a smile.

Sean waved a wooden spoon in Theo's face. "I repeat, where do I find the cheese grater?"

Leone answered. "Bottom left cupboard, second shelf down on the right-hand side."

"What do I have to do to replace this lazy lug with you?" Sean asked her.

Leone scrunched up her nose. "I'd come over. But..."

"But what?" Sean said, grater in hand, eyes riveted on Leone.

"If I correctly guess what she's thinking," Theo said, jumping off the bench. "Can I get out of doing any more cooking?"

"*More* cooking?" Jamie said, frowning at the paper in his hand like it held a puzzle.

"Go on then, tell me," Sean said to Theo. "She'd come over, but what?"

"Roger Petrelli."

Sean calmly set the grater on the board and walked up to Leone. "Is that true?"

Leone pressed her lips together as if to swallow her smile. Theo strutted out of the kitchen as Sean crouched in front of his sister and fluffed his T-shirt. "I do not smell like old man."

"No, you smell of old man and garlic."

"Jamie! How do you put up with her cheekiness?" Sean asked grinning.

"These two Leos are full of it," Jamie said, glancing at Leone and then at Theo. The one-second look made him pause en route to the bedroom. "It grows on you."

Jamie returned to staring at his scrap of paper, and curiosity burned through Theo. He crept around the couch, leaned over the back cushion, and stole the mystery paper from Jamie's hand.

He had been expecting more words, but there were only a handful. *You're the most solid guy in the world.* By the looks of it, Jamie had traced over the words countless times. Why did it make Jamie frown?

Jamie was watching him carefully, his face less than three inches away from Theo's.

"Clearly I was drunk out of my mind," Theo said.

Except he knew alcohol didn't make people lie; it just made them care less about saying the truth.

Theo read the words silently again.

"Keep it," he said, pressing the paper against Jamie's chest. "For days you're feeling *un*solid. Might make you laugh or something."

Jamie kept his gaze on the paper.

"Right then," Theo said, slightly disappointed. He backed toward his bedroom. "Call me when dinner's ready. I've got a date to organize."

∽

JAMIE ACTED OFF ALL WEEK.

He drove them to campus, made dinner, and gave Leone feedback on her thesis, but not with his usual energy. Theo's attempts at luring him into conversation were short-lived.

When Jamie cancelled their Thursday coffee, Theo had had enough.

He ordered two lattes to go and walked to the econ department, where he found Jamie alone in his shared office. He gingerly set the coffee on his desk.

Jamie flickered his gaze from the drink to Theo.

"Read it," Theo said, gesturing to the paper cup.

Jamie picked up his coffee and read: *What's going on with you?* He cleared his throat. "I've been stressed."

"Stressed?" Theo gripped his latte. "Try again, Mr. Jamie Cooper."

Theo thought he saw Jamie's lips twitch, but it was gone too quickly to be sure.

"Did you know your dimples still show when you press your lips like that?" Jamie murmured.

"What's your point?"

"It's hard to stay indifferent toward you."

"Why would you want to stay indifferent to me?" Theo said. "We're friends." And then, a little less sure, "Aren't we?"

An age passed before Jamie responded and Theo feigned—ironically—indifference as he reeled through their last two months. Frustrated bickering, weekly shopping escapades, tight looks Jamie gave when Theo did something spectacularly stupid, like losing Jamie's car keys which they later found under the bathroom sink.

But there were more amused moments than annoyed ones, right?

Jamie set his coffee on the desk and stood up. He cut the two feet between them and twisted Theo's paper cup out of his hand. He produced a Sharpie and wrote on Theo's cup.

After a minute passed, Theo asked, "Writing an essay?"

Jamie paused at the smart-ass comment, and then finished up and set the cup back in Theo's hand. Theo felt his stare as he read the cup.

We are tutor and student. Roommates. Sparring partners. Friends. Anything you want us to be.

A sudden rush of warmth filled Theo's chest, making it difficult to find his voice.

"Knew it," he said, taking all his effort to swallow down his relief.

He took Jamie's Sharpie and added *best* to *friends*. He'd never felt this way with anyone else so from his perspective, it was the truth.

He kept the addition to himself by covering the word with his palm as he sipped. Jamie's face flickered with curiosity when he gazed to Theo's cup, but he didn't speak.

Theo gestured to Jamie's work. "What were you doing, anyway?"

"Reading through an essay on having kids."

"Jumping the gun there, wouldn't you say?" At Jamie's bewildered look, Theo clarified. "First comes love, then marriage, and then the baby in the carriage."

"And before that, there's kissing up in a tree. The essay is an economic argument for having more kids."

"Are you convinced?"

"I enjoy observing the world through economics-tinted lenses. Doesn't mean I want to optimize everything in my own life. Far from it. Even if it were a poor financial decision, and I imagine it would be, I'd still want a few rugrats at my feet one day."

Theo choked on his latte.

"You have a hard time picturing me with kids?" Jamie asked.

That hadn't been why Theo had spluttered all over the place. The term "rugrats" had caught him by surprise. There was a softness to it, like it was wrapped in a deep want.

"No, I don't have a hard time picturing you being a dad." He decided a little nudge in the right direction would not hurt. "Might want to start on that kissing sometime, though."

"Yes, well . . . That's not easy."

"You'll figure it out, smart guy," Theo said, shifting his grip on his cup. He had to step toward Jamie to pass him. As he did, he took a sip where Jamie could read.

Jamie's gaze registered the added word and he nodded.

Theo left his office mumbling, "I know what I have to do."

He stepped into the elevator, already pulling out his phone. He had to help Jamie and bring back the absent smile to his friend's face.

Liz answered on the second ring.

"You mind if we double date on Friday?"

"The worst thing I've done on a date? Ask who her favorite serial killer is. Under a bridge. In the dark."

Theo to Leone, mentally preparing for his date with Liz.

Chapter Nine

Liz soaked up his idea.

Leone needed a little greasing.

Her bedroom was a case study in black-and-white for orientation purposes. Tonight, Leone lay on her bed listening to a book.

Theo set a box of chocolates next to her, swinging onto the bed as she paused her story.

She popped a chocolate in her mouth. "What do you want?"

"You to be happy."

Her brows shot to her hairline. "You suck at lying."

"But I do want you to be happy."

"That's not why you came in here."

"Skating," he blurted. His hands were clammy and his heart beat double-to-one.

"Skating?" She cocked her head. "You've caught my interest."

He waited until she started nibbling on a chocolate truffle. "Thought you might like to go Friday night."

"I knew you were buttering me." She shook her head. "I'm not going on your date."

Theo crossed his arms and slouched back into the fluffy checkered pillow. "Alex manages a small rink, and he owes me. He's keeping it open for us ten to midnight after it's officially closed. I want you there. Liz does too."

She stopped, a chocolate truffle touching her lip. "You asked Liz and she didn't mind?"

"I suggested you and Jamie come for that part of the evening. She was super easy going."

"Me and Jamie," she repeated, then bit her lip. "Has he agreed to this?"

"Not yet, but he will."

Her brows crunched together like she didn't believe it.

Theo would make sure Jamie came. "You know how much you love the thrill of skating."

Leone set the box of chocolates on her lap, tugging them away from Theo when he tried to snag another one.

"I'll come if Jamie does."

THEO TOOK A CUP OF BERRY TEA TO JAMIE'S BEDROOM WHERE HE was working. Jamie typed, deleted, then bounced his finger off the side of the desk when he figured out the perfect phrasing and typed again.

Theo set the cup down on the side of the desk. "Cup of tea for you there," Theo said after a minute. Usually he didn't say anything, but tonight he wanted his attention.

Stating the obvious wasn't cutting it. Jamie didn't so much as glance Theo's way.

"Not even a thank you? Or, how'd you read my mind? Or, you're the best?"

Jamie nodded.

Theo sat on the edge of the desk, tempted to flick Jamie in the ear. "You have no idea what I said, do you?"

Jamie's fingers paused on the keyboard and he slowly lifted that startling gray gaze. "Something about me being the best. But I already got that memo."

Theo swatted the back of Jamie's head. The tea between Theo and the laptop almost spilled over the edge, so Jamie moved the cup to a coaster on the bookshelves that lined the wall to the en suite bathroom door.

Because *of course* that's what his first response would be.

Jamie leaned back. "Two minutes. What's up, Theo?"

Theo scowled. "Fine, all you have to say is yes, anyway."

"Yes?"

Theo jumped off Jamie's desk. "See? How easy was that?"

He made to go and Jamie grabbed his arm. His chair swiveled so they were facing each other. Jamie rested his head back as he looked up and waited.

"You're coming tomorrow," Theo said, "on my date with Liz."

"No."

Theo had expected Jamie to frown but he was not expecting vehement rejection.

"You wouldn't be crashing it. I want you there."

"When will you start making sense, Theo?"

"Let me try again. We have an entire roller skating rink to ourselves tomorrow night. With a little guidance, Leone loves the intense thrill of skating and it would be weird if it were just Liz, Leone, and me. If you came along, it would even things up and be more fun." Theo stared at Jamie's firm lips. It'd be fun *and* Jamie would smile.

"No," Jamie said again.

"What? Why not? Can't you skate or something?"

"That's not the reason."

"What is then?"

"You'll be getting close to a woman. That's not something I want to see."

Theo cocked his head. "I didn't peg you for prudish."

Jamie tugged Theo so sharply, Theo buckled and fell half onto Jamie's lap. One knee slipped between Jamie's thighs and he had to brace his other hand on Jamie's shoulder or else they'd have smacked heads. Jamie squeezed his thighs against his leg. "I am not prudish."

Jamie's strong grip, his steady stare, the heat radiating from him where he pressed against Theo's thigh, the sudden and soft swipe of this thumb over the hairs of Theo's forearm… the deep shiver was difficult to quash.

Theo felt his breath bounce off Jamie's stubble and fan back over his lips. "Prove it then. Come along tomorrow."

"You're impossible."

Jamie let go of his arm and Theo, a little disoriented, pushed to his feet. He blinked at Jamie once, twice before shaking it off. "Is that a yes?"

"Leone is going?"

"Oh, she'll come."

Jamie looked down at his watch. He stood and moved to his door. It was already half open, but Jamie widened it and gestured Theo to come.

Theo followed him onto the balcony outside his room. "So you'll come, then?"

"I shouldn't."

Theo liked the sound of that and grinned. "Shouldn't, but will? Because you're my best friend and that's what best friends do?"

Jamie stepped back into the doorway and stared at him. "Your two minutes are up." He shut the door in Theo's face.

WITH RED HAIR CURLING OVER HER SHOULDERS, A SET OF DARK-BLUE eyes, and a smattering of freckles over her nose, Liz was undoubtedly attractive.

She was all smiles when Theo met her at the pizza parlor next door to the skating rink. The place was thriving with customers, and the stone-baked pizzas smelled amazing.

They had thirty minutes to eat before Jamie and Leone arrived for some skating action. They sat in a window booth and ordered one large pizza.

She was easy to chat with, and he liked that she didn't give a shit about stuffing her face with cheesy meat madness. Theo liked her.

He *did*.

Theo leaned an elbow on the table, fist under his jaw, other hand playing with the straw in his Coke. "Did you vote in the last election."

"Do you ask all your dates that question?" she asked, laughing.

Theo smiled. "It's been a while since I've dated, but yes. This is a stock question."

"I guess it would quickly assess our compatibility."

The word *compatibility* made him think of his horoscope. Aries. He shifted in his seat. "Are you stalling, Ms. 'Lizabeth?"

"I voted. You want to know who I voted?"

"No. I just need to know you did."

"My turn."

Theo slurped his Coke and eyed her as she tucked her hair behind her ears.

"What's your favorite book, and please don't let it be *Catcher in the Rye*."

"Why the hell not?" Theo asked.

"Because that will mean you haven't picked up a book of your own accord since high school."

Theo shook his head. "I haven't picked up a book of my own accord since high school."

"You're kidding."

"I'm not." He grinned. "But I do read all the books Leone tells me to. My favorite? Almost anything by Margaret Atwood, but I'm especially a fan of *Oryx and Crake* and *The Year of the Flood*. I am adding this question to my stock. Now fess up, your favorite book is *Anne of Green Gables*, isn't it?"

Liz punched his shoulder. "Just because I have red hair and I like to read?"

"And your strong personality."

"I take it you've read the books then?"

"Blame it on Leone." He'd read them aloud to her after her sight began to worsen.

"I do love the series," Liz said. "But my absolute favorite book is…"

A familiar car pulling into the parking lot stole Theo's attention. It was dark outside save a row of lamps along the path, but enough light pooled over the side of Jamie's car that Theo could see Jamie as he climbed out. He opened the door for Leone and offered his shoulder.

Leone said something to him and grinned. Jamie looked up

toward the skating rink and rubbed the back of his neck with his free hand.

"…because of the character development and romance."

Theo refocused on Liz and nodded. "Nice."

"Have you read it?"

"Can't say I've had the pleasure."

He inclined his head toward the window. "Romeo and Juliet have arrived."

They shuffled out of their booth, dumping their trash in the bins on the way out. Liz thanked him for dinner and called out Leone's name as they hit the sidewalk around the parking lot.

Leone and Jamie halted ten yards away.

Liz raced ahead, warning Leone she was going in for a hug, and Jamie stepped back as Liz's arms flung out. He watched Liz for a few moments as if trying to figure something out. The flashing neon lights may have skewed Theo's perspective, but Theo thought he saw Jamie's jaw twitch.

Surely the guy wasn't that possessive? Especially since he hadn't yet staked his claim.

Theo winked when Jamie peeked over the girls' heads at him. Jamie frowned and looked away.

"I'm amused so far," Liz said. "Let's see how good he can skate."

"I can skate circles around you," Theo said, sauntering past them as he walked toward a guy in a bright orange cap standing outside the skating rink.

Theo bumped fists with Alex and followed him inside. "Thanks for this," Theo said as they moved to a counter with rentable skates, the others trailing behind.

"No problem. Thanks for building my website. Interest in my work has already doubled." Alex ducked behind the counter. "I'm going to get intimate with this overdue essay until you're done." He hooked his thumb toward a double set of doors where Theo knew the rink and surrounding benches were. "Do you have the music you want me to put on for you? I left the lights and the floor is in good shape."

Liz, Leone, and Jamie walked to the counter. Leone smiled

broadly. "Did someone ask about music? AC/DC will make us buck."

"I made us a playlist," Theo said, handing over a USB stick.

Alex took it and set it on the counter. "Sweet. What sizes are you?"

After they were handed a pair of skates, kneepads, wrist guards and helmet, Theo beckoned them through the double doors to the rink.

A blast of neon lighting and the sweet scent of popcorn greeted them. Liz sidled down one of the benches at the side of the rink. Theo followed and sat next to her. They toed off their shoes and put on their gear. Jamie and Leone sat at the other end of the bench and did the same.

A minute later, music blared from the speakers, filling the rink with pulse and expectation.

Leone squealed when she heard AC/DC's "Thunderstruck," which also slammed the energy into Theo. Leone enthusiastically yelled to the music, Liz tucked her hair under her helmet looking toward the rink with purpose, and Jamie was still removing his shoes. Slow coach.

Theo rolled toward the rink entrance, almost forgetting to take Liz with him. He grabbed her hand and set off, glancing again at Jamie.

As soon as his wheels hit the smooth wooden floors, he and Liz broke apart and skated in earnest. Theo glided across the spacious floors. The second time he hit the oval curve, when Van Halen's "Jump" came on, he hopped around and skated backward.

He stopped with a confident thrust in front of the benches where Leone was still waiting on Jamie who was watching Theo instead of lacing up his skates.

"I know, right?" Theo said. "I can really move." He moved off the rink to his sister. "One round with me while Jamie figures out how to tie his laces?"

Jamie leveled him with a look that promised to make Theo pay for that.

Leone accepted Theo's hand, and he skated with her, slower this time.

"We haven't done this in ages. I forgot how much of a rush it is. How's Liz?"

Liz was confident on the rink. She didn't know how to skate backward and had slowed to watch him as he had shown off, but she was more than steady on her feet.

He looked across the rink at Liz elegantly cutting a corner. "Liz is great," Theo said.

And yet…

"She passed your stock-exam, then?" his sister asked.

"Very funny. But, yes, she passed."

"That sounded unsure."

He agreed, but he could not pinpoint why.

"Can I ask a question?" Leone said. "Are you still comparing everyone you meet to Sam?"

Theo slowed. He hadn't once thought about Sam tonight. "No, I… no."

Leone smiled. "Maybe you'll end up dancing with your date and not caring about their wedding after all."

Liz skated by, flashing him a smile. He forced one back, swallowing hard as he said to Leone, "I guess. You'll be lucky too. Trust me, I'm working on it." Theo squeezed her hand as they rounded a curve. "Now let me deliver you to Jamie and get back to my date."

He almost came to a halt as he caught sight of Jamie at the edge of the rink.

"We're gliding to a stop now," he told Leone, fighting the urge to laugh so he didn't knock them off balance.

Jamie's jeans were tucked into his skates. He wore the kneepads, wrist guards, and helmet. But it was the way he pressed his lips in a flat, determined line as he stared at the shiny wooden floors, white-knuckling the rail that curved around the rink wall that got Theo.

Theo tossed up a laugh-groan. "You don't know how to skate, do you?"

Jamie responded tightly. "I'm sure it can't be too hard."

"I wondered if that was why you didn't want to come."

"It was *a* reason, but not *the* reason."

Theo cocked his head. The frustration peeking through the gaps of Jamie's cool made Theo want to crack a smile.

He planned to milk the moment. Bathe in its rarity. "So this is Mr. Jamie Cooper at a loss."

"Gloating does not look good on you," he said. Then amended tightly. "At least it doesn't get me on the rink."

Jamie step-rolled onto the wooden floor, buckling in half as he tried to balance. He braced himself with a palm to the floor.

Theo chuckled. He led an amused Leone to the wall and moved in front of Jamie, who had pushed himself upright but was bent awkwardly at the knees like he was on a surfboard.

Theo grabbed his forearms, shifting his wheels to share his balance.

Liz rolled up to them. "I'm guessing this hiccup wasn't part of your plan, Theo?"

"Plan?" Jamie asked.

No, it wasn't part of his plan. He'd imagined Jamie dominating the rink like he did the badminton court. He'd thought Jamie would be having the time of his life while cozying up to Leone on his arm. "No way am I having Bambi here leading the blind."

Leone pouted. "The night's already over?"

Jamie tried to straighten, but one leg zipped forward and it took all of Theo's poise and strength to correct him before he fell on his ass.

"I can sit out," Jamie offered, and Theo tightened his grip on him.

"I don't want to be a third wheel," Leone said. "Or, wheels, in this case."

"How about Leone and me skate," Liz suggested, "while Theo shows Jamie a few moves? We can switch it up in a bit."

Leone stretched out an arm and waited for Liz to take her hand, and with that settled, the girls were off.

"I suppose I deserve that smirk," Jamie said.

Theo slid his fingers down Jamie's arm to clutch his warm hand. Jamie gripped him like a lifesaver, wrist guards tapping together.

Theo pulled Jamie into the middle of the rink.

"If you tug me more, I'm going to do the splits. I can't guarantee I'm that flexible."

"Stop, please," Theo said on the tail end of a snicker. "Or I'm gonna piss my pants."

"Might make us even on the humiliation scorecard."

Theo enjoyed taking over the role of teacher, showing Jamie how to use the stoppers on his skates and warning him it was easier to keep moving than stay still. "Push one skate out and lean with the force, then push the other. Make sure your feet move at an angle like this."

Theo circled around slowly for him to watch, then he finished with a cocky little back glide, spinning to a stop an inch from Jamie. "Your turn."

Jamie's gaze slowly swept down him to his skates. "You look… very good at that."

"You look fucking adorable trying not to topple," Theo said, glowing. "Now get moving."

Jamie knocked on his helmet for luck and got moving. It took three Michael Jackson songs, two Prince songs, two Bon Jovi songs —and one spectacular slide on his ass—before Jamie stopped grumbling about how skating ranked up there with his distaste of headless mannequins.

Liz and Leone skated around them with Liz occasionally throwing them a tip. She seemed happy chatting with his sister, which is why Theo encouraged her to keep skating with Leone when she offered to take over guiding Jamie.

Over the last few chords of "Beat It," Theo said to Liz and Leone, "He's not a lost cause. It'll only take a couple more songs."

"A couple," Liz said slowly. "Right."

Jamie tracked Liz as she steered Leone across the floor, holding himself stiffer. He opened his mouth to speak, but Theo had started skating backward, beckoning Jamie to follow.

"I can guarantee after these songs," Theo said, "you'll be semi-proficient at skating."

"My not-bruised ass cheek fears otherwise."

"Tell it to trust me."

Jamie shook his head. "What's the game?"

"Tag me by the end of the next song and I'll cook us dinner

tomorrow night. Like, peeling potatoes, boiling, and mashing them. Without anyone's help."

That caught Jamie's attention. He increased his speed and focus. Theo skated out of his reach, forcing him to try harder.

"What if I manage it by the end of whatever this is that's playing?"

"Let's keep it real."

"Let's say I do, what do I get then?"

"What do you want?"

"I don't know yet. A free truth or dare I can use at any time."

"Next you'll be telling me we should play Spin the Bottle."

Jamie toppled forward, correcting himself before he fell.

"Considering your lack of chances," Theo said, "I should warn you. Fail to tag me on this song and I get the free truth or dare. Fail on the second, you scrub those potatoes."

"Like I wouldn't be anyway. Let's do this."

Theo scanned the rink for Liz and Leone to know where he should be extra careful.

Jamie skated steadily toward him. "They're at the benches watching us."

Good. Better, even. "Hope you don't get performance anxiety."

Jamie's eyes became slits as he lunged at him but Theo scooted out of the way.

Jamie changed tactics, keeping a modest pace. "How do you think your date is going?"

"Fine."

"Sure about that? You've been helping me for most of it."

"Liz seems happy chatting with Leone. She's cool."

Jamie's lurch and outstretched arm Theo predicted, not so much his next question, "Do you like her?"

"She's nice."

"Nice? Just nice, Theo?"

Jamie was trying to make him lose his concentration. It slowed him down a fraction, but Jamie would have to work harder than that.

"I asked her a bunch of compatibility questions over dinner."

"Do you do that with all your dates?"

Another swipe too far to the left.

Theo grinned. "And prospective friends."

That piqued Jamie's interest. "What are the questions?"

"Why, do you want to play?"

"I'm already your friend, according to one particular paper cup. The questions can't apply to me."

"They do, but asking would be like double-checking sheep have wool."

"You know there are breeds of sheep that grow hair, right?"

"Fine. I see what you are saying. Have you ever voted?"

"Yes."

"See, I knew that."

"How did you know that?"

"Because I respect you too much for you not to have voted."

Jamie's glide slowed for a moment before he picked up his pace again. "Next question."

"Really, Mr. Jamie Cooper, there's no point."

Theo knew Jamie grew up with a sister, and their dog passed away the day after his sixteenth birthday, which was the reason he cancelled his party at the last minute. He knew Jamie's dream job would be working as an economics journalist doing podcasts such as *Freakonomics* but wouldn't mind becoming an economics professor. He knew Jamie kicked ass on the badminton court and liked hiking but not running, and was more of a drama-comedy television person than an action movie guy.

He knew Jamie liked music but barring a select few could never remember the titles or artists. If Jamie could only eat one thing for the rest of his life it would be salad sandwiches. Theo knew Jamie's fake pet peeve was when Theo propped his feet up. Jamie loved to drink coffee when he was out and in the morning but fruity teas at home. Theo knew Jamie grew up next door to Sean and they were still best friends.

"What's that look for?" Jamie asked, almost tagging him this time.

The first song began fading out.

Theo anticipated Jamie's last-ditch attempt at grabbing him, scowl morphing to a grin. "That's a free truth-or-dare card for me. How much do you want to see me sweat potatoes?"

Blondie's "One Way or Another" played, and Theo laughed at the way Jamie embodied the song, skating faster and lunging in time to its beat. His intense gaze screamed how much he wanted to tag him.

Theo curled his finger, taunting him. "Come on. Show me what you're made of."

Another ill-timed lunge, but Jamie cleanly readjusted.

"Gonna have to come at me harder than that."

Jamie pushed toward him, gliding on his skates.

"Faster."

Jamie thrust forward and this time it was close. Theo jerked in response. "Yeah, that's what I'm talking about. Again."

Jamie came at him, harder and faster until he was grunting with the effort. Theo felt it too, in his tight limbs and shaky breath.

The song was winding up to its fiery end.

Jamie might not have tagged him, but look at him skate, so smooth and confident, turning corners with the right amount of thrust.

"Theo!" Jamie called out.

Theo stopped skating at his name and Jamie tackled him, body crashing against his. They collapsed to the floor, the wind escaping Theo's lungs. Jamie lay on top of him chest to chest, with Jamie's thigh close to Theo's crotch and Jamie's hands either side of his head.

They were nose to nose, helmets almost touching. "You must really want to see me peel potatoes." Theo scanned Jamie's face, lingering on his mouth, searching for a hint of a smile. "You called out my name." His voice caught and he cleared his throat, wishing his heart would stop beating quite so fast.

"It got me what I wanted."

"I can't promise dinner will taste any good."

"I bet it tastes amazing."

"Amazing enough to get you on your knees and sing my praises?"

Jamie's expression shuttered and he pushed up on his arms.

Theo wasn't ready for him to get up, though. His hands shot up, one balling Jamie's T-shirt and the other covering his mouth, the hard shell of his wrist guard against the stubble at his cheek.

Jamie stilled, gray eyes meeting his, imploring.

"This. I want more of this."

Then, muffled, "What do you mean?"

"This is why I wanted you here tonight. You've been acting off all week, but tonight is the first time you seem yourself again."

Jamie seemed to search Theo's face for something. Sincerity, maybe? If so, he'd find it.

Theo pressed his fingers against Jamie's lips. "You haven't smiled yet, though. I'm going to need you to do that."

The answer came hot on his fingers as Theo felt Jamie's lips twitch. He couldn't see the smile under his hand, but it was there in the sudden deepening of Jamie's eyes, the slight crinkle at their edges, the stray lash on his cheekbone lifting.

"A+, Mr. Jamie Cooper."

Jamie shifted, and that marginal shift against his crotch had Theo releasing Jamie. "You'd better get off me or Liz will get jealous, if you know what I mean."

Jamie pushed to his skates and steadied himself with his stopper. It took a few deep breaths before Theo did the same.

Out the corner of his eye, Theo saw Liz gliding over the rink toward them. "Liz," he said, punching her name with cheer. "Shall we make a few rounds? Jamie, check on Leone, yeah? You should be good enough to skate a slow length with her."

Jamie skated over to the benches and didn't look back.

Theo snagged Liz's hand and held it especially tight, as though it would stop the tremble of his body.

It had just been a while since he'd been laid, was all.

Anything rubbing up against him like that would have triggered the same response.

They made one round without speaking. On the second, when a new song started, he smiled at her. "I put this song on for you."

She scrunched up her face as she listened. "You want money?"

"This is by the Flying Lizards."

A small smile lit her face. "Cute, Theo."

They skated another song before Liz stopped in the middle of the rink in the same spot Jamie had landed on him. Liz smiled up at him, quick and pitiful. Theo braced for bad news. "Look, I had fun tonight."

He laughed. "But . . ." he prompted, knowing it was coming.

"But I don't think we should go out again."

There it was. He sucked in a breath, his pride hurt. Liz glanced at Leone and Jamie, bit her lip, and shrugged. "You don't seem into me and I want someone that is."

Theo stuffed his hands into his pockets. "This was my first real date in a while. Guess I'm rusty."

"You're better at it than you think. Just…" She gestured between them. "I don't think it should be us dating."

Theo didn't know what to say. The spark that should have been there was missing despite the fact he genuinely liked her. "I hope you find that perfect someone. You're pretty great."

Liz lifted onto her stoppers and kissed his cheek. "Right back at you, Theo."

"Be a good idea to dry your hair and put on another layer. It's cold out."

Jamie to Theo on one fucking cold day.

Chapter Ten

A week after a potato-and-mince mash-up with rubbery eggplant that Leone spat out and Jamie chowed through, Theo caught a cold.

It was his own fault. He should have listened to Jamie when he suggested Theo dry his hair and wear another layer before going outside the day before yesterday. But Theo'd been in an obstinate mood and stalked off through the cold, pretending not to feel it.

Now he felt it—runny nose, sore throat, and a cough that threatened to give him away.

He lay on the couch hiding behind the final chapter of his econ book. Leone sat on the armchair next to him, listening to an audiobook on her headphones, while Jamie chopped and tossed fuckloads of vegetables into a large pot.

Theo smuggled another tissue behind his book and discreetly pinched his nose with it. God, his body ached. Was it him or was it freaking cold in here?

He tugged the throw blanket off the back of the couch and draped it over his shivering body. Nothing conspicuous about that. They all used that blanket from time to time.

He rested the book on his face, welcoming the darkness and pressure against his forehead.

He heard Jamie pause his cutting. Jamie's phone chimed with the "*Freakonomics*" theme song.

Whenever Theo heard that ringtone, he started humming or tapping out the tune until Jamie joined in. But tonight he wanted to cover his ears and make it stop.

Jamie answered the call, his deep voice infinitely more soothing than the ringtone. *Damn this headache.*

"Sean, how are you? I'll be home next week as planned...I'm making soup..."

Theo's mouth watered, and a moan slipped out of him—but at least it wasn't that throat-itching cough.

"Can I call you back?" Jamie said down the line. "I've got to wrangle a stubborn someone into his bed."

Theo stilled, then slowly pulled the book down his face. He looked over at Jamie, who was staring right at him as he hung up the phone.

"How much longer were you going to lie there suffering?" Jamie asked.

Theo wanted to talk back, to have that last word he so often sought. Instead, a chest-rattling cough barked into the room. His sister jumped.

She pulled her headphones off. "Damn, Theo, are you okay?"

No, no, and more no.

"He'll be fine," Jamie said to Leone, as he grabbed a bowl and ladled soup into it. Calmly but firmly he said, "Theo, bed. I'll bring this to you."

For once, Theo did as he was told. He even murmured thanks as Jamie tiptoed into his room with a bowl of soup, a bottle of water, and a few Tylenol on a tray.

"You're going to say 'I told you so' aren't you?" Theo's throat sounded pathetic mincing up his words.

"I did tell you so."

Theo aimed for a smirk that might've been a grimace. "You always being right is a pain in my ass."

Jamie dropped his folded arms and stuffed his hands into the pockets of his jeans. He stared down at Theo, a concerned crease between his brows. "Eat your soup and get some sleep."

"Lucky you made soup tonight, huh?" Theo said dipping his spoon into the broth.

Jamie retreated from the room, but not without Theo catching his last words. "Luck had nothing to do with it."

～

"Can I sit here with you?"

Late Tuesday afternoon after three days of self-induced quarantine, Theo dragged himself out of bed. He'd shaved, showered, and dressed in the clean clothes Leone had folded and Jamie had brought him. His sister was having coffee with a friend.

Theo heard Jamie return home and sneak up to his room. Now that he was fresh-faced, Theo decided to head upstairs too. He was bored and he wanted to ask how Jamie's meeting with his advisor went, but one question had been flirting in and out of Theo's mind: Why did Jamie want the truth-or-dare card? What did Jamie want him to admit or do that he couldn't just ask for?

Jamie swiveled on his bedroom desk chair, taking Theo in at his doorway and gesturing to the corner armchair. "Sit? Sure."

Theo bypassed the armchair and threw himself lengthwise on Jamie's plum-and-brown blanketed bed. He wadded a soft cotton pillow under his head and smiled as he took in the newest addition to Jamie's room: three framed prints of *The Emperor's New Clothes*.

Jamie's belongings looked like they were here to stay a while, and Theo liked it.

A small cough escaped him and he sniffed. He expected Jamie to be too engrossed in whatever he was doing to notice or care, but Jamie stopped typing, passed him a box of tissues from the side of his desk, and brought the wastebasket over to the bed.

Theo gripped the box of tissues as Jamie bent over him and planted his palm over his forehead.

"I'm feeling better," Theo said, looking up at a tired-looking Jamie. "I'm just bored."

Jamie hummed. He hurriedly lifted his hand, as if realizing he didn't need to feel his temperature anymore.

Theo's gaze followed Jamie as he moved back to his desk and sat down. He sat there staring blankly at his laptop screen, then peeked at Theo out of the corner of his eyes. He shut his laptop and swiveled toward the bookshelves.

When he turned back around, he was holding a compendium of games.

"Checkers? Chess? Ludo?" Jamie asked.

Theo sat up and leaned against the headboard. He eyed the box, and then eyed Jamie climbing onto the middle of the bed with it.

"There's a deck of cards too," Theo said. "I vote snap."

They split the deck and flipped the cards onto a pile, using the chessboard for a flat surface.

Theo had a habit of speaking first and thinking later. He wished he could call upon the skill today, but for whatever reason, Theo was nervous to ask about truth or dare.

Just a *little*.

Down his king went on Jamie's jack, ten on five, eight on queen.

He sucked in a breath and let it go, saying instead, "I like the prints."

"I want to get a couple more pictures for that wall," Jamie said, nicking his head in the direction of the wall behind Theo.

"Same style?"

"Doesn't have to be."

Theo had a few sketches lying around that would look good above the bed. "Your birthday is coming up soon."

Jamie stopped flipping, thumb resting on the deck of cards. "Twenty-second of March. Shall I keep the wall free?"

"You could at least pretend you had no idea where I was going with that."

"Looking forward to it."

They resumed the game, still no pair in sight.

Eventually it would come though. It had to.

"Spring break is around the corner," Theo said on a second fail to ask the question that had his thoughts spinning at night. "You still up for taking us home?"

"Of course."

Theo slapped the pair of aces and Jamie's hand naturally landed over his own with a solid, warm thump. Theo wiggled his fingers under his palm. "Why do I get such a thrill beating you?"

He drew his hand out from under Jamie's but Jamie tightened his grip. "How about a game you won't win?"

"You're goading me."

"Up for the challenge?"

This challenge, yes. Not the truth-or-dare one, though. Not yet.

Theo watched as Jamie lifted his hand and readjusted his grip so their fingers hooked tightly in a monkey grip. "Are you declaring a thumb war?"

Jamie's gaze sparked.

"You're on," Theo said. He proceeded to utter the initiating rhyme as their thumbs passed over each other in time to the words. "…five, six, seven, eight, try to keep your thumb straight."

Jamie's thumb lunged to pin Theo's. "Hold on. First we bow and kiss before we wrestle."

Jamie looked at him sharply and Theo caught the jut of his Adam's apple as he swallowed.

Theo grinned. "Why yes, Mr. Jamie Cooper, I'm good at this game too."

He bowed his thumb and waited for Jamie to follow. The pads of their thumbs pressed together in a pre-war kiss. Jamie's light touch tickled, and a ripple of goosebumps blossomed on his arm.

The kiss was fleeting though. As soon as Jamie withdrew, the fight was on. They were well-matched but Jamie, damn him, was better. No matter how much Theo twisted his mouth and begged his thumb to overwhelm Jamie's, Jamie was stronger, faster, better. Theo tried playing possum, but it was to no avail. Jamie won every time.

Finally feeling defeated—by the game and his question—Theo dropped his hand and slouched against the headboard. Jamie would say he was pouting, and he might be right. "Your hand is larger. So."

"Fractionally. You had speed on your side, you just weren't quick enough."

"I'm still sick," Theo said, forcing a cough. "Otherwise I would have owned you."

"Give it up, Theo. Let me have this."

Theo stretched out the moment before sliding his foot across the bed and bumping Jamie's knee. "Fine. You won fair and square. You are the master. I'll bow before you forever and always."

"Now that's settled, how do you feel about a trip to the supermarket?"

$\sim$

THEO WAS PUTTING AWAY THEIR CRAZY AMOUNT OF GREEN LEAFY things in the fridge. They'd done the weekly shopping because Jamie wanted to hit the badminton court on Saturday morning with some fellow post-grads.

He didn't even suggest Theo come along.

Not that Theo wanted to subject himself to any more embarrassment on the court. But still.

Leone, back from her coffee, had snagged Jamie into conversation. She was waving her hands about as she spoke, twice clipping Jamie on the chin.

Theo continued unpacking, coming to a halt when he pulled out a peanut butter jar from the paper bag. Smooth.

He narrowed his eyes. Cheeky bastard! This meant war.

Theo searched the cupboards for salted peanuts. He opened the jar, dug out some of the spread, and stirred peanuts into it. He capped the jar and placed it innocently on the condiment shelf.

Take that, Mr. Jamie Cooper.

$\sim$

"I KNOW I'M TALKING DUMB," JAMIE SAID, "BUT I HAVE TO FOR YOU to understand me."

Theo threw the dishtowel in his face. "Some days I wish your mother had sent you back and kept the bird that brought you."

"The stork, Theo. And some days I think I should leave you to Darwin."

Theo tugged at the belt of the cooking apron that Jamie had tied between the belt loops of their jeans. "Did you have to make this leash so short?"

"Yes."

Theo growled and stared at the sliced eggplant on the cutting board in front of them. Jamie had suggested cooking eggplant parmesan for Leone, and since Theo "sorely needed the instruction," Jamie insisted he help.

Theo was beginning to despise the purple vegetable.

Jamie's phone beat out the "*Freakonomics*" theme song and Theo temporarily forgot that he found Jamie infuriating and started slapping the bench to the beat.

Just for Theo, Jamie let it ring a little longer before answering. "Mom. How are you?"

"Hey, Mrs. Cooper," Theo called. "Tell your son to release me from this prison."

Jamie snorted and pointed for him to finish cutting the other eggplant.

"I wouldn't have to keep him chained up if he didn't always slink to the bathroom in an ill attempt to avoid cooking."

"I'm still ill," Theo said and fake-coughed into the crook of his arm.

"Then you won't want dessert," Jamie said.

"There's dessert? Know what? I'm starting to feel better."

To his mom, Jamie said, "Yep, pretty much like always…uh huh…don't ask, I don't know."

"Wait, what?" Theo interrupted. "There's something you *don't* know."

Jamie cupped the back of Theo's neck and gave an exasperated squeeze.

Theo spun up against Jamie and angled the phone, grinning as he said to Mrs. Cooper, "You should have kept the stork."

Leone walked into the living room and plunked herself on the armchair, where she pushed her sunglasses onto her head and pinched her nose.

"I'll call you back, Mom."

Jamie hung up as Theo asked, "You okay, sis?"

"Fine. I just"—she pulled out an envelope from under her arm and set it on the coffee table—"bumped into Derek. He said our invitations should be coming any day. That day's today."

Theo picked at the knot tying him and Jamie together, and this time Jamie let him. When he was free, he walked over to Leone and sat on the arm of her chair. The envelope was cream, embossed in gold. He picked it up.

It was their invite, all right.

"You know," Theo said. "We can always change our minds and not go."

"And wimp out? Hell no. We are going, and we are going with dates."

Too curious for his own good, Jamie asked, "Dates?"

"Yes," Leone said boldly. "You will be one of them."

Not quite the romantic lead-in Theo thought Leone would use, but it was direct and to the point. He liked it.

"Hope you can dance better than you can skate," Theo said to him. "We need to show everyone that we don't care about Derek and Sam anymore."

"Will a waltz be enough?"

"What other dances do you know?"

"Settled then. I'll go with you."

Leone giggled.

"What?" Theo asked.

"Nothing. It's just… never mind. You'll need a nice dinner jacket, Jamie. You too, Theo."

"We'll cross that bridge closer to the event."

Leone leaned into the chair, her ponytail hanging over the back. "I'm hungry."

Jamie looked pointedly at Theo as he rolled a lettuce onto his board. "Dinner is half ready."

Theo grinned back at him as he, once more, slunk toward the bathroom. "Nature calls."

"Economics has never been so fun!"

Theo to the world, because for five minutes it was actually true.

Chapter Eleven

"Theo, come here for a sec?"

Theo strolled into the kitchen, arms overhead in a morning stretch. The aroma of coffee and toasted bread made his stomach rumble.

"What is this?" Jamie asked, and that's when Theo saw it. Two pieces of buttered toast sat on a black plate next to an open jar of peanut butter. Pointed at Theo was a butter knife covered with chunky spread.

Theo stopped an inch from the knife, lifted his hand, and used his index finger to scoop off half the peanut butter.

"This is delicious." He licked it off dramatically with a hearty *mmmm*.

Jamie blinked slowly, then shook his head.

Theo grinned and took the last chunk off the knife. "Either point that somewhere else, or fill it up with more of this goodness."

Jamie set the knife between his two slices of toast. "That's two rounds you've beat me in the peanut butter department," he said. "There won't be a third."

Theo looked at the peanut butter on his finger. "I don't think there should be a third, either. You should give in and learn to love the chunk."

And then, acting on impulse, Theo closed the last foot between them and brought his peanut butter finger against Jamie's lips.

To his surprise, Jamie's mouth parted, and Theo pressed his advantage, sliding his sticky finger along Jamie's bottom lip.

Breath trickled down to the balls of his fingers. He started to withdraw his hand, but Jamie snatched his wrist and held him in place. Their gazes clashed, Jamie's so dark and intent that Theo felt a shiver in his toes.

Wet warmth clamped around Theo's finger as Jamie sucked off the peanut butter. Teeth grazed over his skin before Jamie pulled off with a smack of his lips.

Theo stared, rooted to the spot. "You licked my finger."

"No, I sucked your finger. Still want to force feed me chunky peanut butter?"

Theo didn't answer. Instead he twisted and leaned back against the counter like he had to catch his breath. "You know what, Jamie? That was round three. You won it."

Jamie laughed, found some jam in the fridge, and made his breakfast like nothing had happened.

Nothing *had* happened.

This was what best friends did, although Theo had never been lucky enough to experience this level of tightness he'd yearned for.

He stared at Jamie's fingers as he picked up his toast and took a bite.

Catching him watching, Jamie said, "Do you want this?"

"Yeah," Theo said, plucking the second slice from the plate, but he wasn't talking about the toast. "I do."

THEY GOT UP AT AN INSANE HOUR FOR THE DRIVE TO MINNEAPOLIS.

Five-thirty belonged to overfed roosters and grazing cows not sleep-crusted, yawning Leos.

Still, he let Jamie cajole him out of bed and stumbled into the car.

Leone, curse her, was all cheer and optimism, chatting with Jamie as they drove out of Pittsburgh.

Theo didn't care to join in with that level of animation and closed his eyes. His sister's laugh, the vibration of the car, and

Jamie's voice rumbled through his seat and lulled him back to sleep.

They stopped at the first picnic area they came across after Theo ripped into the cheese crackers. Jamie ordered him and his mess out of the car. Theo laughed. Whatever. It felt great to step out and stretch. They ate crackers and salad sandwiches Jamie woke up extra early to make.

Jamie was still happy to drive, and they continued for a few hours singing to sappy 80s' songs and debating the economic merits of music.

As the sun sank lower on the horizon and they stopped for gas, Jamie didn't climb back into the driver's seat. He came to the passenger door and opened it.

"You can drive, right?"

Theo clicked open his belt. "Are you kidding? I love to drive."

He didn't own a car because he needed the money for his tuition, but he was into driving.

Theo climbed into the driver's seat. Almost the same height as Jamie, there was no need to adjust the seat or mirrors. Theo settled into the warmed seat, gripped the gears, and took off with a decorative burst of speed.

The navigation bleated directions at him but Theo knew this route. They had another five hours before they hit home.

Jamie yawned, murmured something about waking him up if Theo needed anything, and nodded off, chin dropping to his chest. Usually it took a while for Theo to let himself relax like that when someone else was driving. It was a nice feeling knowing Jamie trusted him enough to sink into a slumber so quickly.

Theo chatted softly with Leone for an hour until she succumbed to the motion and slept too. He kept his driving as smooth as possible, wanting Jamie and Leone to get as much shut-eye as they could.

Theo peeked over at Jamie. He looked younger, almost vulnerable, with his head lolling about in the passenger seat. Theo gripped the wheel as protectiveness flooded through him and he slowed down to the speed limit.

Slowing down gave him time to muse over that damn truth-or-dare card he held, and more recently, the sense memory of Jamie sucking his finger, which in turn made him think back to that moment on the skating rink floor…

Theo started counting state license plates. Then how many McDonalds signs he passed.

Jamie and Leone were still sleeping when Wisconsin greeted them with sleet.

The windshield wipers worked overtime as the car ploughed through deep puddles. Theo hoped the sky would hurry and get over it, but the rain worsened to a downpour.

They were still hours away from Minneapolis, and it was getting dark.

"Jamie?"

Jamie stirred. "Hmm?"

"I don't think this rain is letting up any time soon."

Jamie rubbed his eyes with the heels of his hands, stared out of the car and whistled. He picked up his phone that doubled as their navigation. "Take the next exit. We're turning back."

Theo didn't ask, just followed directions and took the next off ramp.

Jamie placed the phone at his ear and a few moments later, smiled. "Hey, Mom. Slight change of plans. I'm coming home tonight and bringing Theo and Leone. Yeah, that would be great. We're twenty-odd minutes off. See you soon."

Theo leaned back in the seat, stretching his arms against the wheel. "Makes the most sense."

"I think so," Jamie said. "Take the second exit at the round-about. I'll drive you up tomorrow."

"Your mom won't mind the last-minute change of plans?"

"Mom's easygoing. My sister doesn't get back until tomorrow, her room is free."

"Brilliant." Theo happily drummed his fingers on the wheel. "I don't know why we didn't think of this to begin with. I can't wait to see how Mr. Jamie Cooper grew up."

"You just want to raid my photo album and give me shit for the rest of the year."

On the one hand, that was *exactly* what Theo wanted.

On the other… "I won't though. Not unless you show me the pics yourself."

Theo felt Jamie's stare and bit his bottom lip. Then got fidgety and played with the radio until NPR came on.

"I don't mind," Jamie said and shrugged. "There are photos all over the house anyway. Besides, that'll give me license when I drop you off at your place."

"Jesus Mom will have told you everything you could ever want to know and more within the first five minutes you walk in the door."

Leone yawned in the backseat. "Are we in a car wash?"

"I wish." Theo gave her a weather update. "We should call Mom and tell her."

"Onto it," she said, and a few moments later she had the phone on speaker.

"Leone, I'm so glad to hear from you," Mom said. "I was just debating whether I should call and check how you're doing. I saw on the news the rain is torrential in many parts of Wisconsin and coupled with my horoscope today, well, I was starting to panic. Your father told me to relax and take a bath, but I didn't have any lavender bath salts left and those are the only ones that work with my nerves."

"Hey, Mom," Theo said loud enough for the phone to pick up.

Leone continued, "We're all safe, but you're right about the weather. We won't make it home tonight."

"This would be the change in plans that might happen today. I'm to see it for its silver lining—and of course I want my Leos safe. Take whatever time you need. Just tell me where you'll stay."

Jamie answered that, not only giving her their address but their landline phone number as well. "We'll call you after breakfast before we hit the road again."

"I hope you can relax now, Mommy," Leone said.

"I think I'll be fine, darlings. Thank you for calling me right away. Oh, and before you go, I was reading the single Leos' horoscope today and thought you might find this interesting—"

"Bye, Mom," Theo called out, hoping Leone would take the hint and end the call.

She didn't.

"Even though today might not be going perfectly, you're finding many things that keep a grin on your face. Feelings that need to be expressed are slowly bubbling to the surface, and since you are single, now might be a good time to catch someone's eye——"

Theo switched on the radio and turned up the volume, drowning out his mom's horoscope. He glanced over at Jamie who was quietly watching him. "What? I'm not being any ruder than I usually am with Mommy dearest."

"I wasn't thinking that," Jamie said, turning down the volume. Leone had switched off the loudspeaker and had the phone pressed to her ear.

"What are you thinking then?"

Jamie pointed for Theo to take the next right. The way he took his time answering, suggested it wasn't his original thought. "She really is something, your mom."

"She loves us Leos to bits." He suspected it would not take long before she loved this Aries as well.

THEY PASSED WOODS, PADDOCKS, AND A FREAKING STABLE BEFORE arriving at Jamie's home. The rain had slowed, but they still ended up dripping water inside the old Victorian farmhouse.

"You'll be sharing Jamie's room, I suppose?" Mrs. Cooper said after welcoming them in.

She was much shorter than Theo had expected, coming up to his chin, but it was clear the moment she looked at him where Jamie had inherited his gray eyes. She also had his sandy hair only hers was streaked white at the temples. Jamie's height and broadness must have come from his father's side of the family.

"Thanks, Mrs. Cooper," Theo said, hooking an arm around his sister. "But I'd rather stay with Leone. It's a new place and that way I can support her more easily."

He quelled a couple of prickly little questions and gave his sister a squeeze.

Mrs. Cooper spoke to Jamie. "I've made up yours and Danielle's bed. Show your friends where they can put their things." She smiled at Theo and Leone, gaze flickering curiously between them. "Get familiar with the place and then come and chat with me in the kitchen."

She left them to it.

Jamie led them upstairs to the bedrooms. "There are twenty carpeted steps," he said for Leone's benefit. "The first door on the left of the hall is the bathroom, the second, the utilities cupboard. Continue and the third door is my dad's office. The first door on the right and almost directly opposite the bathroom is Danielle's room, where you'll be sleeping tonight. My room is the one after that. There are a bunch of family pictures hanging on the walls but the hall is otherwise empty."

Theo and Leone followed Jamie into Danielle's room. The large modern-meets-Victorian room featured a mauve theme. The space was simple enough that Leone would not have trouble navigating it, and the bed looked like it would hold the two of them.

Jamie took Leone by the hand and talked her through the room, making her feel the edges of desks, drawers, night tables, and light switches.

Theo leaned against the bedroom door as he watched Jamie tell Leone everything she needed to know and nothing more. No patronization or unintentional belittling. Simply kindness and respect.

He should be nothing but happy then.

He shifted uneasily and Jamie looked over.

"I'm gonna grab our bags and bring them up," he said, pivoting on his heel and hurrying outside.

Rain drizzled over his face and down his neck. He welcomed it a few minutes longer than warranted before hauling their suitcases back up to Danielle's room. He set their belongings in the closet and told them he was going to chat with Jamie's mom.

Mrs. Cooper greeted him with freshly baked goodness, and Theo fell in love.

"These cookies are delicious," he said, plopping down onto the free space on the bench.

While this was his first time in Jamie's home, he already felt like he knew the family. Mrs. Cooper, librarian of the local library, Mr. Cooper, principal of an elite private school, Danielle, in her senior year of high school. All three badminton addicts.

Jamie had told him heaps of stories already.

"I've heard a lot about you," Mrs. Cooper said, icing more cookies. "Jamie thinks you're quite something."

"You're not just saying that because moms say that type of thing, are you?"

She laughed. "No. I mean it. Jamie's always been solid and dependable, but it's so nice to hear the smile in his voice now."

Theo spotted Jamie guiding Leone past the kitchen. "That'd be the romance."

"My thoughts exactly," she said. "It's beautiful."

Flashing his dimples at Mrs. Cooper, Theo helped himself to a second cookie.

"This place feels homey," he said around a mouthful. "I like it." He swallowed. "I can see myself coming here more often. Days of lounging about on that thick carpet in the living room, deeply fascinated by the backyard the moment chopping onions is required. You're not going to need help with that, are you? Because, remember, I like you."

She gave Theo an amused look, that same splash of sparkle in her eye that her son got. It made Theo wonder more about how Jamie had grown up. How he and his mom might have shared their quiet looks over busy Thanksgiving dinners or in the audience at his sister's recitals. It was a warm insight into their history and he couldn't help but extrapolate how the traits might pass on to a future Cooper family.

"What about peeling potatoes?" Mrs. Cooper asked.

"Peeling potatoes? Chilling way to break a man's daydream, Mrs. Cooper."

"Penny, call me Penny."

"Tell me, Penny," Theo said, sliding off the bench and beelining for the photos stuck to the fridge, "is this Jamie?"

"That's my boy."

"Not quite as intimidating without his front teeth, is he?"

Behind them came a snort, and Theo turned to Jamie who strolled into the kitchen and snagged an apple from the fruit bowl.

"Is Theo always like this?" Mrs. Cooper asked her son.

Jamie looked at him as he polished his apple on his T-shirt and took a bite. "Yes."

"I like him." She smacked Theo's hand lightly as he tried for a third cookie. "How about some dinner first?"

"So that's where Jamie gets it from. He's always harping about eating properly." Theo startled Mrs. Cooper by pulling her into a hug and whispering in her ear, "Don't tell him or I'll never hear the end of it, but it's kinda cute he cares." He turned to Jamie, who looked like he was trying to figure out what Theo had said. Theo waggled his brow at him. "Where's Leone?"

"In Danielle's room taking the time to get used to it. I said I'd come back in ten minutes."

Theo nodded. Leone didn't like anyone watching her fumble around as she took the time to figure out her new surroundings.

"I'm about to start dinner," Mrs. Cooper said. "Got some onions to chop."

That was Theo's cue. "Jamie, can you point me to the backyard?"

Mrs. Cooper laughed, then caught Jamie's eye. "By the way, Sean rang."

Theo stopped his sly mission out of the kitchen. It wasn't his business, but he needed to hear this.

"What'd he want?" Jamie asked, his grin growing when he looked at Theo.

"He wanted to know what time you arrived tomorrow. I told him you three were coming here for the night. Then the usual happened."

The usual?

"He invited himself over for dinner," Jamie explained to Theo.

"He'll be here any minute."

Jamie moved to the kitchen windows and peered outside. Theo looked too, but all he saw were lantern lights and the silhouettes of trees against a dark sky.

"If you plan on meeting him, would you mind checking the rain cover on Ducky?"

Theo followed Jamie to the back door.

He toed into a pair of galoshes that Jamie pushed his way and stepped outside. Lawn stretched either side of a brick path with various bushes lining the fences. There was barely any rain now, but the air felt wet and clung to the back of his neck.

"Why would Sean come through your backyard?" Theo asked, hooking his hands under his armpits to fight off the cold.

"You are not going to like the answer."

Theo almost stopped, almost. Instead, he pushed on, keeping pace with Jamie. "Don't tell me he lives in a back shed or something."

Jamie laughed and slowed down. "No. Look, I didn't mention this, because I didn't want to make you feel uncomfortable, but our property backs onto a lake."

Theo stopped. His throat tightened and his heart pumped faster. He tried to shake it off. It wasn't like he was in the lake or anything. He wasn't even over the water or next to the water, for crying out loud. He needed to suck it up and take this in stride.

He tried for a smile but it felt tight. "A lake, eh?"

They were standing under a lantern, and its soft light spilled over the side of Jamie's face.

Jamie, already standing close, inched closer. With one hand, he clasped the curve between Theo's shoulder and neck, and with the other, he lifted Theo's chin. "You don't have to come on the jetty, but if you decide to, I am right here and I won't let anything happen to you."

"You're a good swimmer?" He hated that he trembled. Hated that Jamie saw this weak part of him. Hated that his stomach felt queasy and flashes of that day filled his mind.

"Yes," Jamie said. It wasn't a cocky, aren't-I-the-best yes, but a reassuring one. Theo would be safe.

He tried not to let his fear of water overwhelm him. Of course, he made a point of not being near large bodies of water unless it was necessary. Views of lakes, rivers, and oceans didn't make him weak at the knees so long as he wasn't near them.

Yet standing with Jamie looking at him supportively like that tempted him.

A wolf-whistle sounded and they both turned. Sean was prancing up the path from the tree line, holding a bottle of wine, his curls bouncing with his jovial saunter.

"Hope I'm not interrupting." He pressed the bottle against Theo's chest, turned to Jamie and pulled him into a hug. "Looking good, Hotstuff."

Theo doubled his grip on the neck of the bottle. If Theo thought about it reasonably, he was the one moving in on Sean's friend, not the other way around. Sean should be jealous, not him.

But he wasn't thinking reasonably.

Jamie clapped Sean over the back of the head and laughed. "Mom and Leone are inside. I need to check if Ducky is still afloat."

"Your boat is good. I docked mine next to it." Sean pulled back and plucked his shirt.

Theo caught a whiff of citrusy cologne, different from the last one he wore. A simple deodorant would have been enough, but it was clear Sean was trying to make a point.

Maybe Theo should warn Leone?

Sean started toward the backdoor. "You two get back to whatever you were up to. I'll help Penny with dinner."

Damn him to hell and back.

Theo glared at Jamie. "He brings wine. Helps cook dinner. I have no chance."

Jamie came forward and gently pried the bottle from his hand. "Let's not take it out on the Merlot."

Whatever moment they'd had before passed. Theo didn't care to walk anywhere near the lake now. In fact, Leone was probably waiting for one of them to escort her. He pivoted on his heel and made for the house.

Jamie called hesitantly after him. "What did you mean, you have no chance?"

Theo looked over his shoulder. "Winning Penny over, of course."

∼

AFTER DINNER AND TWO BOTTLES OF WINE, SEAN LEFT WITH THE promise of bringing his tandem bike to Pittsburgh so Jamie or Theo could cycle Leone around the city.

One thoughtful gesture among tens of others, and it left Theo feeling shitty for disliking him.

By Theo's third glass of wine, he decided to forget his childish animosity and give the guy a chance. He and Sean even paired up against Leone and Jamie—Penny helped Leone with her cards—in a game of Taboo.

Four hours later, he and Leone were lying in Danielle's bed playing tug-of-war with the sheets. Latest status update: Theo = cold, Leone = ever the blanket hog.

"Jeez, Theo! Would you go sleep with Jamie already?"

Theo let go of his corner of the blanket and Leone hit her pillow with an *oof*. "What?"

"I said, go sleep with Jamie."

"I heard you, but you sounded serious."

"Because I am," she said. "I'm more likely to trip over you or these tangled sheets. I'm better off alone."

"Really?" Was he more of a hindrance than a help?

Leone's voice softened. "Really, Theo. Also? Your feet are like ice blocks. Torture Jamie on my behalf, would you? He was totally the reason we lost Taboo tonight."

Kicked out, Theo inched down the hallway to Jamie's room. A bright slit of light under Jamie's room door said he was still awake.

Theo knocked.

After a moment, Jamie called out just loud enough for him to hear, "Come in."

Jamie was in bed, knees bent under the covers, a book on his lap. A lamp above the headboard shed soft light over him and gave the room an amber glow. Unlike Danielle's room, Jamie's showcased modern furniture, simple and bulky and a lot of wood.

Two framed posters decorated the wall above his desk. Not music or sports posters, mind you. No, that wouldn't have made Theo grin as much as he was grinning right now.

One teal poster displayed THE COMMA, and one mauve

poster, THE APOSTROPHE. Underneath each was a smartass caption, and Theo approved.

He looked back at Jamie in bed who was patiently waiting for him to explain why he was slinking in here in nothing but his boxer shorts and singlet.

"That's not a textbook," Theo said instead.

"I read other things."

Theo moved from the rug in the middle of the room to the bed. "Leone kicked me out. Can I crash with you?"

Jamie answered by moving more to one side, making space for him.

A half-beat later, Theo was sliding into the cool, fresh sheets of Jamie's bed. "Murakami fan, are you?"

"Among other things. Will the light disturb you?"

"The light won't. The reading will." Theo pried the book away and set it on the side table. He faced Jamie again, lying on his side. "I can think of better things to do."

Jamie groaned and flicked the light switch, drowning the room in darkness. "You drank too much."

"I don't get drunk on three glasses of red! Just slightly buzzed."

Sheets shifted and Jamie spoke, closer than he was before. Theo could make out the darker outline of his face against the light pillow. Jamie was looking at him. "What better things do you have in mind?"

"You know." *Best friend stuff.* "Shoot the shit. Make you squirm."

"Make me squirm?"

Hairs tickled the balls of Theo's toes as he ran his icy feet up Jamie's shins. Jamie's breath hitched.

"Cold?"

"Hot, Theo. Really fucking hot."

Theo loved Jamie's dry sarcasm. "There's plenty more where that came from."

Jamie hooked his legs around Theo's retreating ones. "You want to borrow some socks?"

"No, stealing your heat works for me."

Jamie's toe bumping against his and the tail end of Jamie's breath hovering over his upper lip dizzied Theo.

"There is something I've wanted to ask for a while now," Theo heard himself admitting.

"Ask."

His feet still hugged between Jamie's, Theo rolled onto his back and stared up where a slither of moonlight cut a diamond of light on the ceiling. "That night roller skating..."

"What about it?"

"Why did you want to win a truth-or-dare card?"

Jamie stilled. Theo felt the tension around his feet.

"I'm glad I didn't win it in the end," Jamie said.

"Why'd you ask for it in the first place, then?"

"I wanted to talk to you about your fear of water. I wanted to make sure you answered. Forcing you like that wouldn't have been right. You have to want to tell me, and when you do, I'll be here to listen."

Theo withdrew his feet and pulled his pillow a bit more under his neck.

He stared at the slither of moonlight and then faced Jamie in the dark. "Next time just ask me. I'd tell you anything."

When Jamie didn't say anything else, Theo prompted him. "Aren't you going to ask then?"

"I want you to tell me when you're ready. I'm not going to ask."

"I was eight at summer camp, splashing around in the lake. I was a weedy boy, not much into roughhousing. I didn't know how to hold myself or fight against it. A couple other boys were having fun dunking us, and it went too far. They held me under so I couldn't cough out the water that was choking me. My lungs spasmed and I inhaled even more water and…"

Theo paused, trying to keep his voice from croaking. Talking about it brought it all back, not just that horrible day but the years of teasing afterward when he wouldn't dare step into a pool.

Jamie squeezed Theo's hand. Theo stared at their knotted fingers between the pillows. He had no idea when that had happened. Had he grabbed Jamie or Jamie him?

"I panicked and my vision tunneled. Strange how quickly the fight went out of me. A bone-deep sadness filled me up."

Jamie whispered, sympathetic and comforting. "Theo."

"Next thing I knew, I was lying on the bank and a teenage life guard was freaking out, banging my chest until I was spitting up water. And that was that. I haven't been in anything bigger than a bathtub ever since. Everyone encouraged me to face my fears and learn how to swim. But…"

"You did what was good for you."

"You think I should suck it up and hit the water?"

Jamie shifted. "I think you should do what you feel is best, but it wouldn't stop me from suggesting water-related activities from time to time. You can say no as often as you like and I'll support that. One day, you might decide you want to jump into the deep end. I'll support that, too."

"Did you swim a lot as a kid?"

"Yes. I also worked as a lifeguard at the local camp. I liked swimming, but more than that I loved rowing. I have a little dinghy I'd take across the lake to visit Sean or go into town. Before I got my driver's license, it was how I got to school."

"When did you get your license?"

"End of senior year."

"That's late."

"I loved rowing."

"When you asked me earlier to follow you to the lake, I was… for the first time, in a long time, tempted." Jamie's breathing changed slightly and Theo made out a smile. Theo untangled their fingers and traced that smile. "What's that about?"

"Halfway between proud and smug."

"Not a good look on you."

"I can swing it one way or another, which is your preferred choice?"

"Smug. So I can sock you in the face."

"With what socks?"

They laughed and the mattress quivered under them.

To hell with it. No more musing or waiting around for the right moment. "Truth or dare?" Theo asked. That shut Jamie up for a few moments. "You have to choose dare."

"Dare, then."

A rush of nausea waved through him, followed by a shiver that dropped through his feet. He shifted his face to the end of the pillow, inches from Jamie. His voice came out strangled and breathy. "I dare you to get me into a lake again."

NOT LONG AFTER JAMIE PROMISED HE'D HELP THEO OVERCOME HIS fear of water, they gave in to sleep. Or at least, Jamie fell asleep. Theo couldn't stop thinking about what he'd done. It hadn't been planned, but he wouldn't take it back. He wanted it to be Jamie encouraging him.

Maybe it was the teacher in Jamie, but Theo felt in good hands.

For a few fleeting moments, he worried. He'd trusted Sam with his story once, and look how that had turned out. Was he stupid to risk another potential punch to his core?

That was the question he drifted off to.

He woke to someone moving around the bedroom. Jamie was already up and showered, his wet hair dripping onto his shoulders. He had already slipped on jeans, but he was shirtless and the sunshine seeping through the crack in the curtains made the stray rivulets of water running down his chest glow.

Theo tucked his hands behind his head and watched until Jamie, without looking, threw his wet towel at him.

"Stop staring and shower before Mom gets in and the hot water runs out."

Theo rolled out of bed with a groan and snapped the towel against Jamie's ass, startling him into a jump. "Now we're even," Theo said as Jamie's lips ticked up.

Theo peered at the shirt options winking at him from the open drawer. "You haven't worn this one before."

He pulled out a red T-shirt encased in plastic tucked at the side of the drawer. He tugged it out of the plastic, the material soft and the color a never-been-worn vibrant red with a splash of black lettering. JLM. He'd never seen Jamie wear red. He measured the shirt against Jamie. "You're not religious are you, or have I missed something?"

Jamie snatched the T-shirt, but not in the playful way Theo was expecting. With a frown, he stuffed it under the others in his drawer.

Theo spared him a questioning look.

"Not religious," Jamie said.

"So… JLM? Just Like Me?"

Jamie stared at his T-shirts. "Yes. That one doesn't fit right."

Theo didn't believe him. "Would fit me, though. Maybe I can borrow it?"

Jamie visibly tensed.

"Alternatively," Theo said, gesturing to his nicely shaped torso, "forget the shirt and wear only that. Leone would approve."

Jamie snapped out of whatever painful reverie he had been sucked into. "I'm sure my mother wouldn't."

"Pity. Now where do I find a dry towel?"

"Well aren't you just exuding masculinity today."

Theo catching Jamie doing push-ups in the living room.

Chapter Twelve

Upon stepping inside Theo and Leone's cluttered, incense-filled home, Mom led Jamie down a hall of crystal cabinets and ushered him into the floral armchair that Theo had once purposely peed on as a kid.

The pee story was the first out of their mom's mouth. Theo shrugged. Whatever. He'd been four. Mom should have given him the cookie.

Mom ended the story by hugging Theo tight against her side, a strand of her dyed chestnut hair sweeping across his nose.

Their dad, who barely left the matching armchair in the corner of the room near the potted orchids, had called Leone over to his lap for a hug. Later, Theo would present him with cigars he'd bought and do the same.

For now, his mother had commandeered him into her game of Who Is Jamie Cooper? What was his star sign? What year and time of day was he born? What three words would he use to define himself? How was it living with her Leos?

She filed his answers away for now, but Theo could tell she struggled to hold back.

His mom also sensed the connection between Jamie and Leone. How could the queen of busybody not? The clues were difficult to miss. Jamie had carried Leone's bags to the door and dropped them to catch her elbow when Theo, leading her, stupidly stumbled over the threshold.

"This is my favorite question. You tell me to mind my own business if you don't want to answer, but I've always said you don't get anywhere if you don't at least ask."

Jamie lifted his hand from the arm of the chair and curled his finger. "Hit me, Crystal."

"If a fortune teller could tell you one thing about your future, what would you ask?"

Jamie settled back against the armchair, sweeping his gaze from Mom to him.

Theo felt too warm in the small living room and extracted himself from the hold. He was unexplainably nervous to hear Jamie's answer. His mom had once said this simple question said so much about a person and sadly too many people only wanted to know whether they'd be wealthy. "We need to open a window in here."

"Just a sec, Theo," Jamie said. Then he refocused on Mom. "I'm happy to answer that question if you and your children return the favor."

Mom smiled widely. "I'd ask whether there is anything I can do to help my kids live a happy life."

Leone, listening from Dad's lap, piped up. "I'd ask about my life purpose. What am I here to do and how can I do it well."

Jamie raised an eyebrow at Theo.

"I'd ask when I'll beat your ass at badminton."

"Theo!" Mom said.

"That's fine, Crystal," Jamie said with a slight shake of his head in Theo's direction. "I'd ask whether I'll be lucky enough to have kids someday."

Mom beamed, while Jamie shared a look with him that suggested neither had told the whole truth. "Of course you'll have kids, and it'll be the adventure of a lifetime."

The questions continued through lunch until Dad told her to quit harassing "the kids" and give them time to settle in. Theo took the chance to show Jamie through the house before he headed home.

He'd hoped Jamie would stay the night at their place as they'd originally planned, but because of the weather mishap it no longer fit. Jamie was happy to stay the afternoon, but he wanted to drive back before Danielle and his dad arrived home. He also needed to help Sean pack for the move to Pittsburgh.

Theo's room had a double bed, desk, drawers, a narrow strip of floorboards, a lone bush-shadowed window, and thirty-seven ribbons he'd won in high school. Twelve running medals were also nailed over his desk.

"This puts the A+ into perspective," Jamie said, taking a seat on the side of his bed.

"I earned one B. Worst day of my life."

A bemused look lit up Jamie's face.

"Anyway," Theo said. "This was my room junior and senior year after we moved from Pittsburgh."

Jamie had already known this fact since asking why Theo had chosen to study in the steel capital instead of Minnesota. While home was now Minneapolis, Pittsburgh had been home for longer. He'd always dreamed of studying there and Leone moved with him to make it happen.

When Theo asked Jamie the same question—why not Wisconsin?—the answer had been simple. His uncle worked as a professor there and Jamie wanted to go.

"It makes me wonder…" Jamie said slowly, as if not sure to continue or not. "Tell me if I'm overstepping."

"It's not like you to be coy." Theo plunked himself on the bed next to Jamie and flung himself back against the sheets. "Spit it out."

Jamie twisted and stretched out on his side, propping himself up on an elbow. "Do you have big loans for university?"

"Right. Because my place is a matchbox compared to yours, I have to have loans."

"I overstepped. I'm sorry."

Theo shrugged. "I didn't have loans until this semester. I used my savings and I've been working to pay my way. I do well with my design work, but it wasn't enough."

"If you got this far on your own, hard-earned dime, that's pretty damn impressive."

"You think so, Mr. Jamie Cooper?"

"I know so. And I have a degree in this stuff."

"I take it you don't have loans then?"

"No, I don't. But that's because my parents paid for my undergraduate."

"And now?"

"Like you, I saved."

"All that hair-pulling work teaching brats like me econ, huh?"

"Precisely."

"That was your opportunity to tell me you secretly loved having me in your classes."

"I grew to tolerate you, Theo. Trust me, it didn't happen at first sight."

Theo felt for a pillow and swung it into Jamie's face. "Get out of here. Leone wants to chat with you before you head back."

Jamie hugged the pillow between his knees. "You lied about what you'd ask the fortune teller."

"No I didn't. I do want to know when I'll beat your ass at badminton."

"Tell me the truth."

"After you."

Jamie pressed his lips together, thoughtful. "I'd ask if I should risk the roommate thing again, even though the first time was such a disaster."

Theo choked on his breath. Finally, an admission. Jamie was considering dating his roommate. Something special was happening between him and Leone. Now Theo understood why it was taking them forever to hook up. "Did things get awkward with your ex?"

"Yes."

Theo wanted to press for more information, but he was just being a nosey bastard. If Jamie wanted to give him more details, he would have. Besides, as he had to remind himself regarding Sam, the past was a lost hand. One could only hope to play the next hand better.

Jamie needed to focus on this round. "That's your cue," Jamie prompted.

Theo chuckled nervously. He risked sounding especially sappy admitting this. Still, fair was fair. "I'd ask whether our friendship is one for the ages," he said. *And why it is so important that it is?*

He should have spoken the last part, but his throat seized and left the words rattling in his chest.

A heavy quiet stretched between them. And then, not what he expected, Jamie said, "Close your eyes."

Theo closed them.

"I want you to imagine something for me."

"Paint it for me, Mr. Jamie Cooper."

"We are on the lake sitting in my dinghy. Deep water surrounds us, and the rapidly darkening sky looks like it's about to storm. We can't see land."

Theo opened his eyes again. Jamie was staring at him, ready to stop describing the scenario at Theo's request. He opened his mouth to do just that, and instead heard himself say, "Go on."

"Rain falls thick and heavy, churning up the lake, rocking the boat."

A shiver unfurled in Theo's belly and spread to the tips of his fingers and toes.

"I try to row us through it, but a heavy wave slaps against the side of the boat and I lose my grip on the oars. They disappear overboard."

"I hate this picture, Jamie. But… keep painting."

"I wrap my arms around your waist and you press back against my chest. You are trembling. The waves toss the boat about, then a swell lifts us high and drops suddenly. Seconds stretch as we free fall. But I still have you locked in my arms, and I'm ready for anything. Over the hiss of the storm, I tell you as much, and you squeeze my hands."

Jamie pressed against Theo's stomach above his belly button, where he would be holding him. Theo closed his eyes, imagining himself in Jamie's picture, concentrating on the warm tickle of Jamie's touch.

"As the rocking intensifies," Jamie said, "you give in to the fear. Your stomach fills with thrashing butterflies. But you feel a rush too. The boat lifts and plummets, over and over, and a thrill slides through your body. Part of you wants the waves to grow bigger so the rush never ends.

"Like this"—Jamie scooted against him, nudging Theo on his side and curling an arm over his waist—"you relax against me and we rock through the ever-pounding storm. When the boat tips, a wave of soul-shattering fear sweeps through you."

The story paused. "Don't stop, Jamie."

"Fear rolls through you but it lasts only a moment because you remember that I'm here and I'm ready. I've readjusted our hold, taking your hand."

Theo felt for Jamie's hand resting palm up on his stomach. As soon as he touched it, Jamie curled their fingers together.

"The boat jerks wildly and we are tossed from it with one final exhilarating fall that submerges us in water.

"For a moment, you're disoriented and water presses you from all sides. But I haven't let go of your hand and I won't. We kick to the surface. Before I do anything else, I make sure that you're okay and breathing, and when I'm sure you're good, we swim to shore."

"And if I can't swim?"

"I swim for both of us."

I swim for both of us. Theo's breath caught.

"We make it to shore and I take you home and dry us up."

"Have you finished?"

"Not quite. The next time I ask if you want to come out on my dinghy, you say—"

"Yes. I say yes." Theo opened his eyes. Jamie's smile was breathtaking.

"That's your answer, Theo."

He was about to throw *What do you mean?* back at him, but stopped himself. The point of the story was trusting Jamie.

He could trust in their friendship too.

"Nicely played. Now get your ass to Leone's room. Check out the fridge on your way. I wrote a quote in red marker while Mom was informing you how best to live your life and what to do with cumin pods."

≈

It was almost time to head back home. Pittsburgh, home.

The few days with his mom and dad flew by and there he was, promising to return for the 4th of July. Leone had left to spend the afternoon with her old girlfriends before they headed back to the city of steel. It was just he and Mom.

She cleared their plates from the dining table, and Theo popped the milk back into the refrigerator. Across the front in washable marker was the quote of the day: *Don't step off the pedal, Aries, you're so close to your destination.*

Under that, in Jamie's scrawled handwriting: *Mrs. Wallace. I intend to listen!*

It'd been there for days. Theo liked looking at the writing and knowing the owner of the scrawl was a few hours away, doing his thing in his corner of the woods.

"Do you need any money?" Mom asked, turning on the dishwasher.

Seemed this weekend he couldn't run away from his financial… tightness. "I have the loan now, so I'm fine. Paying it back is what sucks, but I'll have it under control."

"I wish I could help you more," Mom said, staring sadly at him as she leaned back against the dishwasher.

"You've given me so much already." Theo wrapped an arm around her neck before planting a kiss on the cheek. "Besides, I'll have enough credits to finish my double degree by the end of summer."

"But I know you. You want to do a master's like your sister."

"If I decide to, I can apply for a small loan. Really. I have it good compared to other students."

She accepted that. "When are you applying to graduate?"

"I thought I would try for the one in December. Leone's thinking of applying too, that way you only have to come down once."

"Just do your best, love. There will be all sorts of twists and turns along the road."

"Be nice to have a life-GPS, wouldn't it?"

"That's what the horoscopes are. But even then, you have to use common sense or you could end up in a rut."

Theo squeezed her into a hug. "Sign me up for your quarterly newsletter."

"I wish I could take the knob off. Make it easier to clean."

Theo, about the *shower*head, dammit!

Chapter Thirteen

Four days back at home and Sean had already dropped off his tandem bike and invited himself over for dinner. Twice. Badminton evenings were the newest activity, although Leone begged herself out of participating, while Theo played despite his complicated relationship with birdies.

Jamie fell right back into a routine of carpool, office, work, cook, play. Leone was the only one able to distract him when she put on dance music and ordered him to lead her around the room.

Well, almost the only one.

Nights, when they lay in bed and the house hummed with quiet, Theo had gotten into the habit of sending Jamie a quick one-liner over chat.

Theo: Gotobed.

Jamie: If I didn't so badly want you to say goodnight, I might call you out on that shit.

Theo: Goodnight.

~

Theo had not stopped thinking about their moment in his bedroom in Minneapolis; the story of the lake, of Jamie being there for him, promising him a friendship for the ages.

It made what he needed to say both harder and easier. Theo wanted Jamie happy, after all.

Thursday morning, Theo traipsed into the kitchen in shorts and a T-shirt, ready for his daily run and to *finally say it*. He passed Jamie preparing their daily sandwiches and opened his mouth.

He faked a yawn instead.

A drink of water later, he maneuvered to the coffee table to stretch his legs. *Just spit it out.*

Jamie's iPad blared the "*Freakonomics*" theme song. Theo smirked as Jamie used his butter knife on the cutting board to the beat.

It urged Theo's voice to the surface. "The roommate relationship thing…"

Jamie looked up sharply and blinked. Like he was surprised Theo had broached the subject. "Excuse me?"

"Give it another shot. You'll regret it if you don't try."

Jamie took a moment, watching him. Then he turned the volume of his podcast down and spoke carefully. "It wouldn't be a big deal for you?"

It was time to get over this weird jealousy and give Jamie the green light. When had this possessive streak happened, anyway?

Jamie continued, "It wouldn't be awkward?"

Was he referring to him banging his sister? He wasn't thrilled to picture them together, but happy Jamie was his favorite. "Good thing about this Victorian, she has solid walls." He swallowed. "Make a move."

"I got the impression friendship was more important than romance."

"Sure it is. Why not have both?"

"I wasn't sure about just going for it."

"Are you blind? The signals are all there."

"I didn't think I was the blind one in this relationship. But yes, I have seen signals." Jamie studied him. "You just come right out and say it, don't you?"

"I've been waiting for weeks. I'm starting to get impatient."

A dorky smile crossed Jamie's face. "So it's up to me to make the first move?"

A door squeaked open, and in walked the woman in question, dressed in a charcoal pencil skirt, matching jacket and a peach blouse. Her hair was twisted up and her cheeks bunched with a smile. "Morning! I smell coffee," she said. "Gimme some."

Jamie poured her a cup right away.

Theo said, "The answer to your question is yes. Make it memorable."

"The whole dance so far has been memorable."

"Keep it up. And, *yes*, pressure." Leone deserved all the romance. All of it.

His sister took the coffee Jamie handed her with a happy sigh. "I could kiss you right now." She proceeded to take in a moaning mouthful of caffeine.

Theo flung an arm over his head and gripped his elbow, stretching his bicep.

Leone's phone rang from her bedroom, and she whisked her and her mug toward the sound.

Jamie added an apple to each lunch bag. He looked at Theo again, his expression blatantly pleased. "So. Bye, then?"

Theo followed the sweep of Jamie's finger and stared down at his running clothes. *Oh.* He wanted Theo to get the hell out of here to work his magic.

"Ah, yeah. Bye. Meet you for coffee later?"

"With your usual side of econ?"

"You know me so well."

Leone waltzed back out of her room with the phone pressed to her ear. Theo flashed some good-luck dimples to Jamie.

As he retreated, Jamie muttered, "I love memorable."

THEO HAD TO CANCEL ON THEIR COFFEE.

The store where Theo was having a couple pictures framed hadn't finished preparing them when he arrived to pick them up. The earliest they'd be ready was that afternoon.

Instead of their usual coffee and bicker, Theo picked up the pictures and raced home to wrap them before Jamie got home. Leone was there with a visitor.

"Sean," Theo said. "Fancy seeing you here."

"Get used to this mug, man. I'll be over a lot."

"Make yourself useful and pass me some scissors."

Sean grew quiet when he saw the sketches.

"You think he'll like them?" Theo asked.

"He will."

"Why are you frowning then?"

"No reason." Sean helped Theo wrap the pictures, then suggested hiding them under the couch.

"Give me your number," Theo said, shaking his phone like that might recharge the battery. He plugged his phone into the kitchen socket. "Hit me."

Sean rattled off his number and Theo returned the favor with a message.

Theo: You here for dinner?

"Not tonight," Sean said. "I have a Skype date."

"When are you coming by tomorrow?"

"Unless you or Leone are able to make pancakes, breakfast."

"Breakfast it is then."

Sean left to find Leone who had slipped away, and Theo over-heard snippets of conversation. Something about Sean wanting to bike ride with Leone again sometime.

Jamie returned home. He ducked under the strap of his satchel, set it on the coffee table, and collapsed onto the couch.

"You look like you missed our coffee in more ways than one," Theo said.

Jamie beckoned him over. Theo pushed the satchel aside and perched on the coffee table.

Jamie shifted forward, arms on his knees, new energy seeming to fold into him. "Theo—"

Leone and Sean walked out. Judging by the grin on his sister's face, she had cut him to size again.

Jamie murmured, "It's fun when we all hang out, but I'd like some alone time. Some us time."

Theo forced himself to smile. "Gotcha. Try dinner tonight then?"

Sean would be on his Skype date and Theo, well, Theo could spend some time in the library studying.

"Tonight?" Jamie said.

"Can't think of a better way to start your twenty-fourth year."

"I'm turning twenty-four. That makes it the start of my twenty-fifth year."

"Good luck on your date."

Jamie laughed then rocked to his feet. He said goodbye to Sean and disappeared upstairs. Theo followed Sean out of the house.

"You're leaving with Sean?" Leone said.

"Hitting the book palace. Got a couple of papers to research. More design work." He doubled back and gave his sister a hug. "Have a …" His voice croaked and he covered it with a chuckle. "Have a nice night."

THEO DIDN'T MAKE IT FAR INTO THE LIBRARY.

In the foyer, a familiar voice called out his name and Theo swiveled to find two blond guys striding toward him grinning. Ben, slightly smaller than Kyle, dumped his bag into Kyle's arms and yanked Theo into a quick embrace. "Funny, we were just talking about you."

Theo pulled back, readjusting the bag strap that was cutting into his neck. "Do I want to know?"

Pray to God it didn't have anything to do with him and Sam.

"Actually we were talking about your mother. Same diff."

"Agree to disagree on that one."

Kyle snickered and fondly knocked Ben on the back of his head. "What my boyfriend here wants to say is your mom sent out our quarter-yearly horoscope."

Theo groaned, clueless they had signed up. Usually only her drama students dared do that.

"How long have you been getting them?" he asked, moving aside to allow the more studious people into the library.

"Since your mom visited during freshman year."

Theo balked. Ben had kept that tidbit under wraps. "You still read them?"

"Sagittarius has to spend his energy on others today, and Leo's in for a surprise." Ben mouthed something to his boyfriend. Then to Theo, "Want to have a drink with us at the bar around the corner?"

It wasn't like Theo was in the right place for cracking open his books—the right place mentally, that was. He had barely managed to drag himself here. After getting off the bus, he'd rummaged through his bag for his phone, but all he could do was curse; he'd left his damn phone on the charger at home.

That left him unable to drown out the images of Leone and Jamie on their date.

Only Ben's voice had snapped him free of his thoughts.

"A drink sounds fucking perfect."

The rustic, old-timey bar featured a wall of old tins and low-hanging table lanterns. Theo slung himself onto a booth bench and Kyle stretched out on the opposite side, propping his back against the wall, one knee bent and his wrist resting on it.

Ben, standing at the table, slow-eyed Kyle, his lip curling. "I'll get this round. What's your poison?"

"Whiskey. Double, no ice."

Kyle sighed as Ben swaggered toward the bar. The dancing crowd swallowed him from view halfway. "How the fuck did I ever get so lucky?"

"Figure out that secret, then by all means, share."

Kyle tapped his knee to the beat of the country rock music. "I was such a dick before him. You know how we met?"

"No."

"Nineteen and no money, in a bar like this. My friends had piled into a taxi while I was in the john and I needed a Hamilton to get back to my dorm." A sly smile. "There was only one thing to do. I eyed the bar, saw this hot-as-fuck guy nursing a tequila sunrise, apparently alone. I slapped him on the back with a hearty *Hey, man, it's me, Kyle. God it's been a while.* I almost felt sorry for him as he tried to figure out where the hell he knew me from. I mentioned I was a dick, right? Then he smiled and lightly punched my arm and fucking went with it. *Too long. What're you up to now?* he said. So began the bullshit. Then I hit him up for a loan. Know what happened then?"

"He told you to piss off?"

"Heart of gold, you know. But clever sucker too. He slapped a ten into my hand, then pulled me close and whispered, *Nice to meet you, Kyle.* Then he melted into a line of sashaying students and left me speechless."

"He'd cottoned on to your game from the start, then?"

"For a whole week I replayed the moment and felt shitty about using him. I wanted to pay him back and apologize but I didn't have his number. Only clues to his general whereabouts. With a little creativity, I tracked him down."

"And that was it?" Theo asked, amused. "You were a thing?"

Kyle snorted. "Nope. Took a while before he realized he wanted some of this."

"Why was that?"

"I'm demisexual," came the answer from the guy in question. Ben set two whiskeys and a tequila sunrise on the table and slid onto the bench next to Theo.

Theo snagged a whiskey. "Demisexual?"

Ben shrugged. "I'll sum it up for you: I'm an emotional lover. I only get turned on after getting to know someone—and liking them, of course."

"And he likes me. See?" Kyle tapped his chest. "Lucky son of a bitch."

They smiled at each other like they were reliving a memory.

Theo swigged a large mouthful of whiskey. The universe sure was rubbing it in his face.

He scanned the bar. Everyone seemed to be here with someone. Another gulp of whiskey.

Ben elbowed him in the side. "You're drinking like you saw Sam on the dance floor. Do we need to buy a bottle?"

"Tempting," Theo said, then shook his head. He couldn't drink more than a couple of drinks tonight. Jamie didn't deserve to have him hungover at his birthday breakfast.

"So…" Ben prompted. "Are you going to tell us?"

"Nothing to tell."

"Feel free to change your mind any time."

Theo sighed. The thing was… he felt sad. Like Leone and Jamie hooking up meant Jamie wouldn't need him so much anymore. He enjoyed the bond they shared, and losing it... Maybe he was looking at the situation wrong. Maybe the universe wasn't rubbing love in his face. Maybe it was offering him more pieces of the friendship pie.

This time Theo sipped his whiskey. "Do either of you play badminton?" he asked, and when Kyle nodded, Theo smiled. "I have a favor to ask you…"

"I've one hell of a to-do list. Just need someone to do it."

Theo at the dinner table procrastinating.

Chapter Fourteen

It was close to midnight when Theo returned home.

He made a racket at the door, purposely dropping his keys and swearing before jiggling the door handle. That should give everyone enough time to get decent.

Bit by bit he pushed the door open. No lights.

Maybe they were in bed. Jamie was too classy to have sex on the first official date, so Theo probably wouldn't need to crank up music when he reached his bedroom.

Theo carefully slipped his shoes off and hung up his jacket. He didn't bother with the lights as he stole across the living room to his bedroom. He didn't particularly want to draw them from their rooms.

Theo quietly shut his bedroom door. He let out a relieved breath and turned into the room, automatically reaching for the light switch.

A movement caught his eye and Theo shrieked. His bag slipped off his shoulder and hit the floor.

Jamie was lying on his bed cloaked in darkness.

"You almost gave me a fucking heart attack. What the hell are you doing in here?"

Jamie swung off the bed and strolled through a patch of window-shaped moonlight toward him. "I've been here a while. Waiting. Pondering how best to do this."

"How best to do what?"

"Make something abundantly clear."

It happened too fast.

Jamie moved toward him and Theo's shoulders hit the hard door. Jamie pushed against him, chest to chest, one leg slipping between his, snug at his crotch. Jamie's hand threaded through Theo's hair, his other on the curve of his neck. Jamie pressed his thumb against Theo's rapid-fire pulse. Theo barely had time to suck in a surprised breath when Jamie kissed him.

A maelstrom of sensation had Theo bracing himself against the door, palms suctioned on to the paneling. Jamie's warm, firm mouth teased his and when Theo instinctively parted his lips, Jamie hummed. Low and deep, the vibrations tingled the bow of Theo's lips. The rasp of Jamie's stubble over his chin was foreign and a flare of goosebumps tickled down Theo's neck, pooling where Jamie was now stroking his thumb.

Jamie pulled back and his tone was displeased. "I'm gay, Theo."

Theo brought his fingers to his swollen lips. The kiss was still dancing on his bottom lip, and yet his brain hadn't caught up. "You're not."

"I am."

"You are not."

"Darwin would've loved you as a test case."

"You can't be."

A frustrated growl. "This isn't like peanut butter. You can't just add nuts and make me chunky. I'm gay."

"There's a joke in there somewhere." For later though, because right now his brain was still processing. "Seriously? You're gay?"

"I could throttle you," he said through clenched teeth.

"Get in line. I could throttle myself." Then, because it just slipped out, "So you're gay?"

"Need me to kiss you again, do you?"

Theo paused and dropped the fingers still playing at his lips. "I'm confused."

"You don't say."

"But I thought… you and Leone…"

Jamie crossed his arms. "Believe me. I understood what you thought tonight."

"But you've been flirting with her from the beginning."

A dry laugh. "Leone is amazing and we get along well. But I was flirting with you."

"Really?"

"I'm starting to question every A you've ever scored."

"Me too." Theo frowned. "I never even thought…I just assumed you were…well, shit. You should have told me you were gay in the beginning."

"Hey, Theo, I'm Jamie. I'm gay. No. Gay isn't who I am. I thought my actions spoke of my attraction to you." He dropped his arms at his side and sat on the end of the bed.

"You find me attractive?" Theo couldn't keep the pleasure out of his voice. Compliments always did wonders to his ego. He was a Leo, after all.

Jamie let out a strangled laugh. "You're crazy cute, Theo. I've wanted to get into your pants since you first propped your feet up in my tutorial and yelled."

He wasn't sure what to think, but his whole body felt strung taut. He was suddenly aware of his breath and the way he kept swallowing and the faint stir of arousal lingering from their kiss.

Theo didn't trust himself to move away from the door and rested his head against it. "I mistook your flirting for friendship," he said softly. "I've had friends before but never one like you. It felt— feels—special."

Jamie lifted his gaze from his threaded fingers. "It is. It was one of the many reasons I wasn't sure if I should make a move. I want to suck you senseless—at least, more senseless than you apparently are —but more than that, I want to keep the comradery."

Theo snickered. "One of the many reasons? The roommate thing, and…?"

"You were, and quite frankly still are, hard to get a read on. When you mentioned going on a date with a girl, it surprised me. I guess I made as many assumptions as you did." His mouth twitched. "Maybe you should have told me you were straight from the beginning?"

"Point driven home, Mr. Jamie Cooper. But, yeah, I date girls."

"I'd give you my apologies for the kiss, but consider it payback for trying to set me up with your sister. Who is not into me, by the way. What possessed you to think of hooking us up?"

"We're finding each other dates for Derek and Sam's wedding. You came into our lives all charming and together, and I thought, yeah, this is a worthy guy."

Jamie stood and stepped toward Theo, gesturing for him to free the door. "I'll take the compliment."

"Here's another one for you," Theo said, still not moving.

"What's that?"

"You're a good kisser."

Jamie raised an eyebrow.

"I'm not homophobic."

"I didn't think you were."

"I'm not sexually repressed. A lot of things get me off."

Jamie slammed his eyes shut and palmed his crotch. "You are not helping right now, straight guy."

"I just… I can't imagine myself falling in love with another man."

Again, Jamie motioned to leave. This time Theo turned the knob and pulled the door open for him. A whoosh of air fanned Theo's heated face, heated neck, heated everything.

"Goodnight, Theo," Jamie said on his way out. He didn't look back but his casual words drifted over his shoulder. "Who said anything about falling in love?"

THERE WAS A HUGE POTENTIAL FOR AWKWARDNESS.

Theo might feel strange around Jamie and back off a bit because Jamie was gay and wanted to do the dirty with him.

Jamie might feel exposed and embarrassed after admitting the truth, and wish he had never said a word.

There was the potential for things to feel weird.

Except, they weren't.

The next morning, Theo glided into the kitchen where Sean was making pancakes and hummed the "*Freakonomics*" theme song as he poured himself a hot mug of coffee. He had slept like a log and after a long, hot shower, he felt chipper.

When the birthday boy descended the stairs—well after eight o'clock—in a button-down shirt with the sleeves rolled to the elbows and dark gray khakis, he breezed up to Theo and stole his coffee. Theo saw the slightest curve to his mouth just before it disappeared behind the cup as he drank.

"If it's that easy to make you happy," Theo drawled. "I wouldn't have bothered with gifts."

Sean flipped a pancake, then side-tackled Jamie into a hug. Coffee sloshed over the side of the cup and onto the floor, and Theo, next to the paper towels on the bench, dropped some on the floor and stepped on the mess.

"Happy birthday, Hotstuff," Sean said. Theo stiffened for a moment and then let it slide. Mostly. "Leone! Jamie's up."

Leone, dressed for the occasion in a black sleeveless trench coat and jeans, came into the living room with a phone pressed to her ear. "Mom, I'm passing you to Jamie now."

Theo scooped up the sopping paper towels and trashed them.

Jamie, phone jammed between ear and shoulder and murmuring, sidled next to Sean and pinched a pancake right out of the pan. He juggled it until it didn't burn his fingers and took a large bite. Theo stared. Pancakes were not Jamie's normal start to the day. As if reading his mind, Jamie cupped the receiver and said, "Moderation, Theo. I like to indulge sometimes."

Theo picked his jaw up off the floor and helped set the table.

"Your mom says good morning and she'll call you later," Jamie said, dropping into his usual seat by the window.

Theo continued to lay out plates, cutlery, glasses, and birthday-themed napkins.

"I could get used to being waited on like this," Jamie said. "Did you say something about gifts? Hand them over."

It was as though last night never happened.

Theo swept an eye down Jamie, taking in the casual way he leaned in his chair and stopping at his mouth where a pancake crumb rested on the bow of his upper lip.

Jamie cocked his head.

"Out of curiosity," Theo said, shifting from one foot to the other. "Were you and Sean…?"

Jamie did not look surprised. "Together? No."

"Did you—"

"Seriously crush on him for a year in high school? Have you seen the guy?"

"And—"

"Did I get over it because he is straight? Yes to that too."

Theo threw up his arms in exasperation. "What am I thinking now, Hotstuff?"

Jamie laughed. "You know he calls me that because it's the truth. I don't need it, but I don't need it to stop, either. Unless… does it bother you?"

Theo stepped back from the table, flipping him off. He fished for Jamie's gifts under the couch. Jamie smugly took the wrapped parcels out of Theo's hands. "I have no idea what these could be."

It deserved a smack on the back of the head, so Theo gave him one. "I don't care if it's your birthday, there's more where that came from."

Theo swung a seat around and straddled it, resting his arms on the back.

Jamie carefully peeled away the wrapping. His cool superiority dissolved when he took in the bold black-and-white sketches—a roaring Leo and a charging Aries—framed in dark wood. Jamie traced over the lion's mane with his finger.

"Thank you, Theo. They're… A+."

Jamie gingerly set the pictures on the windowsill, then pulled the back of Theo's chair, causing it to tilt on two legs. "Whoa. Pull anymore and I'll catapult into your lap."

"Was that your argument to *dissuade* me?"

Okay, Theo deserved that.

He stared at Jamie's mouth. He needed to take stock of this new situation, because the images flashing in his mind were oddly arousing. The knowing curl of Jamie's lip brought him back down to earth.

"I'm not gay," he said.

"I didn't say you were."

"You're thinking it, though."

Jamie leaned forward, dropping his voice to a whisper. "I'm thinking you are, Leo."

"What does that mean?"

"You know what they say about cats and curiosity."

Theo's head fell back as he laughed. "You're killing me, Mr. Jamie Cooper. Killing me."

"I rather hope I am."

Sean slipped between them with a plate of piled pancakes. He set it on the middle of the table then clapped his hands on Jamie and Theo's shoulders. "Seat yourself, Leone," he said. "Breakfast is served."

"If you want to understand the principle of scarcity, just look in the fridge for vegetables after your brother has gone shopping."

Jamie to Leone and a scowling Theo.

Chapter Fifteen

Theo had two papers due by Friday. He holed himself away in the library most nights.

By Thursday he had finished one paper but was struggling with the second. His economics-of-the-health-care-system outline would pass with a B, but some part of the argument he hadn't explored in depth enough was missing.

He trudged home at eleven and popped into Leone's room. Now that he wasn't reading aloud to her anymore, they shared less time together.

"Miss you," he said, and flopped on her bed. Leone paused her audiobook and sat back against the headboard.

"What's up?" she asked.

"I have to rework my paper. I messed something up." He had emailed Jamie on the off chance he might give him feedback, but Theo had left it so last-minute that Jamie wouldn't have time to do it. Especially seeing he was taking over a lecture tomorrow on short notice and needed every free minute preparing for it. "Give me two more minutes procrastinating with you first."

"Should I make tea? The water is probably still hot, I heard Jamie making a drink a few minutes ago."

Theo shook his head. He wondered if Jamie's drink would be consumed warm or forgotten at the side of his desk until later. "Did you know he's gay?"

"Okay."

"Okay? Just okay?" Shouldn't she be upset that the guy she was into would never be into her?

"What else do you want me to say?" Leone said.

"I don't know. That's a shame?"

"Why a shame? Jamie's awesome——"

"Because you liked him!"

"Who said that?"

"I have eyes."

"And yours are working! I suspected Jamie might be gay almost from the beginning. How have you not noticed the way he acts toward you?"

Heat flared in his cheeks and he was glad she wouldn't see it. "Why didn't you tell me?"

"It's not my news to tell."

That shut him up and unleashed a ribbon of guilt in his belly.

"Well," Theo mumbled, twisting as if he could scratch the itch building inside of him. "He can't be your date to the wedding."

THEO SPENT ANOTHER TWENTY MINUTES WITH LEONE BEFORE HE wished her goodnight and left. He contemplated climbing the stairs to Jamie's room but decided to drag his ass to his bedroom instead.

Tucked in bed with his laptop and econ book, he checked his email. Nothing.

He reopened his essay, some online resource materials, and his econ book.

There were not enough resources in the health care system to meet every health need, so his essay detailed the opportunity costs in determining which needs were met.

One important criterion for resource allocation was efficiency, whether technical, economic, or social. But he couldn't quite put a finger on it.

With a frustrated growl, he chucked the econ book across the room. Immediately, he got out of bed to pick it up, shoving it roughly on his shelf. Even though he was tired, he wouldn't be able to sleep until the paper was just right.

Ding.

Theo scrambled back into bed and checked his inbox.

Jamie: What's with the racket?

Theo: Did I wake you?

Jamie: No. I've been reading over your paper.

Theo: *groans* okay, lay it on me.

Jamie: I'm sending you my annotations.

Theo: It's B material, isn't it?

Jamie: Your paper overlooks equity.

Theo: EQUITY!

Jamie: Yes.

Theo: That noise is me banging my head against the wall. Equity, of course. People would place more importance in equity in health services than with other goods.

Jamie: It is difficult to measure equity, though. This is where things get interesting. A tip for you: look at equal need and equal access, and maybe contrast those with other definitions of equity.

Theo: Such as use and willingness to pay?

Jamie: There's your A. Send me the final draft when you're done.

Theo: Might need an hour.

Jamie: I'm running through my lecture once more and taking a shower. I'll give it a once-over before bed.

Theo: I could kiss you right now.

Jamie: You know where my room is, right?

Theo: Make it a cold shower, Jamie.

After a grueling evening with Kyle on the badminton court, Theo went home and took a much-needed shower. He lifted his face into the streaming water as he rinsed off his soapy body. His hand worked through the suds around his dick, and a knuckle shuffle was in order.

He fisted his rapidly hardening dick and closed his eyes, imagining instead of a tight wet hand, a warm mouth sucking him and gazing at him with lust-filled gray eyes.

Theo's eyes pinged open. Those were Jamie's gray eyes. Jamie's lips. Jamie's tongue.

Fuck! The image made his dick throb. He stroked faster, picturing Jamie on his knees before him, taking him all the way down his throat.

He gasped and his cock pulsed as thick ropes of come shot over the white tiles. His whole body trembled as he imagined Jamie swallowing his come, tasting him, then flashing him that cocky grin. *Curious Leo.*

Theo let out a shaky laugh and leaned against the wall until he'd collected himself. Well. That was interesting.

He dressed and collapsed on the sofa. A strange emptiness filled the house with Leone at her book club and Jamie off gallivanting with Sean.

He was not sure what to do with himself. The moment in the

shower slammed once more to the forefront of his mind, and he shook his head. What else to do with himself, dammit.

Dinner was a pizza he shoved in the oven, and entertainment was finishing some websites. But by 8:30 he'd finished and was twiddling his fingers.

Channeling his inner Jamie, he sorted the laundry before the situation grew critical and even swung a vacuum over the living room.

After finding a dry-erase marker while tidying his desk, Theo snuck up to Jamie's en suite bathroom. He uncapped the marker, wrote a quote on the mirror, then exited the bathroom and took in Jamie's room. His framed sketches caught his eye and—fuck it—he jumped on Jamie's bed, rearranged a pillow under his neck, and started messaging.

Theo: Whatcha up to?

It didn't take long before his phone pinged.

Jamie: At a bar.

Theo: And you didn't invite me?

Jamie: It's a gay bar. You want to join us?

Theo: Does that mean I need to vacate your bed?

Jamie: You're in my bed?

Theo: Yep.

Jamie: I think I need another drink.

Theo: Mr. Jamie Cooper drinking? Send me the address. I've got to see this.

An hour later, Theo rocked up to a stone-brick building with massive wooden doors and a lantern-lit KRAVE sign. Clumps of people milled about the pavement smoking cigarettes. Were they all gay? Did it matter? He tugged the hem of his thin hoodie that had ridden up under his fitted jacket on the bumpy bus ride.

Enough gawking. Get in there.

Theo rolled his shoulders back and strode inside.

Guys weren't dry humping on the dance floor like he'd expected. In fact, most guys were sitting in booths talking over pitchers of beer. The place was quiet and only half full, although it was still early. A few others sat on stools at the bar making furtive glances around the room, but it was far less boisterous than he'd imagined.

It was almost disappointing.

A heavy hand thumped his shoulder blades and Theo jerked his head to a grinning Sean. "Couldn't give me a single night alone with my man, could you?"

"Twenty-odd years' worth not enough for you?"

Sean hitched a thumb toward the bar. "Whiskey?"

"Soda. Not drinking tonight."

"And here I hoped you'd indulge in another whiskey-fest."

"You feel free to take your time, Sean."

They parted ways, Sean toward a couple flannel-loving dudes, and Theo toward an observant Jamie in the corner booth. He played with the metal strap of his watch as he gave Theo an appreciative once-over, eyes deepening with what Theo would now label desire.

Theo slowed and bathed in the attention. "I expected you to look more drunk."

"I expected you to look more bed-rumpled." Jamie released his watch and sipped the last of his beer. "One might think you dressed up for me."

Theo noted Sean's empty glass opposite Jamie and shuffled into his spot anyway, sliding the empty glass to the end of the table. "If I leave tonight without at least one more person checking me out, then I've done the gay bar experience wrong."

Jamie scanned the crowd, jaw twitching. "I'm quite happy for you to do it wrong."

Theo laughed and rubbed his palms over his jeans.

He had come here hoping to catch Jamie with his guard down. He loved how strong Jamie was, how much he held his life together; how much he helped others too; strict, but only in the sense that he cared deeply. But Jamie drunk, able to let go and not be responsible for a night?

Theo wanted him to have that freedom and know someone would have his back. "Did you bring your car?"

Jamie answered by arching his hips and drawing out keys from his pocket. Then he jiggled them to snap Theo's gaze away from his crotch.

"Good." Theo hit the underside of Jamie's hand and snagged the keys as they went airborne. "Thanks for teaching me that trick. Handy as hell."

"I've had two small beers in two hours. I'm under the limit."

"Now you don't have to be." Theo continued, saying the first thing that came to his mind. "So, a week out of the closet. How does it feel?"

"I didn't come out of the closet. You just opened your eyes."

"Technically, you opened them for me. I'd still be oblivious if you hadn't shoved your tongue down my throat."

"I'm almost regretting that."

"Sounds like a fun conversation," Sean said, passing them their drinks.

Theo thanked him for the soda. "That wasn't taking your time."

"What can I say? I nearly got groped by Paul Bunyan over there."

Theo tilted his head at Sean, who looked pointedly at Jamie and motioned their surroundings. "See, he's doing the bar thing right."

Jamie accepted his beer and shook his head. "Think I'll buy the next and all subsequent rounds."

A hearty laugh left Theo. "Want some hearty groping of your own, do you?"

"Whatever it takes to save your virtue."

"Ever the gentleman. You don't happen to know any decent straight guys, do you?"

Sean made a noise.

Jamie said, "Too many."

"I need to find a date for Leone to take to the wedding."

Sean made an even louder noise.

"I'd love to help," Jamie said, "but I'm trying to find a nice guy of my own, right now."

"Thought you weren't looking for love?"

Jamie leveled those slate gray eyes on him and a shiver zipped through Theo right to his crotch. "Tell me, Theo, do you make a habit of fucking people you don't find nice?"

"Touché," he croaked. And then, "Is that why you're here? To find someone to fuck?"

Sean snorted, and Theo rounded on him all curiosity. "Jamie," Sean said, "you haven't told him why you come here?"

Jamie took a long drink of his beer.

"One of you is going to tell me," Theo said, resting his arms on the table and looking at Jamie.

Sean said, "Does Theodory know anything about your exes?"

Jamie's gaze flickered to Sean and then back to him. "Almost as much as I know of his."

Which was almost nothing. He knew that Sam was getting hitched to Leone's ex, though.

"I think you should start," Theo said. "In fact, let's make it a game. For every factoid you tell me, I'll return the favor."

"Both of you will need to drink during this game," Sean said flatly.

"I'm the designated driver," Theo said, jangling the keys like Jamie had.

In the same maneuver as Theo had stolen them, he was robbed.

"How about I'm the designated driver and I watch this highly entertaining show?" Sean swapped Theo's soda for his Long Island Iced Tea.

Theo wanted to be the one Jamie counted on tonight. Just as he opened his mouth to protest, Jamie hummed, "I like this idea."

In a stage whisper, Theo said, "This isn't a ploy to get me drunk so you can have your wicked way with me, is it?"

A marginal shift of his eyebrow. "You called me a gentleman, you tell me."

Theo lifted the cocktail and took a gulp. Not his drink of choice, but it was cold and potent. He didn't beat around the bush. "How many boyfriends have you had?"

"Three. John in junior year, albeit briefly then"—his voice hitched—"Charlie. And after, Wesley, the roommate."

"Which one was the most serious?" Judging by the break in his voice, Theo guessed the answer. He took another sip.

"You first. Girlfriends."

"Also three. Sarah, at 16. Lost my v-card to her. Anna for the rest of high school, and then—"

"Sam," Jamie finished for him. Theo nodded, watching Jamie gulp his drink. That one little motion made this whole talk easier.

"Charlie and I were together two and a half years. We met at the end of senior year."

"What happened?" Remembering it was his turn, he said as succinctly as he could, "I wasn't enough for Sam. Derek had something I didn't."

That deserved a long drink.

Jamie's arm jerked, like he wanted to reach across the table and take his hand. "I told you I came to Pittsburgh because my uncle teaches here. But mostly I came for him."

He already didn't like Charlie. Talking about him made Jamie's voice pinch.

Jamie continued, "We came to this bar, even sat in this booth."

"You come here to torture yourself?" Theo drained his cocktail.

"I come here to remind myself good things come to an end. And to see there are plenty of fish in the sea."

That bristled.

"Did you love him?" Theo heard himself ask the ultimate question, the one they both had known hovered between them.

Jamie reciprocated. "Did you love her?"

"I thought I did."

"Me too."

One cocktail and he already felt off-center. *Fuck.* He stood abruptly, causing a few heads around the amber-lit bar to look their way.

Jamie watched him carefully. Theo thought the look was all too probing. Like maybe Jamie knew better than he did what he was about to say.

"We need to leave."

"But you just got here," Sean said.

Theo ignored him. "I mean it. Right now. We need to leave."

Theo couldn't stand witnessing Jamie sitting in the bar telling himself good things wouldn't last.

Funny. He'd come tonight hoping for Jamie to lose control; within ten minutes, Theo was the one making a scene. But dammit, this whole discussion grated on his nerves.

He took Jamie's beer and chugged the rest of that too. "No excuses. Let's go home."

No doubt trying to make a joke, Sean said, "But he hasn't a 'nice guy' to take home yet."

"The only 'nice guy' Jamie is taking home tonight is me."

Jamie's brow quirked. Just a fraction.

Theo whirled around to Sean. "Drive us home, would you?"

Sean raised his arms, slid off the bench, and freed Theo.

The problem with storming off is this: It looks ridiculous when you head in the wrong direction.

Sean trotted after him and bravely grabbed his arm, motioning toward the other end of the street. "The car's that way."

Theo stopped, then kicked at a stray bottle cap.

Sean slung an arm around his shoulder. "Dude, do you want to talk about it?"

"I shouldn't have drunk tonight. I was meant to be the solid one."

"Why?"

Theo stared at where Jamie was waiting for them at the car, poised and together, and far too reasonably giving Theo some space.

"How could you let him come to this bar if you knew why he comes here?"

"Jamie always knows what's right for him, and I support that."

Theo pressed his lips together in displeasure. So many competing emotions were ripping through him right now and he couldn't grasp them all. He wanted to punch something. Preferably Jamie. Because he deserved better than this. Better than Charlie.

Theo pegged Sean with a stare. "You like Leone, don't you? Your snarky chit-chat is just for show."

"You'd know," Sean threw back.

"You want to be her date to the wedding."

"Well I don't want to be yours."

Theo looked at him. "Do me one thing. Don't let him come here again."

ON THE RIDE HOME, THE LONG ISLAND ICED TEA KICKED IN WITH A mellow buzz. By the time Sean dropped them off and disappeared, Theo's freak out was well behind him. Leaving the bar helped.

Really fucking helped.

Jamie, composed as ever, tracked him as he moved into the kitchen and grabbed a drink of orange juice. He'd have drunk from the bottle had Jamie not followed him and plucked it out of his hands a second before the rim met his lips.

Jamie poured him a glass. Theo jumped up on the bench and lifted one leg, blocking Jamie when he tried to leave. Then he lifted the other, caging him.

Jamie could've gone around his feet, but he stayed put, facing him.

"You were right," Theo said when that gray stare began burning shivers into him. "I am curious."

Jamie's eyes, usually clear and focused, darkened. Theo could tell it took him every ounce of restraint not to move.

Silently, Theo begged Jamie to lose control. Let him take something for himself.

When he didn't, Theo put his emptied glass in the sink and said lightly, "Do you want to mess around with me?"

That met a pause. "You're drunk."

"Tipsy, not drunk. And if drunk, then I'm more blatantly honest."

"You're straight."

Theo snagged Jamie's shirt and pulled him close. "I told you I'm not sexually repressed. I meant it when I said a lot of things can get me off. Would it screw with your head if we did the whole friends-with-benefits thing? Or"—Theo swung a finger over his length and tapped his temple—"are you head over heels for all this?"

Jamie nipped at Theo's lips, the barest scrape of his teeth against his bottom lip and then it was gone. "I wanted to get in your pants, not marry your arrogant ass."

"Then let's do it. Sex me up."

"Just like that, you want me?"

Theo could only stare at those lips. How would they feel on his neck, his chest, his dick? The memory of his earlier session in the shower flooded him with arousal.

"This is just sex, Jamie. Not science. We don't have to think so hard."

"Theo," Jamie said as a warning.

But when did Theo ever listen to Jamie's warnings?

Theo locked his legs around Jamie's waist, bringing him snug against him. Jamie was just as hard as he was. Theo cocked his hips into that revelation. His words whispered along Jamie's stubble and Theo chased after them with open-mouthed kisses. "You're an Aries. I'm a Leo. Apparently, we are extremely sexually compatible." He whispered in Jamie's ear, "I've been thinking about that a lot since you kissed me. Maybe even before."

Jamie swiveled his hips and his hand snaked to the back of Theo's neck and squeezed. "As much as I love hearing you admit that, tonight Aries tells Leo to get his drunk ass to bed."

"Your bed?"

Jamie picked him up off the bench, hands firmly gripping Theo's ass as he twisted and set him on unsteady feet. "Go."

"It smells good in here."
"Well, it did.*"*

Sean and Leone when Sean comes over for dinner.

Chapter Sixteen

Theo woke remembering every line he had said to Jamie, which wasn't a surprise because he had only been tipsy. He wanted to commend Jamie for not taking advantage of him.

Mostly though, he wanted to curse him for leaving him strung high and freaking dry. Twice he'd woken to sort himself out and neither time had sated him.

His bedroom door creaked open and Theo rolled on his side. For a moment, his heart leaped into his throat thinking Jamie was waltzing into his room about to tell him this was going to happen.

Pink-pajamaed Leone shuffled in instead, hesitating in the doorway.

"Floor's clear," he said.

Leone found her way to his bed. He reached for her hand and helped her find a good spot on the side of his bed.

"How was book club, yesterday?"

"Good. Liz says hello."

"I like that you and her are friends," Theo said. "She's pretty freaking cool."

"That she is." Leone bit her lip. "Theo..."

Theo pushed himself up and rested against the headboard. The pink blush shading her cheeks suggested she had something to tell him.

"About our dates—"

"I haven't forgotten our deal," Theo said. "In fact, I think I've found you the perfect match."

"You have?"

"That sounded decidedly disappointed."

"I think I found someone I'd like to take myself."

Theo tugged her fingers. "Sean?"

Her blush deepened. "Half the time I want to punch him, the other half… not so much."

"At least this time I *know* it's reciprocated."

"You think?" she sounded very pleased.

"I'm not about to make the same mistake twice. Sean likes you. Possibly adores you."

She laughed. "I wouldn't put it behind you to misread."

"Hush."

She laughed harder. "I hope you open your eyes before you hurt yourself. Stop scowling."

How did she always know when he did that!

Leone's laughed subsided. "What about you?" She pointed up to the ceiling toward Jamie's room. "Is there any point in me looking for someone?"

"We said we'd take our own dates, that we'd dance and laugh at their wedding and not care that they left us. I can do all those things with Jamie."

"Because you are…best friends?"

Would he ever tire of hearing that? "That's right."

She stood. "I'm happy for you. If you ever want to talk about… best friend stuff, you can always chat with me."

She left and Theo dressed for a run. On his way, he turned on his heel and charged into Jamie's room instead.

Jamie was sitting in bed, typing on his phone. He didn't look up, just smiled. "Your footsteps could wake an entire neighborhood."

Theo climbed onto the bed and stole Jamie's pillow, making his head fall back. Lying lengthwise, he propped his head up with an elbow, pillow between them, and looked down at Jamie's face. Tousled hair, red skin at his neck where he'd slept on his crinkly pillow, a rip at the neck of an old T-shirt.

"You look wrecked," Theo said.

"Such the charmer. Also, Sean is the answer." He waved a hand toward the bathroom, and Theo remembered the quote he'd marked on the mirror. *Would a young Yoda have curly hair? Straight hair? Any hair?*

"I figured it was time to add him into our game."

"You two friends now?"

A snort, then a shrug. "I figured I'd better get used to him." Theo fingered the tear at Jamie's T-shirt, nail lightly scratching the red part of his neck when Jamie hooked his gaze. Theo's voice dropped. "I meant what I said last night."

"I know."

"You should have jumped me."

"And here I thought I'd get points for protecting your virtue."

"Stop being so decent."

Jamie shifted onto his elbow and stared right at Theo, mirroring the two pictures of Aries and Leo above them on the wall. "Trust me, last night I was one breath away from being as indecent as it gets."

Theo moved forward so their noses grazed. He exhaled, long and slow over his lips. Then Theo rolled off the bed, and a pillow hit him as he sauntered out of the room.

THEO RAN HARD AND FAST, WIND WHIPPING THROUGH HIS HAIR AND drying his sweat. As always, when he hit his stride, his thoughts wandered. This time, they wandered right to Jamie.

Had he been wrong last night? Should he be thinking more about what it meant to have sex with a guy? Was it odd for him not to care?

He'd never been turned on by any other guy before. He was confident when he said he wasn't gay. The thought of getting off with Jamie didn't make him question his identity or make him curl into a ball of angst. Sex didn't define who he was.

Of course, he had the luxury not to care.

His mom, his dad, his sister, and his friends were as rainbow-supporting as they came. He lived in a bubble of acceptance he hoped would eventually cover the world. This was why he didn't have to care. It was a luxury he was quite happy to milk.

Past the cemetery, through the local park, slight detour around construction, Theo ran. When he approached the derelict bus stop and boarded houses where he'd bumped into Sam, his thoughts pivoted to her. Why wasn't he enough for Sam? Could something change in their future? What was real love, anyway?

Neither the blue sky, the daffodils, nor the stray ginger cat he passed gave him answers. Understanding seemed beyond his reach.

Sex with Jamie meant he wouldn't have to worry about the love stuff. Theo wouldn't have to feel like he was stringing someone along or disappointing them. The girls he'd had flings with, while physically satisfying, had always left him feeling like an asshole. He didn't want to be an asshole.

For him, sex and emotion were separate.

Even with Sam, who he thought he loved, sex was a tangent of their relationship, a hot, sexy, dirty tangent that was all about getting off; their emotions never crossed into that passion.

A few anatomical differences aside, he had no reason to assume sex with Jamie would be any different. They were both economists. Mutually releasing themselves made economic sense. Supply and demand and all that.

Intro-level econ.

Theo slowed to a walk as he turned onto their street and was unsurprised to see Sean knocking on their door. He looked like he'd rolled out of bed before hiking over here.

"Here for breakfast?" Theo said, sidling next to him.

The door opened and Leone smiled out at them. Smelling like vanilla shower gel, Leone was dressed in jeans and a blouse, hair hanging in locks, sunglasses resting on top of her head.

Sean stared at her and then pressed his hands to his hair, trying to flatten the kinks. "Actually, I'm here to take your sister on a tandem bike ride."

Theo studied the two smiling stupidly at each other. There was a nervous tick in Sean's throat and Leone incessantly rubbed her thighs. Sparks were flying.

It was electric. It'd never been like that with Jamie and Leone. What had he been thinking?

Theo slapped a hand on Sean's shoulder blades. A little harder than he needed to, but Sean would understand. "Take care of my sis."

"Take a shower, Theo," Leone said, blushing. "You reek of *run*."

Theo did just that then raided the kitchen for anything to eat other than full-grain muesli.

Air stirred behind him and Theo spun around. Jamie breezed into the kitchen in a charcoal crew-neck T-shirt and tan shorts. Their gazes snagged. Theo didn't let a single second settle between them. He grabbed the back of Jamie's head and kissed him. Jamie sucked in a sharp breath, drew back to search Theo's face, and then grabbed Theo's hips and pulled him in again.

There was nothing shy about this kiss. Nothing that questioned where Theo expected this to lead. He was hard and he swiveled his hips to make sure Jamie felt him.

"Get me off, Mr. Jamie Cooper."

Jamie took his time kissing him. His thumb drew circles on Theo's throat like it was calling his lust to unleash itself.

"Get me off, please?"

Jamie's lips curved against his, and then he pivoted their bodies, pressing Theo up against the kitchen island. "I want you here."

Here? flashed through his mind but the question fled as Jamie rucked up Theo's T-shirt, clutching it to his shoulder. Jamie swept a hand across Theo's chest, then bowed his head until he captured a nipple between his lips and sucked.

Theo grabbed at the side of the kitchen island and Jamie's shoulder. "More. I like it."

Theo felt Jamie's lips turn up at the edges as he kissed his way over his stomach and lower, where his arousal tugged at his balance, threatening to topple him.

On his knees, Jamie thumbed open the buttons of Theo's fly and shoved his pants to his ankles. He guided Theo's feet free and peeled his socks off. Theo would have been fine keeping them on, but Jamie probably had his reasons. Grip, perhaps.

He grinned at that.

But not for long.

Jamie slipped his hands under the waistband of Theo's boxers and squeezed his ass. He sucked the tip of Theo's throbbing dick. The heat of Jamie's breath through the fabric stole all the air.

Jamie looked up at him then. A studious gaze, like Jamie were committing this moment to memory.

"Damn dimples," he murmured, and pulled off Theo's underwear.

Theo snapped his head back as Jamie's warm mouth closed around him. Theo was glad he wasn't wearing socks then, because he was boneless as Jamie took him all the way down his throat. It felt like he was trying to suck every tickle he'd ever had out of his dick. Jesus.

"You're kidding me," Theo said.

Jamie torturously pulled off him. "Please explain."

"Please keep going."

Sex in the past was passion that transported him from the here-and-now to Horny-As-Fuck Forest. A magical place filled with filthy desires that even stripped of all inhibition he would never share with anyone.

Jamie, mouth swollen, sucked his cock like he would happily worship it all day. Horny-As-Fuck Forest had sprouted right there in their kitchen. On the spot where Jamie had licked peanut butter off his finger; where Jamie had leashed them together to cook; where every weekday morning Jamie prepared sandwiches for them, and at night, dinner.

That's why Jamie wanted him *here*. This was where he controlled the kitchen, where he was controlling every one of Theo's cursing groans.

A devilish spark lit Jamie's eye and Theo knew, just *knew* the meaning of that smug look.

"You win," Theo gasped. "Finally found a way to keep me in the kitchen."

Theo threaded a hand in Jamie's hair and his hips bucked. He watched his dick disappear into that mouth—that smart, funny, demanding, always right mouth.

And Jesus, it was *so right*.

"I'm..."

Theo lost all sense as his orgasm slammed through him. He tensed, riding the seconds of bliss as Jamie swallowed it all.

Then Jamie was standing, holding him steady, and Theo was clutching him as he let out ragged breaths on Jamie's shoulder.

Theo pulled back. He could feel Jamie's no-doubt painfully hard dick against his hip, yet Jamie kept his composure, scanning Theo's face. When he was satisfied, he hitched an eyebrow. "What did you mean, 'you're kidding me'?"

"To think we could have been doing this from the start of the year!"

He felt more than heard Jamie's responding laugh.

With a crooked finger, he drew Jamie's mouth to his. Instead of kissing him, Theo said, "Jesus, Jamie. I'm never going to look at your mouth the same way again."

"I'm glad to hear it. Now, if you don't mind," He pulled away. "I need to visit the bathroom."

Jamie was already halfway across the room before Theo had pulled up his underwear.

"Have you met me?" Theo abandoned his pants, caught up to and dragged Jamie back into the living room. "Classic Leo, remember?" He shoved Jamie's pants to his knees and toppled him lengthwise on the couch. "I'm arrogant in bed too. I have to know I'm good enough to get you off too."

Theo laid on him and Jamie instinctively grabbed his hips.

"You just want to see me undone," Jamie said, and there was an edge to his voice promising it would not take long.

Theo grinned. "I told you this is more for me than you."

Jamie shut his eyes, chin lifting as he rutted against Theo. His neck, stretched out like that, so bare...

Theo pistoned his hips, offering more friction, and Jamie. Let. Go. His mouth pinched in a groan, his eyelids flickered, and the more they ground together, the more he panted. Wispy, needy breaths of air. Fingers bore into Theo's ass cheeks as Jamie thrust hard and harder.

Theo couldn't stop himself. He slanted his lips over Jamie's and tangled their tongues together, breathing in Jamie's next frantic moan.

Jamie stilled, and Theo swallowed the hitch in Jamie's voice as he came.

The whole thing was so vulnerable and trusting, and it might have been the first time his partner had fully given into the moment. Jamie didn't care about looking pretty or screaming because that's what sex was supposed to look like. He just fucking enjoyed himself, bodily noise be damned.

Theo was turned on as hell.

Come seeped between them where Jamie's shirt had slipped up, warm and sticky. Theo slipped a hand between them and skated his finger through it. What would he taste like?

Healthy, probably.

Jamie focused on him, flushed and *done*. Theo rewarded him by flashing his dimples. "What a happy coincidence Sean took Leone out this morning."

Jamie's hand trailed up Theo's back and tickled the hairs at his neck. "Coincidence, Theo? Is that what you think?"

"Wait, you messaged Sean to occupy my sister?"

Jamie lifted his head, stopping a breath away from kissing. "And I did it before you dived onto my bed this morning."

"I'm a lean, mean, quoting machine."

Theo. He should have been drunker. Enough said.

Chapter Seventeen

S o. They'd done the dirty.
It had been great.

Promptly afterward Jamie had suggested Theo crack open his books.

That? Not so great, but in true Jamie fashion, Theo's only possible response was to laugh—and then actually get his books.

Showered and changed, Jamie worked at his spot at the dining table while Theo lounged with his laptop at the site of their passion. It was impossible to concentrate on whatever commerce bullshit he was supposed to be studying.

He faked it like a pro.

It was just. Damn. Jamie should let go like that all the time.

Theo liked how married to composure Jamie was, but seeing that side of him…

Ding!

Jamie: You haven't stopped grinning. What are you thinking?

Theo: Wouldn't you like to know.

Jamie: Yes, that's usually why one asks, Theo.

Theo: I was thinking that next time, I'm sucking you off.

Jamie's expression was steady, though he did shift in his chair a fraction.

Jamie: Get your commerce paper done, and we'll see.

Theo snapped his head up. "What are you, superhuman? I just offered to blow you."

Jamie leaned back in his chair. "Look who cracked first."

That shut Theo up. And then, conceding, "Point, Jamie."

"But I meant it. Paper first."

"Of course you did."

IT WAS A DAMN SHAME THEO'S ESSAY WAS A BITCH AND A HALF. HE needed three days working around the clock to finish it. Despite an unhealthy amount of innuendo, Jamie stuck to his guns.

Theo was beginning to think Jamie was enjoying the tease.

Two could play at that game.

The day he finished writing his essay, Theo came home to the mouth-watering smell of salami pizza. He passed Leone at the dinner table and slipped his arms around her for a quick hug, and then slunk to Jamie cutting the pizza.

It was home-baked, the dough and everything. Trust Jamie to make pizza from scratch.

Theo jumped up on the counter next to the wooden board.

He reached for a slice and Jamie batted his hand with the spatula. "Did you make this for me?"

"I made it for all of us."

"Yeah, but you made it for me."

Jamie ignored the large smile on Theo's face and whisked the pizza to the dining table. But his next words were softer, maybe even a little husky? "Did you finish your paper?"

Theo followed the hot yumminess—and the pizza. He stifled a sly grin and focused on scooping up a slice as he answered. "It was so hard, you know? I kept working and working on it but I thought I'd never finish."

Jamie paused, holding the tip of his slice to his twitching lips. He took a bite.

Theo continued, "Maybe you'd like to look at it? Work your magic? I'm happy to return the favor, of course. In fact, I insist."

Leone nodded. "You're always doing it for me. Theo and I can work on it together to give you different perspectives."

Theo choked on a mouthful of pizza. Jamie pinned Theo with a look and shook his head, while Theo stuffed his mouth full of pizza and tried not to giggle.

They demolished dinner and washed it down with chilled water. Theo leaned back in his chair and lifted his feet onto Jamie's lap.

Again, Jamie took it in stride, his expression twitching as he squeezed Theo's feet between his thighs.

"What are you up to tonight, Leone?" Theo asked, worming his big toe along the seam of Jamie's jeans. He smiled smugly as Jamie swelled and hardened.

"Not much. Probably listen to an audiobook and call it an early night."

"And you?" Theo asked Jamie.

"Helping you out. Come up to my room after you've washed up and we'll get started."

Gotcha right where I want you. "How about I email you the paper? I have somewhere I need to be."

That earned a hard pinch to his toe. "And where's that?"

THE BADMINTON COURT WITH BEN AND KYLE.

That's where he had gone after washing up. He'd even been cheeky enough to ask Jamie to borrow his car, citing research at the library. Jamie acquiesced, albeit with the stiffest nod he'd given Theo all week.

That made him light and giddy, laughter bubbling inside of him. It gave him new energy in his games, too.

Jamie still had no idea Theo met with Ben and Kyle on a semiregular basis to sweat on the court. After three sessions, he was clearly improving.

Kyle had taught him the basics of hitting the birdie on its sweet spot and at the top of its arc. How he should always stay on his toes and work from the middle of the court. No laziness allowed for this Leo.

Ben played too, helping to demonstrate, but Kyle was the more skilled.

"Are you thinking of joining a social team?" Ben asked as they packed up.

Theo zipped up the racket Kyle had lent him and retied his laces, foot propped on the bleacher. "Social team? Hadn't thought about it." But badminton, once he'd gotten the swing of things— was fun. "Maybe."

"Wait," Kyle said, taking his and Ben's sports bags and throwing them casually over his shoulder. "Why are you learning the game?"

"To piss Jamie off."

Jamie came up in conversation from time to time during their sessions. Throwaway banter. How Jamie wasn't a fan of playing games on his phone because it was a waste of time, but whenever Theo started one, Jamie would find an excuse to peer over his shoulder and watch. Or how he'd caught Jamie listening to one of Leone's audiobooks when he thought he was home alone, and he'd been smiling while calling out the fictional character for being so stupid.

"Jamie?" Ben asked, smirking at Kyle. "I should have guessed."

"He has a habit of being good at everything. I have a habit of hating to lose."

"I find myself wanting to meet this Jamie," Kyle said. "Properly this time. Though coming to pick up your and Leone's drunk asses made quite an impression."

"You want to meet him?" Theo asked.

"Don't you think your friends should meet your other friends?"

A hard lump formed in his throat. Sure, he'd hoped this was where things were heading with Ben and Kyle, but hearing the words made Theo want to do the happy dance.

Life was so much better with people to share in it.

And this time, Sam could not take it away.

But that wasn't right, was it? Sam had never taken the guys away, that had been all him. He'd let hurt feelings sever the good ones. He'd told himself over and over that Ben's waves in class were out of pity, but they hadn't been. Theo had fed himself the lie as an excuse to wallow in his misery.

Next time it looked like he might lose a friend, he intended to fight harder for them.

"Let's give it until after finals, then I'll lure him onto the court, and you can watch as I wow him."

THEO PARKED JAMIE'S CAR AND GAVE IT A ONCE-OVER MAKING SURE he hadn't dropped any of the chocolate or wrapping that he'd stolen from the glove compartment. Satisfied, he made his way up the darkened path toward home. All the lights were out, even the ones upstairs.

It wasn't even eleven yet.

Jamie should have still been up.

Maybe this made it easier? Theo wasn't sure he'd be any good at blowing Jamie, and the cover of night might hide the rough edges. Besides, things always felt better in the dark.

He entered Jamie's room, not too quietly—he didn't want to frighten him—but softly. The closing door, the churr of his socks over the rug, the sound of his clothes hitting the floor. Jamie stirred.

"In bed already." Theo *tsk*ed. "You won't stop trying to outlast me, will you?"

Jamie's response sounded too loud in the dark room. "I happen to be tired."

Theo lifted the blankets at the base of the bed and climbed between Jamie's naked legs, running his palms over his hairs. Jamie was already hard.

"Still tired?" Theo said pulling on Jamie's cock. He was determined to make this good. It was already too hot under the blankets and Theo whipped them off to the side, exposing Jamie's starfished nakedness. One might think he'd been hoping this would happen.

"Feel free to instruct me. I might not be good at this."

"Trust me. You can't go—"

Theo twirled his tongue around the head of Jamie's cock.

Jamie forgot what he was saying, ending on a pleasure-filled *hiss*. One hand gripped Theo's head and the other the sheets. Theo's erection rubbed against Jamie's leg and it was hard not to thrust. But this was his turn to please Jamie.

He pulled off with a pop and grinned up at Jamie. "I just realized I once said this was never going to happen. I take it all back, I don't mind being on my knees, singing your praises."

A light laugh morphed to a groan as Theo fed Jamie's length into his mouth, gripping the base. He liked a hot, sucking friction and tried his best to do it right. Jamie's hand in his hair helped steer the whole show—not pushing, but nudging how he liked it. Theo liked that level of honesty in bed. It made the whole experience hotter and freeing.

Theo relaxed his throat muscles as Jamie pumped in his mouth and made Theo promptly gag. He drew back. Deep throating? Probably a little ambitious.

Jamie let out a deep guttural moan that rumbled through Theo. It was such a turn on that two bucks against Jamie's leg and he was coming too. He thought about lifting off Jamie for about .001 seconds and then swallowed every drop of Jamie's release.

He used tissues to clean up his mess as Jamie needed a thorough moment to recover.

"I'm going to need a do over," Theo said, trashing the rubbish. "I want to score an A on this next time."

Jamie pulled Theo up and rolled him onto his side of the bed. "It was fucking hot, Theo."

He glanced at Theo's lips, but then he pulled away and rested on his pillow.

They enjoyed the post-sex bliss for a few moments, and then Jamie spoke in his teacher voice. "Teasing you was an excuse. That's not to say it wasn't fun, but it was an excuse."

"Excuse?"

"Hell, I almost gave in to your charm the moment you called me superhuman." Jamie stroked a thumb over Theo's arm to the tip of his middle finger. "But I wanted to give you the chance to change your mind—and see how awkward things got."

"Because of what happened with your last roommate?"

"That meant nothing. The stakes are higher with you. I don't need the sex. Just everything else."

Theo's belly flip-flopped. "Hmm, now that I've had the sex? I need the sex."

Jamie tossed a pillow at him but it didn't smother Theo's laughter, and Jamie was grinning too. "Fine. We can have the sex."

Theo pushed the pillow under his elbow and looked down at Jamie. "You can also fuck me, too. Just so you know, I wouldn't mind."

"Shh, Theo. Let's just take it easy."

"I'm just saying it wouldn't be a big deal for me."

"Well, it would for me."

Theo scratched the back of his neck. "I thought …" What had he thought? That Jamie wouldn't mind screwing him up the ass? That it might be fun to try? That it was just fucking?

Jamie touched his cheek, thumb brushing over the bow of his lips. "Get some sleep. It's past midnight and we are up in six hours."

"Are you insane? I'm sleeping until seven."

"Your choice." Jamie swatted his ass. "But you can't complain when there's no time for morning fun."

"Six hours is good. Know what? So is five and a half."

SIX HOURS LATER, JAMIE ROLLED HIS WARM, SOLID WEIGHT OFF Theo after a hot, headboard-bumping frottage session.

"There's the bed-rumpled Theo I've fantasized about."

Theo was satisfied. He wanted to curl up and stay in bed with Jamie all day. But their come was quickly growing cold on his belly and starting to seep down his sides, and unfortunately he had class.

Downstairs, Leone was banging around in the kitchen. Theo wasn't sure she'd like this arrangement he had with Jamie and her opinion meant a lot to him. Better to keep it secret. It was just sex, after all. She didn't need to know how he got off with his friend.

Jamie gently wiped up their mess off him with a satisfied smirk.

"Can I use your shower?" Theo said, shaking his head. Grinning too.

Their gazes caught and Jamie swooped in for a kiss. Pulled back. "But after me. I need to make our lunches."

While Theo waited, he stretched in bed and observed Jamie's room.

It was nice up here with these bold colors and books. Everywhere he looked made Theo want to laugh, sigh, or both. There was the desk where Jamie took studying to new levels. The olive armchair Theo often curled into with notes trying to steal Jamie's attention. Theo's framed sketches that had rattled during their morning passion. The frayed piece of paper stuck to a small corkboard with Theo's words: *You're the most solid guy in the world.* And this soft-blanketed bed that smelled like dark vanilla and sex.

The room was so Jamie.

But it was also, more and more, so Theo too.

"Shower's free."

Theo sat up as a towel flew into his face. "To save time we should have jumped in together."

"I don't know how you think that would save time." Jamie opened a drawer and pulled out underwear and Theo was treated to a view of firm, dimpled buttocks as Jamie dropped his towel and slid them on. "But I like the idea."

Theo showered quickly. Usually he loved soaking in the steam and hot water, but he was too jumpy. He needed to get moving. Needed to … something.

He took the towel and walked into Jamie's room as he scrubbed his wet hair. Jamie was dressed in black jeans and a gray T-shirt, and he was packing his laptop into his shoulder bag.

"You're not shy, are you?"

"Even less now," Theo said with a glance at the bed's tangled sheets. He dropped the towel on the armchair and slipped on yesterday's jeans sans underwear.

"The self-control one needs… I should get a medal."

Theo opened Jamie's drawers where he'd seen him put away

nicely stacked piles of T-shirts. He glanced over at a curiously watching Jamie. "You don't mind, do you?"

"Your room is downstairs."

"Have you seen how full my laundry hamper is?"

Jamie shook his head, but he was grinning.

Theo stared at the options but it was the red one in the corner that caught his eye. He recognized the shirt from Jamie's home in Wisconsin. He had brought it to Pittsburgh, then. Why? Theo picked it up. The material unfolded, until his fingers had it only pegged at the collar. Three letters stretched in bold at the chest: JLM. *Just Like Me.*

Jamie curled his hand around the strap of his bag as if frozen the second before slinging it on.

"Isn't this too tight on you?" Theo asked.

A slew of emotions passed over Jamie's face, but they came too quick for Theo to make any sense.

"I'll put it back—"

"Wear it." Their gazes connected. Jamie voice was rough. "I'd like you to wear it."

Theo held the soft material against his chest. "I do like it."

Jamie swallowed. "See you downstairs."

Theo shook off the moment, slid into the shirt, and crept downstairs while Jamie engaged Leone in morning conversation. Jamie sounded different, bigger somehow, like he was also filled with this jumpy energy.

Theo grinned.

It was the sex.

It had to be.

"Smells like guy in here. Crack a window?"

Leone coming home just after Jamie and Theo's couch fun.

Chapter Eighteen

Their friends-with-benefits status continued, possibly the only highlight of the next two weeks. Final exams were coming up fast, and most of his time was spent working toward excellent grades, finishing some website design, and thinking about whether he could afford to complete a master's degree or whether he should start working.

At night, tired, stressed, and no closer to making any life-changing decision, he ended up in Jamie's arms, ragged breath in his ear, their naked bodies thrusting toward a shattering release.

They only kissed during sex. Then it was fine—more than fine. Theo loved the feel of Jamie's tongue twisting against his—but without sex, there was an unspoken agreement that kissing crossed a line.

This sex was all just for fun.

If they had any energy left, they set up the laptop between them and watched re-runs of *Community*, or they worked side by side under their respective Aries and Leo sketches. If they were tired, Theo crashed with Jamie, too lazy to drag himself to his own room.

Most mornings, Theo woke in Jamie's bed.

Sometimes they had time to suck each other to a hard and fast release, but usually he slipped downstairs when Jamie jumped in the shower, leaving a card on Jamie's pillow with a quote of the day.

Other than nights, the ride to campus, and their one coffee date each week, they barely saw each other. Even communal dinners were sporadic affairs. He usually ate on the way to or from the library.

Leone he saw more often. She caught rides with them and Theo walked her to the history department and hung out in her office or studied alongside her until tutorials began. He also lunched with her most days, and when it wasn't raining, they took their packed sandwiches to the park and chilled.

Like they did today.

A warm spring breeze and blue skies graced the squirrel-frolicking park. Theo leaned back in the park bench and soaked in the fresh scent of new beginnings.

His phone buzzed. He fished it out of his pants like it might catch fire. Jamie had said he'd message if he could not make their usual coffee date.

Theo read, let out the breath he'd been holding, and replied.

Kyle: We on for practice again tonight?

Theo: Sure. See you at 7.

"Who got you so excited?" Leone took out one of Jamie's sandwiches from a container.

Theo snorted. "You see too much for a blind girl."

"You have no idea. Who, then?"

"Kyle about meeting for badminton this evening."

Leone smirked. "When are you going to tell Jamie? I think he suspects something's up."

"Why do you say that?"

"This sudden interest in the library, perhaps?"

"I use the library!"

"Not this much."

"Finals are next week."

"Are you prepared?" Leone asked around a mouthful of tuna sandwich.

Theo hummed. "Prepared for finals. Just not what comes after."

192

"You haven't decided on a Masters' project? You have the summer."

"I'm not sure I can afford it. I've been offered some freelance work for a few local startups, but it won't pull in enough for another year, and I don't want to take on another bank loan."

He realized the moment he said it that it was a mistake. He'd not meant to involve Leone in his financial affairs.

"You have a loan?" Leone said tightly.

"I didn't get scholarships like you, sis."

Leone punched him in the arm, hard. Theo sat up sharply, rubbing the tender spot. She sure had a swing on her. "What was that for?"

"Does Mom know?"

"She signed some of the papers."

Leone's face was red and her jaw twitched. "Why didn't you tell me? How did Mom keep that quiet? She blabs about everything!"

"I asked her not to. I didn't want to worry you or make you feel guilty."

"I could punch you again." And she proceeded to do just that.

Theo caught her balled hand before it connected a third time. "I'm sorry, I didn't want to upset you."

"How much do you need to do your master's?"

"I can scrape most of it. Maybe a couple thousand?"

"God, Theo. I hate you sometimes. I love you, and it hurts me that you didn't ask me to help. I can give you money."

"What about when your scholarships run out? I know you're hankering to do a PhD."

Leone pushed up the sunglasses sliding down her nose. "I've been offered some research assistant work over the summer, so take the damn money."

But by Theo's calculation it would make things more than tight. No matter how much Leone wished to help him, it wouldn't be enough. "It won't be enough."

"We'll figure it out. Promise me."

Theo rubbed the back of his neck and put himself in her shoes. If Leone needed the money, he would be pissed as hell if she didn't come to him first. Someway, somehow, he would have found a way to help. He sighed. "Okay. We'll figure it out."

⁓

THEO STILL FELT SHITTY ABOUT HIS LACK OF FINANCIAL togetherness when he met Jamie for their usual Thursday coffee.

They sat in their outside spot, the sunshine even warmer here than it had been in the park. Theo shrugged out of his leather jacket and slung it over the back of his chair. Jamie, in his usual head-resting-against-the-wall pose, peeked over at him, gaze dipping to the red JLM T-shirt.

By a mutual, unspoken agreement, the T-shirt had become one that Theo regularly wore. The bamboo and cotton mix created the most comfortable and cuddly T-shirt Theo owned. Also, he liked himself in red.

And liked the way Jamie looked at him when he wore it.

Like he was looking at him now, lips softly curled at the edges.

This pleasant but momentary reprieve almost made Theo shrug off the tension from his lunch with Leone. Almost.

Theo sipped the latte Jamie had bought him. He was thankful Jamie grabbed both of their drinks, which he did most of the time, but today it hit a tender spot in his pride. Jamie was always taking care of him like that. Without question.

Even when Theo had crashed Jamie and Sean's gay-bar outing, Jamie had covered for him; he hadn't even thought about it.

Theo wanted to buy Jamie something too.

"You're quieter than usual today," Jamie said, closing his eyes.

"A lot on my mind. Finals." *Finance.* "You've been busy too."

Jamie had been preparing lectures for a summer econ course. He had reviewed his Keynesian economics notes and reworked the examples that students hadn't grasped. Theo had looked over it briefly after they'd rolled around naked last night.

"Would you kiss me?" Jamie had asked.

Theo had known that he meant *Would you find the examples too convoluted and yell out to Keep It Simple, Stupid in class*, but the question had left his lips on a whisper, laden with double meaning, and it had made Theo prickle—

"Theodore?"

At the sound of his name, Theo swiveled.

Sam was coming over to him, a bright smile topping off her outfit of teal jeans, strappy sandals, and a black-and-white top under a navy cardigan. She held her takeaway coffee cup in her left hand, highlighting the glittering rock on her finger.

Theo returned the smile, He felt nothing for her. Nothing. "Hey, Sam."

She stopped at the end of their table and looked around for a chair.

Theo was glad there were no chairs free.

"How are you doing?" she asked, swirling her cappuccino—she always ordered cappuccino. "Set for finals?"

"Not much has changed, Sam." Of course he was set for his final exams. Did she know him at all?

He remembered her failure to warn him about the pontooning. Perhaps she had never known him at all.

Theo noticed Jamie shift in his seat, alert, eyes trained on Sam, hand clutching his latte. He gestured to Jamie. "Sam, Jamie. Jamie, Sam."

Sam gave a small smile and drummed her fingers on her coffee cup in a half wave. "I feel like I've seen you before," she said to Jamie. "Econ department, maybe?"

It took a moment for Jamie to find his voice. When he did, he spoke deeper than normal with a blunter edge. "The econ department is my second home, my first being Theo's."

Theo choked on a mouthful of coffee.

"You're the new roommate, then," Sam said.

Jamie smiled. Perhaps a little too tightly. "Not so new anymore."

Sam tucked a lock of hair behind her ear and laughed softly. "I hope he isn't driving you crazy. He's a hard one to live with, that one."

Theo knocked out a self-deprecating laugh but before he could throw a half-joke back, Jamie spoke.

"Theo is relaxed, good-humored, gives as good as he gets. He's no Gordon Ramsay in the kitchen but he always washes up. He knows how to work a laugh out of anyone who comes near him. Hands down easiest person I ever lived with."

Surprise flickered over Sam's face, followed shortly by an embarrassed blush, but it was nothing compared to the heat flaring in Theo's cheeks. He was taken aback by the burst of sincerity. Taken more aback by how weighted in jealousy it was.

It made him flutter.

Sam gave a nervous giggle, took a sip of coffee, and looked to Theo for a bit of support. But Theo was stuck grinning, taking in the flat stare Jamie was giving Sam as he leaned forward on his chair as if ready to jump between them and shout *My Leo!*

Jamie glanced at Theo's widening smile and instantly, his shoulders dropped and he stopped choking his latte.

"Yeah," Sam said. "He always did make our friends laugh." She rolled her shoulders back and looked at Theo. "I definitely miss that."

Theo's smile softened. It meant something that she'd said "our" friends and not "my" friends.

They'd grown up since the breakup, and he sensed something might be rekindled. Nothing romantic—Jesus, no. But maybe they could one day be friends.

He said, "We should catch up properly sometime."

"I'd like that."

Jamie made a sound in the back of his throat that said he wouldn't like that.

Theo stretched his legs under the table, bumping his foot gently against Jamie's.

"Well," Sam said, backing up. "It was nice to run into you again, Theodore. Jamie, it was…something. Maybe we could try again, sometime?"

"You will," Theo said. "He's my date to your wedding."

"He is?"

"I am?"

Theo looked from a bewildered Sam to Jamie, whose confusion was warring with satisfaction.

Theo frowned at him. "You knew that."

"I assumed you'd changed your mind since discovering I'm not Leone's best option."

"You're my best option, though. You still want to come?" To Sam he said, "That's cool, right?"

"Of… of course. Bring whoever you want." Her smile returned. "Maybe we can chat again at the wedding then, Jamie?"

She left the question hovering, spun on her heel, and wove through the tables and out of sight.

Jamie was still eyeing him

"What?" Theo said.

Jamie took a moment, then locked Theo's foot with both of his. When he spoke, it was quiet, curious. "What did you see in her?"

"Our interests aligned. We're both studying for a business degree, we enjoy running, and she could drink me under the table, which I guess isn't that hard. She was sweet and liked to squish up her nose when she was talking and"—Jamie's coffee spilled over the table, weeping over the edge onto Theo's pants—"she can skate like a pro."

Jamie grabbed their napkins and threw them atop the puddle. Clearly, they needed more. He bolted up and made his way into the store. Theo distinctly heard him mutter, "Anyone can skate!"

"I've got a bit of a wood thingy in my heel."
"A splinter?"

Theo and Jamie before Jamie begins surgery with tweezers.

Chapter Nineteen

Theo barely recognized how he got home that evening. There was a bus, and some walking, and a stop at the supermarket, but he was so deep in thought it startled him to find he was unlocking the front door. He put his shoes in the rack, swung his book-heavy bag off his shoulder onto the couch, and set his groceries on his and Jamie's spot on the kitchen island.

He called out for Leone but no answer came. It was just him, which wasn't bad right now. His head was still spinning. He'd been amused by Jamie's no-so-subtle jealousy and had told Jamie before they'd parted that he was not-so-secretly flattered.

All that was true, but other stuff churned underneath the surface. The restlessness and frustration that had been lurking in him for weeks only started voicing itself after meeting Sam.

He pulled out two items from the paper bag.

A jar of smooth peanut butter and a packet of yoghurt-covered raisins.

He picked up the jar and rubbed his thumb over the side of the lid. A flare of excitement cut through his swirling confusion as he jotted out a quote of the day, stuck it on the jar, and slipped the jar into the shelf where Jamie would see it.

He sat on the bench and threw the raisin packet up and down as he pinpointed what the hell it was that made it feel like his insides were being pulled in all directions.

It was just…

Romance had fucked him twice, the nice way and the horrible way. When Sam left him, it felt like Theo had lost everything: someone to count on, the people he thought were his friends, the future he'd hoped for. This was why he hadn't been interested in dating for so long, why it hadn't worked with Lizard.

Boundaries were good. They kept him safe and sound.

Theo tossed the raisins to the ceiling and caught them with the clap of both hands.

The sound of the door opening was followed by a laugh and urgent footsteps. Theo jumped off the bench and turned to see Sean backing his sister into the living room against the wooden beam she often used for yoga. His hands cradled the back of her head as he pressed himself close and kissed her.

Theo clutched his yoghurt raisins to his chest as surprise glued him to the scene.

Leone had her arms wrapped around his neck, one leg hooked over his hip. "Sean," she said with a suggestive note that had Theo clearing his throat. They both stiffened and looked over at him. Sean stepped back from Leone but didn't let her go.

"When did that happen?" Theo joked, though he had seen it coming.

Leone pulled up her sunglasses. "I thought you had your library date?"

"Soon."

Theo dropped the packet of raisins onto the counter and glanced at Sean. A large, goofy smile lit up his face as he pecked Leone on her temple. "Can that happen any sooner?"

He swung his gaze on Theo and dropped to his chest. Immediately, his smile vanished and his cheeks reddened furiously. He let go of Leone and moved into the kitchen where he grabbed a handful of Theo's red T-shirt and yanked him close. "Why are you wearing this?"

"Jamie let me." Theo jabbed Sean's fingers. "Do you mind?"

Sean reeled back, dropping his arm.

"I gave that to him," Sean said, and then, quietly, jaw twitching, "if you ever hurt him I will kick your ass."

"What's going on?" Leone asked.

"That's what I would like to know," Theo said, glaring back at Sean who carded a hand through his hair.

"Never mind," Sean muttered, pulling out his phone. "I need a word with Hotstuff."

∾

THEO MADE IT A SHORT BADMINTON SESSION. HE SHOULD HAVE canceled considering he was too caught up in his head to pay attention, but he hadn't wanted to put Kyle out. He wanted to know where Sean's macho-aggressiveness had come from and he wanted to know now.

When he got home, he bypassed Leone and Sean cuddled up on the couch with barely a hello, and jogged up to Jamie's room.

Jamie must have sensed him—or his footsteps were loud—because he swiveled on his chair as Theo came through the door.

"I assume you and Sean had your chat?"

"We did." Jamie stood, grabbed his sweater lying on the back of the chair, and shrugged it on while crossing over to him. He gently tugged Theo's bag off his shoulder and tossed it onto his bed. "Come for a drive?"

"I hope that is code for *Let me tell you what's going on.*"

In the living room, Sean turned his head and watched them walk downstairs. His eyes seemed to be having a silent conversation with Jamie, and Theo wished he were privy to it.

Jamie pressed a hand to the small of Theo's back and swept him to the front door. Theo hadn't taken off his shoes, and Jamie needed less than ten seconds to stuff his feet into his boots and grab his leather jacket.

They didn't speak much in the car. Jamie seemed lost in his thoughts and Theo had clammed up, nerves prickling like they had last night.

They parked downtown on a lamp-lit side street crammed with brick buildings and jutting metal pipes.

Jamie sat back and banged his head against the headrest. He

clutched the wheel and stared into the distance, where the city opened to the snaking river, silver in the moonlight.

Theo focused on Jamie and tried to find a joke to lighten the mood, because that was their thing. They bantered, they didn't have serious conversations.

"Jamie, you're freaking me out. What's going on?"

Jamie's body heaved with a breath, but then it deflated. He clicked open his belt and got out of the car.

Theo did the same.

Jamie kicked off down the pedestrian path at a pace that had Theo scrambling to catch up.

Theo caught his elbow and squeezed. Jamie slowed.

"Sean…" Jamie pressed his lips together and didn't speak again until they'd turned onto the street flanking the river. Theo shivered, but he wasn't sure if it was coming from the anticipation of their talk or the flowing river. "He found out about us sleeping together."

"How?"

"Yesterday he came upstairs to chat about him and Leone, and he saw us together in bed."

Theo played with the hem of the red T-shirt underneath his sweater. "Oh. Wearing your shirt triggered it. He thought we were secret boyfriends and needed to give me the whole *Hurt my friend, and I'll hurt you* lecture." He was probably pissed Jamie hadn't told him earlier. "You explained, though, right? That it's just sex, and that's why you didn't tell him. Same why I haven't told Leone. Surely he can't be too mad at you?"

Jamie looked away from him toward the glittering river. He cleared his throat. "Right. Yes. I told him of our arrangement."

"Then he knows I am not going to hurt you and you can't hurt me."

Jamie slowed, and a frown appeared between his brows as he glanced at Theo. "Are you still happy with this?"

His emphasis on *this* made it clear he meant the friends-with-benefits thing. Theo was quick to nod. A bit too quick maybe. His stomach still hadn't settled down. He shivered and walked closer to Jamie.

"Being this close to the river is freaking me out," Theo said. "I feel strange. Sick. Like I'm so light I'm going to be whisked away on a breeze and dropped like a stone into the river."

"Do you want me to hold you, Theo?"

Yes, yes, he wanted Jamie's strong arm around his waist, drawing him tight to safety. "Well, I don't want to fly and sink."

Jamie wrapped an arm around him. His old wood-and-vanilla scent mixed with his warmth enveloped Theo.

"Better?" Jamie asked.

Theo sighed. "I think I could walk to the middle of the bridge like this."

Jamie's fingers on his arm tightened a fraction, and he steered them closer to the river. A small slip of anxiety threaded through him but when Jamie turned his head in and asked in his ear if they should go back, Theo sank more into Jamie.

"My finals will be done by next Friday."

"I'm sure you'll do well."

"I thought we could book a badminton court for that night? Try another game?"

Theo felt Jamie's chuckle rumble through him. "You sure? You didn't seem to like it the last time."

"Is that why you didn't invite me again?"

"Yes." He stopped. "Wait, why do you think I didn't invite you?"

"Because I sucked."

"You do suck."

Theo pinched his thigh.

Jamie didn't jerk away, he pressed closer. "But it wasn't the reason."

"Then next Friday?" Theo said. "How about it? I promise it'll be fun."

"You and fun."

Jamie stopped moving and Theo looked around. They were standing on the Andy Warhol Bridge where only a decorated steel railing separated them from dark, rippling water.

"Are you okay? Sounds like you are holding your breath."

Theo pivoted and Jamie did the same so they were standing face to face, Jamie's arm still curled around his back. "Tell me again how well you swim?"

"You're safe, Theo."

Theo, trembling, shifted away from Jamie and walked over to the rail. His stomach felt like it was falling through his feet, but it was an almost-familiar feeling now seeing how often he experienced it around Jamie.

Theo gripped the steel and stared down at the water, focusing on how it reflected the lights.

He hissed in a breath. He looked over his shoulder at Jamie, who slid up behind him and weighted him down with both arms around his waist, tight, solid, secure.

"Tell me the story again, Jamie," Theo said quietly. "The one with us in your dinghy."

"I was having such a shitty day until you came home."

Theo reclining on Jamie's bed. Naked.

Chapter Twenty

The hours before each final exam seemed to stretch as he re-read his notes and made Jamie or Leone throw test questions at him. When the exams began, time passed faster than Theo liked. He tried not to think too much afterward how he could have done better.

Applied econ was his last final and he spent the evening before pacing Jamie's room, making Jamie test him from every possible angle.

Then Jamie stopped throwing questions at him and pushed him to his bed where they tested all sorts of other angles.

He answered all those correctly, his body arching when Jamie fingered him, brushing over his prostate. His deep, hungry groans clouded Jamie with lust. His hands bruised Jamie's ass as they mimicked fucking—still a limit for Jamie. Theo respected that it crossed their boundaries even if he was close to yelling how much he wanted Jamie inside him.

When Theo rolled out of bed afterward to study more, Jamie cuffed his wrist and pulled him back in.

"If you don't know your stuff by now, you won't," he said, pinching a stray hair from Theo's cheek. "I'm confident you know it, though."

Theo grinned. "How would you grade me, Mr. Jamie Cooper?"

"Your ego needs another boost, does it?"

"Yep."

Jamie laughed. They fell asleep soon after and woke shortly before the alarm, warm and comfortable in each other's arms. Theo relished the feel of Jamie cocooning him and didn't want to get out of bed.

"Who'd have thought naked cuddling could be this good?" Theo said to a stirring Jamie.

Jamie drawled, "Just about any man with drive."

"Who would have thought naked cuddling without wanting sex could be this good?"

Jamie cracked an eye open. His voice was husky from sleep. "You don't want sex?"

He shook his head. "While I love making you roll your eyes back and shudder, I think five minutes of this is all I need this morning." With the exam nerves fluttering in his belly, being close felt more grounding than sex.

Jamie had studied his face closely, his hand cupping Theo's neck, thumb tapping his temple as if he were trying to read his thoughts.

An hour later on his way to his exam, Theo was still thinking how Jamie's gaze seemed to bore right through him, throwing him off kilter.

Theo powered through his last final, thinking—hoping—Jamie would have been proud at his answers. When he submitted the exam, the first thing he had to do was find Jamie and tell him all about it. He bought coffees and headed to the econ department where Jamie was busy outlining summer lectures and tutorials.

The smile Jamie gave him made that prickling feeling flare. It had been steadily growing, this reaction he had whenever he saw Jamie. This time it reached to Theo's fingertips and toes. Coming near him was almost too much to bear.

They only had a few minutes together before Jamie had a meeting with his advisor. Theo swallowed down the disappointment. It wasn't like they weren't going to see each other for ages. They were meeting tonight for badminton.

Jesus, what is wrong with me?

Theo left the office crashing into the girl who had flirted with him the first time he'd come to the econ department to find Jamie. It seemed like an eon ago, not four months. It almost made him laugh how much had changed in only four months. Who would have thought his ex-tutor would become his best friend and the guy he slept with every night?

He swept a look over the girl like he had that first day. She was still pretty with her bangs and wavy hair, but this time there was no desire. Not the slightest stir.

"Sorry," Theo said, releasing her arm where he'd grabbed her to stop her falling over. "I wasn't paying attention."

She gave him a sweet smile. "You come up here a lot," she said, glancing behind Theo toward Jamie's office door.

Funny how he hadn't noticed her at all other than that first time and this one.

"It's Jamie's second home, so…" He shrugged.

"He's been so different this year," she said.

"What do you mean?"

"He was always so focused and to-the-point with a quiet humor, you know? Like he found things amusing but didn't want to share. But lately we've caught him staring out of his window, smiling. He laughs more, shares more too." She leaned forward and lowered her voice, "Half the department thinks he has found a boyfriend."

Theo gripped the strap of his bag at his chest where he could feel his heart drumming.

"And," she continued, "most of them think it's you."

He shook his head and fought a stammer. "We're friends. Nothing else."

Theo left, banging his way out of the building and marched to the history department. The sickness he had had at the river slammed into him. He found Leone and dragged her to their lunch park.

She pressed her sunglasses up her nose, waiting for him to explain the abduction.

Theo paced the bench before her, stepping on gravel that had been kicked off the path into the grass. "I'm sleeping with Jamie."

Leone sucked in her bottom lip, but she didn't seem as shocked as he expected.

"Did Sean tell you?" Theo asked.

"No," she said slowly, "but—"

"It's just sex," Theo blurted, shoving his hands in his pockets, still pacing. "Friends with benefits."

"Is it?"

"What is that supposed to mean?"

"I was just curious, Theo." The breeze blew a lock of hair across her face and she tucked it back. "But what is the difference between friends who have sex and boyfriends? Do you date others? Does Jamie?"

"He wouldn't. Or at least he'd tell me if he was interested in someone else."

"Let me get this straight," she said and smiled wryly. "You are friends, who are exclusively having sex?"

"I know what you're getting at, but there's a difference, okay?"

"By all means, enlighten me."

"Sex with Jamie is fun." And playful and strong and sensual and raw. It was the cherry on top, but one he'd willingly decimate into a million pieces so long as their friendship remained. "Having more than sex would get complicated."

"Sounds complicated enough, if you ask me."

He shook his head. She didn't understand. His friendship with Jamie was deeper than anything he'd ever had before, so deep it felt like a core part of him. "What we have is safe."

She was quiet for a long minute. When she spoke, she quoted, "Fear not rejection and heartbreak, Leo."

Theo laughed. "You can't honestly believe in that stuff! Horoscopes are just for shits and giggles, they're not a manual for how to live life."

"There is a kernel of truth there, though. If I hadn't taken it to heart, I wouldn't have opened myself to the possibility of Sean."

Theo hooked a piece of gravel on the tip of his shoe and sent it skipping over the grass.

"Another question," she said. "How will you feel when Jamie finds a real boyfriend?"

That sickness just wouldn't go away, would it? "I'd be happy for him. Because he's my friend. The sex is just for now and just for fun."

Leone stood and beckoned him over. When she gripped his shoulder, she told him to head back to the history department.

Theo led her there, unsatisfied, still restless. More than restless. Much more.

It was like he was choking inside and close to drowning. His throat was closing in, and it made him desperate to find Jamie, because he was a good swimmer and he would not let anything happen to him.

He hugged Leone and told her she and Sean should come to the badminton court tonight.

Just as he was leaving, Leone called out softly. "If it's just for fun, why the urgency to talk to me? Why tell me at all?"

Theo didn't answer, but her question haunted him the rest of the day.

ALL OF THEM TURNED UP FOR BADMINTON. BEN AND KYLE, SEAN and Leone, and he and Jamie. Ben and Leone sat on the bleachers at the sidelines watching as the rest of them started a doubles set. Kyle and Theo against Sean and Jamie. Best of three games of twenty-one points.

Jamie had tried to suggest Sean or him pair up with Theo to "even things out", but that was out of the question. Theo was about to prove a point.

Or score one, at any rate.

Theo served first and did it flawlessly, almost catching Jamie by surprise. Jamie returned the hit and Kyle snapped it back. The birdie flew hard and fast over the net, and Theo swished and flicked, definitely catching Jamie by surprise.

The birdie soared past his startled face and Sean did a gymnastic stunt to reach it—and failed.

Point, Theo.

Kyle high-fived him with their rackets. Ben cheered and Leone frowned, believing Ben mistaken when he told her Theo had made it happen. "Theo? My Theo?"

Theo smirked and waggled his brows. "Bring it on, Mr. Jamie Cooper."

Surprise morphed to a smirking determination as Jamie brought it.

Theo, though much improved, was still no match for Jamie and Sean. Yet, he was determined to win their side one more point. Determined to see that genuine surprise flicker over Jamie's face, his eyes glittering with awe. He flicked his racket and smashed the birdie. He drove, he cleared, he carried—

and he killed.

The birdie cracked against the floor at Jamie's feet and Jamie shook his head in disbelief. Sean scooped up the birdie with his racket and gave it back to Kyle.

"Break," Jamie called and stepped off the court. Instead of going directly to his sports bag for his water, he rounded the net and snagged Theo by the arm.

Theo let Jamie drag him, grip rather gentle on his upper arm, to their bags a birdie-serve away from Ben and Leone. It was as private as it got for the open court.

Jamie fished out two water bottles and passed Theo one. They took a few sips, Theo unable to hide a cocky smirk as he counted down the time it took for Jamie to crack. Ten seconds.

"Got something you want to share, Theo?"

Theo let the tension mount before he spoke, making sure his dimples deepened the way Jamie liked. With a shrug, he said nonchalantly, "I told you anyone could play badminton."

When Jamie had picked up his racket, Theo had no idea, but he sure felt it as it lightly flicked against his ass.

A laugh bubbled through the off-kilter frustration of the day— month?—as he capped his bottle. "Kyle has been teaching me."

"Wait…library nights? I knew your dedication to studying was too good to be true."

It was Theo's turn to swat Jamie, but Jamie was backing toward a gawking Sean before he grabbed his racket. "Let's make this inter-esting," Theo said. "Next one to score a point—"

"Does the laundry for a month."

"Laundry? That's what you come up with?"

Jamie raised a brow. "How else will I get you to tackle that chock-full hamper of yours?"

"You think you're going to win."

"It will be fun watching you fold my T-shirts and pair up my socks."

Jamie got off on that torture, didn't he? "You're on."

They faced each other on the court, rackets at the ready, and the air cracked with their thirst to win the next point.

～

"You sure wowed him," Ben said to Theo as they ordered the first round of drinks for everyone.

The bar had been Ben and Kyle's choice. Likely because they lived around the corner and would not have to worry about getting home later. Considering the wink Kyle had given Ben, Theo wondered if it was the same bar where they had met.

It was a hip place, with exposed brick walls, rough wooden furniture, and mellow purple spotlights that cast a warm glow over the L-shaped rooms. Theo liked it because it wasn't Jamie's usual haunt.

Music vibrated through the floors, louder here than in their corner booth, and he had to lean in to talk. "Didn't wow enough, though."

Theo had lost the bet to Jamie after a long and hard rally. Fair was fair and he should suck it up and do their laundry, but he still made it his mission tonight to weasel out of it.

"Pfft," Ben said, "he had his eyes on you the whole game. And after, too."

They had used the changing room facilities to shower and dress in casual clothes, and Ben had darted in to hand over a towel Kyle had left in the hall.

The way Ben hadn't stopped watching the two of them since made Theo sure he caught a stolen moment between him and Jamie. He probably thought something was going on.

Which there was. But not… well.

He stuffed back those thoughts and lifted the first drink tray the waiter slid over to them. Ben grabbed the second and they carted the beer, cocktails, and soda to the quieter corner of the bar where Leone and Sean, Kyle and Jamie sat on a three-sided booth.

Ben did not hesitate in climbing around Jamie to get to his boyfriend after they had doled out everyone's drink.

Leone and Sean were discussing the merits of blindness, and Kyle seemed to find Leone's outtakes funny as hell. Jamie took his beer and sipped, quietly amused, and Theo slid onto the sweater he had laid over the sticky leather seat and cradled his soda. Tonight, he was definitely the designated driver; he wasn't going to mess it up like the last time.

Theo's arm brushed against Jamie's, the cool wedge of his wrist-watch hitting Theo's wrist, hairs tickling his forearm. They peeked at one another at the same time, and Theo's toes curled.

He purposely bumped their arms together as he twisted his soda. Under his breath, he said, "Is there any way I can get out of this whole laundry thing?"

"Ha. No."

Theo scowled, then decided playing harder for it. He rested his hand on Jamie's thigh under the table and inched upwards. "Sure about that?"

"You're unbelievable."

"I know."

Jamie found Theo's groping hand and pegged it to his thigh, fingers sliding together. It was the closest they had come to holding hands post sex-arrangement and suddenly Theo's palm grew clammy and nervous. Hopefully he didn't soak a handprint into Jamie's jeans. Jesus.

"Still not going to change my mind. A lost bet is still a bet."

"Double or nothing? You could have me slaving over an ironing board for two months. Hell, let's make it the entire summer."

Jamie took interest. He tapped his thumb against the back of Theo's small finger. "Tempting. I'll think about it."

Theo squeezed Jamie's thigh and slipped his hand free, cooling it on his glass that pearled with condensation.

"...No line-ups at the airport is great too. But the best part?" Leone said, "I have a permanent excuse to avoid other people's chores. You need help moving your shit to a new apartment? Sorry, can't help. Blind."

Sean scoffed. "I've seen how resourceful you are. I'm not letting you escape helping me move."

"Planning on moving again so soon, are you?" she said.

"My roommate chants for three hours every night. I hadn't slept through the night until I started sleeping at yours, gorgeous."

"If that's your idea of sleep, then—"

Sean laughed and cut her off with a kiss, sparing Theo the details, thank God.

Ben snuggled into Kyle. Comfortable, relaxed. "You guys ready for the wedding?" Theo groaned at the reminder. The wedding was only two weeks away. "Find a dress, Leone?"

"This is another advantage," she said. "I can wear whatever the hell I want. What kind of asshole is going to tell me I look shit?"

"Well…" Sean started, earning himself a punch to the shoulder. Any higher and Leone would have clocked his jaw—another advantage of being blind? Oops, I didn't *mean* to kick you in the nuts?

The quick-fire banter continued like they'd all been friends for ages. Kyle and Jamie discussed the best badminton rackets and whether they should join the local club. Ben and Sean chatted about some game Theo had never heard of, while Leone got Theo to be a gentleman and lead her to the bathrooms.

When Theo and Leone returned, it was to an almost vacated booth. Only Kyle lounged on the seat with his arms stretched over the back taking in the scene.

He looked at Theo and said, "You and Jamie are totally doing it."

Theo didn't bother to deny it.

Leone spat out her greedy sip of Jack and Coke. "How do you know?"

Kyle shrugged. "Intuition. The fuckload of sex pheromones pouring out of them on the badminton court. Or maybe I caught the two groping under the table."

"Theo!" Leone said, shocked.

Theo flashed Kyle a grin and said to Leone, "Well, he *is* my Aries. Highly sexually compatible and all that."

Leone rang out a laugh. "Mom would be pleased."

"Is it serious?" Kyle asked.

Theo's grin disappeared. "No."

"Friends with benefits," Leone said. "Right, Theo?"

Theo swallowed. "Right."

Ben came back to the table and Theo let him past. Sean and Jamie followed with hot fries and dip. Sean didn't bother sitting to enjoy it. A new song started and he took Leone by the hand and led her to the dance area

Theo hooked a finger in the belt loop of Jamie's jeans to force him to sit, but Jamie didn't budge. His gaze had fixed across the room and his Adam's apple jutted as he swallowed.

Theo followed his gaze. "What is it?"

Jamie's sigh sent ice hurtling through Theo's veins. "Charlie."

His ex-boyfriend was here when they had avoided going to Jamie's bar? What type of fucked-up shit was that? Was the universe flipping their finger at them or what?

"Oh," Theo said, throat clogged.

"I'm going over to say hello."

Theo didn't like it. "Is that a good idea?"

Jamie flashed him a small, half-reassuring smile. "You set a good example the other day with your ex. It's high time I also left the past behind. Maybe we can be friends again too."

Theo didn't like this at all.

He tried to find something to say to make Jamie stay, but let out a shaky breath instead. "Okay, sure."

He gripped the lip of their pockmarked table until his fingers hurt, watching as Jamie waltzed over to a cute copper-haired, preppy dressed guy, whose guy friends seemed enthralled. What was up with his sparkling eyes? Had to be drugged.

Ben slid over to him and tracked Charlie. "Cute guy. What's your man doing approaching him? Is that part of your deal?"

He shut his eyes for a moment hoping when he reopened them Jamie would have finished chatting with Charlie.

No such luck.

Theo couldn't stomach any fries. He drank all his soda, the fizz burning his throat.

Theo narrowed his eyes as Jamie and Charlie hugged. Jamie motioned to the bar behind him and Charlie pointed to a free booth his friends were piling into. Jamie was going to get him a drink so they could talk.

Theo edged his way around the dance floor and made for Jamie, then he changed course and made for Charlie and company instead. He wanted to size him up and hear his voice. Wanted to know who it was Jamie had thought he was in love with.

He wished he'd taken his drink. It would make lurking near their table less weird. Thankfully, behind their booth was a framed board of drunken quotes and a thick brick column to lean back against. Theo feigned interest in reading the quotes, while surreptitiously eyeing Charlie.

He wasn't that cute up close. His nose turned up too much at the end, his ears stuck out, and… who was he kidding? Charlie looked good, and the way he absorbed his friends' attention said he knew it.

Theo stilled, pretending to read a lengthy quote, when he heard one of Charlie's boys say, "Who is that guy?"

"My ex."

"He's hot."

"Yeah, but once I got over that, there was nothing to keep me there."

Theo stopped pretending to read and pivoted, watching Charlie flick a bang from his eyes.

"You broke up with him, then?"

Charlie shrugged. "He was really boring, you know?"

A familiar green T-shirt flickered in Theo's eye and he looked over to see Jamie standing there with couple of beers. He'd stilled a few paces from the booth, and the tension in his stance made Theo ache. He had heard Charlie. The light in Jamie's eyes blacked out and he stared for a moment at the beers before turning and heading back toward their booth.

Thanks to the brick column, he didn't think Jamie had seen him. He wasn't sure whether to be relieved or not. He had meant to pry, but he hadn't expected that insight into their painful breakup.

Theo's throat felt raw and his fists closed into tight balls. How dare Charlie say that about Jamie. How *dare* he.

Charlie was still talking. "Always about eating well and cleaning and studying. The only interesting thing about him was how he shuddered every time we went into a store that had mannequins. I guess he'd make an okay friend, but he wasn't a good lover."

Theo fumed. A blinding rage twisted in his gut. He emerged from behind the column and stepped right up to booth, glaring at the copper-haired, sparkly-eyed dickface. "Are you talking about Jamie Cooper?"

Charlie gave him a startled once-over. "That's none of your business."

"Actually, it is my business. That's my best friend and if you're talking shit about him, I have a problem with it."

"Well I have a problem with you butting in on a private conversation."

"You're in a bar, nothing's private." Through a mist of red, Theo leaned forward, bracing his hands on the table not to fucking punch that cold sneer off Charlie's face. "Let me set the record straight."

One of the boys snorted, further cementing his dislike for Charlie.

Theo went on. "Jamie is the most caring, protective, determined, genuine, all-around most amazing guy I have ever met. He would do anything for those he cares about, and making sure you eat well and take care of yourself and reach your potential makes him the best person you could ever have in your life."

"Nice sonnet. Sing it to him."

Theo sucked in the boiling need to punch Charlie's stupid face.

It might have been almost unnoticeable for anyone else but Theo knew Jamie. That slight deadening of his gaze meant Jamie felt sad.

Charlie had to take his words back, dammit.

"I feel sorry Jamie wasted his time with you. You didn't deserve him."

Charlie shot up and shoved Theo in the chest, making him reel a half-step back. In the distance, Theo vaguely heard his name, but he kept his eyes glued on Charlie.

"Fuck off back to Mr. Dreary, would ya?"

Theo threw back a balled hand ready to sock the guy in his stupid nose, but someone caught his elbow and dragged him back. "Whoa. Theodory, calm."

Sean hooked Theo's other elbow and pulled him from Charlie through the glitter-covered dance floor.

"Fuck!" He wrenched free of Sean's hold and slammed his eyes shut as he forced his rational side to take over.

He caught a whiff of old wood and dark vanilla, and the hairs on his arms and neck lifted with a shiver.

Jamie pressed the small of his back and herded him through the crush of newcomers outside.

Theo had the car keys in his pocket, but he walked to a path at the side of the bar and leaned back against the brick façade. He let his head fall back.

"What were you thinking?" Jamie said tightly.

Theo's eyes welled with heat. "He insulted you."

Jamie stared at him, long and hard. Was he pissed off at Theo? Finally, Jamie closed and rubbed his eyes. "Come. Sean is leading Leone to the car."

"You heard him," Theo croaked. This was the worst part in it all.

"Yes."

"I wish you hadn't," Theo said.

"That's my line."

Theo reached out and balled Jamie's T-shirt, then he drew him close, then closer still until Jamie's breath hitched over Theo's chin. "He is not worth pining over."

A tilt of his head. "Who said I was pining?"

"Aren't you?"

"About Charlie? No."

"I still want to punch him."

"How about we get home so you can entertain me with more double-or-nothing shenanigans? Or better yet, start a load of laundry."

∾

THEY GOT HOME AND LEONE SET THE TEA KETTLE ON, ORDERING Sean to grab the cookies from the bottom cupboard. Jamie busied himself putting away his badminton gear in the utility closet.

Theo couldn't stomach eating anything and waved the offer of cookies away. He sat on the couch and stared at Jamie when he came back with a fixed smile that didn't reach his eyes and Theo hated it. The smile was a lie.

Theo felt the tenderness of Jamie's hurt like it was his own.

Sean slumped next to Theo, grabbed him around the neck, and knuckled his head. "I've decided I like you, man."

Theo peeled Sean's bony knuckles off him. "I'm still undecided."

Sean laughed, and Jamie watched briefly as he helped Leone squeeze out the tea bags from their mugs. Theo knew it took everything Jamie had to act normal and he wished Jamie would drop the fucking act.

"Honestly, for a second I hesitated before pulling you back," Sean said. "I wanted you to hit the fucker."

Leone chimed in, "I'm glad no one will be able to press charges. Theo, why?"

Theo kept his mouth shut. He refused to bring up Charlie's words. The way Jamie stared at their finished tea, the memories were close enough to the surface.

"I'm shattered," Jamie said and clamped a hand on Leone's shoulder. "I wish you all a good night. Sean, you're on breakfast tomorrow."

Then, with the barest glance at each of them, he trudged up to his room.

Sean planted a hot mug in Theo's hand. A few minutes later, Theo still hadn't sipped his tea. Sean clicked his fingers, forcing Theo's attention from the balcony and Jamie's closed door back to the living room.

"You've been practicing badminton on the sly. Tell me about that."

"Know what? I'm tired too." Theo stood, poured his untouched drink down the sink, and headed up the stairs.

"Your bedroom's that way," Sean joked. Theo flipped him off and continued up to Jamie's room.

Theo slipped inside and shut the door softly. The reading lamp at the side of Jamie's bed was on, casting a soft glow over the room. Jamie wasn't reading, though. He lay in bed, one arm crooked over his upward turned face. He had forgotten to take off his watch, but the folded clothes on the armchair suggested he'd undressed.

Jamie shifted his arm as if to peek out from under it and then changed his mind. Theo gritted his teeth, wishing he had clocked Charlie. Jamie might be good at pretending he'd be fine and he sure as hell would be reasonable, but that wasn't enough for Theo. He needed to take the hurt away. Needed Jamie to know it wasn't true.

Needed him to know he was the most incredible guy Theo had ever known.

Theo pinched the hem of his shirt and drew it over his head. He tossed it over the back of the armchair and did the same with his pants. He shirked his underwear too.

Theo slid into the crisp, cool sheets, rolling on his side.

Neither of them spoke.

Theo carefully unclasped the latch of Jamie's watch, drew it off him, and placed it on the side table.

Jamie still didn't remove his arm, but his fingers twitched.

Resting his head on Jamie's shoulder, Theo put a hand on his chest, fingers skimming over Jamie's light hairs.

Jamie curled Theo closer, palm grazing Theo's back and hip. Arousal thickened his cock, but Theo ignored it. The edge of his lips was against Jamie's skin, and he pressed them against the warmth, feeling Jamie's heart pulse and his quick intake of breath.

Finally, that arm dropped and Jamie cupped the back of Theo's neck. Their eyes met, the seconds spinning and tangling until Theo was caught and couldn't look away. Didn't want to.

Theo pushed a foot against Jamie's and hooked a leg over his waist, propping himself up. He fit himself against Jamie, their erections pressing together with a burst of want. He restrained from thrusting and combed his fingers through Jamie's hair, settling his grip at the side of Jamie's neck. He urged Jamie's chin up with his thumb and dipped his head.

The kiss was tender, unhurried.

Theo's breath shuddered when they pulled apart, and then he kissed him again, relishing the way Jamie clutched and arched into him. Shivers slingshot through him as their tongues touched.

Feeling Jamie's need, Theo wrapped his hand around both their dicks and he stroked slowly, pulling out every grunt and gasp and shudder from Jamie as he could. Every time Jamie let go, Theo soaked it up.

Theo kissed down Jamie's neck to the spot on his shoulder that made Jamie buck and rumble with a moan, and Theo returned each grunt, gasp and puff of breath until he didn't know whose was whose anymore.

Theo felt Jamie's pleasure crescendo and because of it, his own. He dropped another kiss, and then another and another. He couldn't get enough.

Jamie was close, and Theo felt the short, urgent bursts of breath tickle the seam of his mouth. Their gazes locked. A moment of connection—startling awareness—passed before orgasm plunged through them and they stilled, croaking together as their warm seed spilled over their stomachs.

Boneless, Theo collapsed against Jamie as they caught their breath, mingling their release over their treasure trails. Jamie flexed under him as he shifted, reaching for the tissues.

Theo pushed up with a shy smile and took over, cleaning both of them. He caught the flush in Jamie's cheeks as he reached for his lamp. Theo had made that happen.

He climbed back into bed and Jamie doused the light. Without hesitation, he tucked Theo against his side.

Jamie shut his eyes and sighed. The feeling vibrated through Theo's hand lying against Jamie's belly. That sick lightness surged inside, filling him up violently, insisting Theo face what it was.

He trembled at Jamie's side.

Oh.

Fuck.

"And, Leos? Don't forget to smile."

Crystal giving Theo and Leone their daily horoscope.

Chapter Twenty-One

This time things got awkward.

Theo felt extremely… aware. So aware that everything he did seemed exaggerated. All that mattered was making Jamie laugh. Making Jamie banter. Making Jamie *anything*.

Yet he seemed to be fucking it up, because over the following week, Jamie grew distant.

If Theo didn't know better, he'd think Jamie was avoiding him.

Jamie was still there, but he kept a ring of space around him. When Theo flopped down on the couch next to him, Jamie got up to make tea. When Theo touched his arm, Jamie pulled away to check the time on his watch. When Theo climbed up to his room at night, Jamie would not come to bed until Theo had fallen asleep—and he'd be up first in the morning.

When Theo masked a sudden ache and joked about Jamie not being *hot for him*, Jamie grew silent. He swallowed a lot. Then he told Theo he had a lot on his mind. Summer courses started next week and he had too much planning to do. To be fair, every time Theo glanced at Jamie's laptop he was working on economics slideshows.

Turned out Theo fretted about being with a guy after all.

He ran, navigating potholes while trying to sort out the pitfalls of his new situation, but he didn't get far. That sickness kept stinging him like a manic, evil wasp. Twice he even stopped, bent over a gutter.

All he could imagine was the horrible hollowness that would consume him if he lost his friend.

~

FINAL GRADES WERE IN.

Theo checked his results online while Leone tried on a dress. "Can't go too short or too flashy, keep that in mind."

Leone tugged at the separating curtain and Theo stopped looking at his screen and helped. Leone wore a navy tank dress with splits up to the low thigh. "Looks classy to me."

"This one? Or the twisty dress one? Which one works better with my cleavage?"

"Shouldn't your boyfriend be here for this?"

"I want to surprise him. We should hurry because my alarm just beeped. He'll be outside any minute now."

"Fine, the one you have on. It covers more."

"The other one it is."

Theo huffed out a laugh and helped her to the cashier to pay. Once they were out of the store and into the early evening sunshine, Leone handed him her bag. "Take that home with you and shove it in my closet? And maybe do something about whatever's making you restless?"

"I'm not restless." He was restless.

Sean made his presence known with a whistle, then slung an arm around Leone's shoulder and pulled her in for a kiss.

"That's my cue to leave," Theo said. "Enjoy your dinner."

At the bus stop, Theo continued checking his grades. He almost missed his ride when he saw an A+ next to applied econ.

He punched the sky and dashed into the bus. He couldn't wait to tell Jamie. No matter what awkwardness was happening between them, Jamie would be thrilled. Proud too, as he should be. Without Jamie, it never would have happened.

He spotted Jamie's car at the curb. He entered the house too excited to care about taking off his shoes or dumping his satchel. He darted to Leone's closet and put her dress away, and then bounced up the stairs calling Jamie's name.

He heard the shower running and parked himself on the desk chair, setting his bag on Jamie's desk. For a moment, he considered stripping and joining Jamie, but he decided against it.

Theo searched Jamie's desk for a piece of paper to scribble a quote of the day on. He opened Jamie's desk drawer and pulled out some wrinkled paper.

Theo blinked. Looked at the second piece of paper and the third. He swallowed hard as he set the paper on the desk in the shoddy puddle of evening light coming through the window.

The shower shut off. He heard Jamie's footsteps.

His throat had seized up and heat burned his eyes. He pinched the lip of the desk with his fingers as if that might ground him.

It didn't.

The air stirred behind him.

"Theo," Jamie said. A drawer opened and closed. The wet towel *thwapped* over the top of the door. "I thought you were meeting Ben and Kyle tonight?"

"Something came up," Theo said stiffly. "I came home instead." He swiveled around slowly, hoping his stomach would come with him. "You're looking for a new place?"

Jamie had one leg in his pants when he froze. He looked over at Theo and then past him at the papers on the desk. Roommate Wanted notices pulled from pin boards. Slowly, Jamie pulled up and buttoned his pants. "I was thinking about it. In case."

Theo numbly nodded. "You were thinking about it," he repeated, a new bloom of pain hurtling through him. "Thinking of how you will up and leave us."

Jamie abandoned his T-shirt and sat on the edge of the bed facing Theo. He tried to take his hand, but Theo leaned away. "It's not like that. I just –"

"Want to leave us."

"No. Yes. It might be best, but—"

Theo gasped the second Jamie uttered yes. He shoved off the chair and grabbed his satchel. "Might be best?"

Jamie stood, reaching for him again. Theo jerked out of reach. "Don't touch me."

"You need to calm down so we can talk about this properly."

"You want to talk? You want to be mature about this? Here's what I think: you're wrong. You, Jamie, who are always right, are so fucking wrong."

Jamie kept himself in control, tempered, waiting for a break so he might slip in a word. He wasn't going to get one.

"Fuck you, Mr. Jamie Cooper. Fuck you." But his voice betrayed him.

Theo fled the bedroom without looking back. He couldn't bear to see Jamie's sudden realization followed by the gentle way he would let Theo down.

With a pounding heart, he took the stairs three at a time.

"I lied, Theo," Jamie yelled from the balcony, but the words bounced off Theo. He was too anguished, sad, and embarrassed. He couldn't take any more. "From the beginning, I lied. About that T-shirt, I lied."

Theo slammed the front door and ran.

∾

JAMIE: PLEASE COME BACK SO WE CAN WORK THIS OUT.

Theo: Stop being so damn reasonable!

Jamie: Pretty please?

Theo: Let a Leo lose some steam, would you?

Jamie: Does that mean you are coming back eventually? Or do I have to bribe you with promises to do your laundry over summer?

Theo: But you won't be here over summer.

Jamie: It's complicated. Let's have this conversation in person.

Theo: I know talking is the sensible thing to do. But I want to lick my wounds in private.

Jamie: I never meant to hurt you. That is the last thing I want. Can I help lick your wounds at least?

Theo: Stop it.

Jamie: Stop what?

Theo: Making me laugh. Clearly I'm meant to be cursing you right now.

Jamie: You can curse me to my face, I won't stop you. I'd prefer it.

Theo: I'm turning my phone off now, Jamie. I will message you later.

Before switching off his phone, he sent two more messages. One to Sean and one to Leone. Theo bussed to the pizza parlor where he had gone out with Liz and close to where Sean was dining with Leone.

He ate a slice of pepperoni pizza as he stared out the window at the parking lot. Every time a car parked, his stomach flipped and he watched, each time reliving that moment Jamie had arrived during his date. That sudden tingling elation.

The pizza sat heavy and greasy in his stomach. Maybe this was why most people opted for ice cream in these situations. The coolness would help numb the flaring nerves and frustration and the waves of nausea.

Just the idea Jamie had been looking for another room…

He chucked his used napkin in the trash and shouldered out of the restaurant.

Time for part two of his moping hour.

Alex at the skating rink wasn't working tonight and Theo almost winced handing over the money for his gear. Families and groups of friends skated and laughed as they made rounds to snappy music.

As he rolled over the polished wood, Capital Cities' "Safe and Sound" jumbled the butterflies in his stomach as he thought of Jamie's first economics lecture and the first time he and Jamie met when he'd interviewed Jamie for the room.

He threaded through other skaters, making fast rounds, determined to rid himself of this pent-up energy. But the more he skated, the more he pictured Jamie on the rink. How he had stumbled and slipped. How his unnerving determination won out as he practiced and bettered himself. How Theo had teased him. How they'd made that truth-or-dare bet.

Theo spun to a halt on the spot where Jamie had startled him by yelling his name and they had tumbled together. It had been so important that Theo not let Jamie up until he had smiled.

That had also been the first time he'd been aroused by Jamie— and he'd pegged it on friction!

Really, Theo. You're an idiot. That's an F on the paper of life.

"Theo!"

At the edge of the rink, Sean and Leone were waving at him.

Thanking his lucky stars, he skated over and off the rink, beckoning them to a free bench at the back wall. Sean helped Leone maneuver the tight aisle and they sat next to him, Leone frowning, Sean with an expectant stare.

"You said you needed us?" Sean said, his fingers playing with a loose lock of Leone's pinned hair.

Theo rested his helmet between him and Leone on the bench. He leaned back against the wall. "Tell me about the red T-shirt." Sean stopped twirling Leone's hair. "Maybe Jamie should."

"No. You said you gave it to him. Why? Tell me everything."

Leone rested her head on Sean's shoulder. Theo had told her how he had practically annexed the soft shirt and how people looked at him like he was a religious freak when he wore it. She knew he loved it. Apparently, she knew more. "You should tell him, Sean."

Sean sucked in his bottom lip. "I told Jamie to tell you this. He said he would."

"The night you threatened to kick my ass?""

"Yes."

"He told me you found out about us sleeping together."

"That's not all of it and he knows it."

"So tell me." Goosebumps prickled as Theo took a nerve-wracking breath. "JLM. It doesn't stand for Just Like Me, does it?" His voice hitched. "And it doesn't stand for Jesus Loves Me."

It hit him hard and heavy like a bat to his gut, knocking the air from his lungs.

Oh, God.

Jamie!

Tears swelled at the edges of his eyes, and he choked as an enormous smile filled him up on the inside.

Sean hummed, studying him before relenting. "We were in our last year of high school and I fancied myself in love with this girl Rebecca. I didn't know what to do with the crazy jumpy energy inside me—I wanted to show her how I felt. But I was relatively clueless what I should do.

"So one day, on the middle of the lake after racing our dinghies to Jamie's place—for dinner, of course—I asked him what I should do. Turned out Jamie was a notch more clueless. *Buy her a T-shirt or something?* he'd suggested. I laughed so hard I nearly fell into the lake. That had to be the least romantic gesture I had ever heard of and I told him so.

"That Christmas I bought him that red T-shirt with the lettering JLM. As a joke, I made him promise that he would give this to the guy he fell in love with."

Through his blurry gaze, Theo concentrated on the middle of the rink, on him and Jamie looking at each other, Theo's hand at Jamie's lips. Staring so hard, he could almost feel Jamie's warm, heavy weight and the whisper of his smile over his fingertips.

Sean continued, "Jamie had it in his drawer for a long time. He told me he was going to give it to Charlie. He had it in his bag the evening Charlie broke up with him."

"Fucking Charlie," Theo muttered, gripping the bench with vengeance.

"See why I almost let you punch him?"

"See him again, and I will."

Sean shook his head. "No, you won't because Charlie never got the T-shirt."

No, he hadn't.

"That's why I flipped when I saw you wearing it. I'd seen you tangled together in bed, but I hadn't known what it meant until seeing JLM over your chest."

Jamie Loves Me.

"You've been wearing that shirt for a while now," Leone said.

"Yes," he somehow managed to say, though it came out a hiccup.

"Jamie promised he'd tell you how he feels."

Theo scrubbed his face. The Roommate Wanted notices. Jamie's *I was thinking about it. In case. It's complicated.*

How many times had Theo told him they were just friends with benefits? No wonder he had a Plan B.

Jamie loves me.

What had he yelled at him on his way out? That'd he'd lied from the beginning. From their first kiss, that cavalier *Who said anything about love?*

Theo couldn't hold it in. He grabbed his phone, turned it on, and punched out a message.

Theo: I know about the T-shirt.

Jamie: I'd rather not talk about this over text.

Jamie was right. His response couldn't merely come through a few lousy words that zipped through the air to Jamie's phone. "It has to be memorable," he said to himself. "I have to make it memorable."

"What do you mean?" Leone said.

She had a soft, relieved smile on her face like she'd been waiting for this moment for a long while. "You knew, didn't you?" he said.

Leone inclined her head. "I thought so."

"Why didn't you say something?"

"That's not for me to say, is it? You had to figure it out for yourselves."

"I've been so blind."

"Blindest of us all," she said. "What do you mean, memorable?"

Theo ran a hand through his helmet-matted hair. "I don't want to be a lazy Leo about what comes next."

Leone's eyebrows shot up as Sean's bunched together.

The sick, light, twisty feeling in his gut now felt like it was shooting though his feet. He was sure he would fall if he tried to stand, but at the same time, it made him want to laugh. "I'm giving him two days."

"Two days?" Sean asked.

"Before I speak to him."

"That's torture."

"No." Theo clapped his hands over his phone, fingers entwining, and outlined a rough plan. Leone loved it. Sean looked a bit leery, but then nodded and said he liked the idea. "That's my version of a red T-shirt."

∽

THEO: DO YOU TRUST ME?

Jamie: Yes.

Theo: Good.

Jamie: Why?

Theo: Give me two days and follow two rules. No touching. No talking.

Jamie: Only listening?

Theo: And watching.

"Remember your good friend Darwin, Theo?"

Jamie after Theo did another dumb thing.

Chapter Twenty-Two

Theo: I wake up wishing you were already looking at me.

THEO FOLDED JAMIE'S LAUNDRY AT THE KITCHEN TABLE. HE HAD four neat piles when Jamie emerged from his room. In gray and black, Jamie stared down at him from the balcony. A tingle under his skin had Theo dropping Jamie's shirt. He whipped it back up before it fell to the floor.

Twice Theo caught Jamie's chest swelling as if he were about to speak, and twice Theo steeled a look until Jamie let it go, rested his arms against the wooden railing, and simply watched.

An iron and board came out, and that's when things got tricky. Theo didn't usually iron. He knew how it was done. In theory. He just couldn't remember the last time he'd done it. Still, couldn't be too hard.

Steam sprayed in a cloud misting all over Jamie's shirt—the one he'd mentioned wearing for his first summer lecture.

"Shit!" he yelped and held one finger up to stop Jamie from running down and saving him, while praying that running the iron over the wet drops would solve the problem.

No matter how hard he worked the iron, there were still creases and he'd ironed a fold down the back of the shirt. Fuck.

Theo's phone buzzed in his pocket. He glanced up at a bemused Jamie holding his phone.

Setting the iron down, he checked the message.

Jamie: No touching. No talking. Is laughing allowed?

Theo glanced at him and scowled, then nodded. Laughter softly rumbled from the balcony. When he was done, he gathered Jamie's clean laundry and climbed the stairs to his room.

Jamie hesitated, but stepped aside and let him put everything where it belonged.

It took every inch of willpower for Theo to resist dropping the clothes and jumping into Jamie's arms, but he powered through. He had something to say, and he was saying it.

～

Theo: You make me want to be a better person, who eats actual vegetables.

～

Theo had gone shopping during the afternoon while Leone and Sean took Jamie out for an afternoon at the park, and now he was back at home staring at a fuckload of fresh vegetables.

"Mrs. Cooper?" Theo said down the line. "It's Theo here. Jamie's—"

"I know who you are." Mrs. Cooper chuckled. "Please, it's Penny."

"I'm lost, Penny."

"Metaphorically or literally?"

"I'm in the kitchen."

"Oh dear." She laughed. "Where's my son?"

Theo heard the telltale signs of a key sliding into the lock and the front door opening. Leone, Sean, and Jamie were talking quietly.

"He just got home."

"He can't help you?"

"Here's the thing, Penny," he said as Jamie walked into the house alone. Leone and Sean had scampered off. Theo hooked Jamie's gaze and fought another burst of need to hurdle over the kitchen island and attack Jamie on the couch. "Jamie once showed me how to make a vegetable lasagna—the non-microwave variety."

Jamie's eyebrows shot up as he leaned back in the couch.

"Only," Theo continued, "I sort of wasn't paying attention."

Jamie shook his head, a small twitch at the corner of his mouth.

"I was hoping you might assist me this time?"

"Tell me where you are," she said.

He stared at the produce on the island before him. "I have vegetables."

Mrs. Cooper sighed, but Theo sensed a smile too. "What vegetables, Theo?"

Painstakingly, Theo followed Penny's instructions, keeping the phone on speaker so they could talk while he worked. Once, Jamie tried to speak to his mom, but Theo pointed a wooden spoon at him and he backed down, throwing his hands up, amusement and affection blazing in his eyes.

Between instructions, Theo asked how Mrs. Cooper was, and what she'd been up to since they'd visited. What her plans were over the summer.

"Leone and I are up in Minneapolis at the end of July. I don't know Jamie's plans, but maybe I can bus down for a night? You can make those delicious cookies. And I can eat them."

She laughed, so hearty and happy. "I take it you two have figured things out, then."

Theo felt Jamie's stare burn into him. When he looked over, Jamie was still, possibly holding his breath. "Let's just say I'm glad you didn't keep the stork."

~

THEO: I WANT TO ALWAYS PROTECT YOU FROM DICKS THAT **insult you.**

THEO SPENT SUNDAY EVENING LOCKED IN HIS ROOM, STRETCHED ON his bed. He ended one of the calls he had to make and made the other. The upstairs floorboards creaked and groaned. Theo pictured Jamie walking to and from his desk to the balcony.

Theo smirked. Phone pressed to his ear, silence met his announcement. He fingered the open packet of yoghurt raisins next to him and plucked out the last two. He rolled them in his mouth and savored the sweet flavor.

After a few minutes, he said his goodbyes and hung up. A soft laugh left him as he rolled over and trashed the packaging. He flopped onto his back, one arm flung out toward the nightstand, his bare heels skidding over the comforter as he snow-angeled in the sheets.

He slipped his hand under the pillow and drew out the envelope he had tucked there. He had found it taped to his bedroom door after coming home from the supermarket this afternoon. A blue envelope with his name on it—Sean's writing, by the looks of it.

The contents were all Leone. He rolled his eyes as he drew out the folded paper once more.

Staring back at him was a section of the yearly horoscope their mom had sent at the beginning of the year.

Fear not rejection and heartbreak, Leo. Hold your head up high, be your glowing, fiery self and the right people will gravitate to you, maybe even a soul mate among them.

Theo read and reread it. This was the part he feared most. Jamie's friendship was the most important thing to him and he didn't want to lose it. Those fleeting thoughts of *what if* made him nervous but Leone was right. Leaping was the most exciting, terrifying, and hopefully rewarding thing he would do.

Theo switched off the lamp, tucked his restless fingers under his head, and smiled toward the still creaking floorboards above.

THEO: YOU ARE NOT THE BEST PART OF MY DAY, YOU MAKE MY DAY.

~

THIS WAS THE SECOND TIME THEO SAT THROUGH A KEYNESIAN economics lecture, and the second time he kept both feet firmly planted to the floor—though his left was lightly tapping the frayed carpet in anticipation. He rubbed his palms over his thighs for the millionth time.

It helped that he hid in the last row of the lecture hall and didn't think Jamie had spotted him yet.

It didn't help that Jamie looked so damn good in the front of the class full of summer students. He wore khakis and the shirt that Theo had pressed, undone at the collar. Casual and confident. He was engaging and he sparked curiosity. The room swelled with collective excitement—economics had never been so fun.

Jamie's lecture flowed, his passion radiated, and he respected students as they answered questions and he carefully helped them navigate the trickier concepts.

"You can adapt and apply this theory to many facets of life," Jamie said. Like the first time he gave the lecture, he outlined a few examples, using students from the audience to keep the lecture interactive.

This was his cue.

Theo raised his hand and waved just enough to catch Jamie's attention. When Jamie saw him, his posture stiffened, he blinked rapidly then openly stared at him, his mouth parting—and then he gave a spontaneous laugh that stirred the class and made them glance at Theo.

Jamie gawked at the JLM T-shirt peeking out of Theo's leather jacket and his face glowed. "Yes, *I-L-Y*?"

The rush of those spoken letters down his middle almost rendered him speechless. "I have another area of life the multiplier effect could be adapted to," he somehow managed.

A wide smile. "Please, enlighten me."

Theo leaned back in his seat and took a steadying breath. He flashed his dimples at Jamie. "Love."

"Love. Please elaborate." There was an edge of desperation in the way he stressed *please*, telling Theo he needed to hear this.

"Imagine a person invests a lot into a relationship; for example, cooks, cleans, and tutors to show they care and help make the other the best they can be. They show what they believe the meaning of love is. This person inspires trust that encourages them to want to do your laundry and cook and make you smile."

"Are you suggesting a Keynesian love approach could work?" Jamie asked. He came a few steps up the aisle, his voice carrying throughout the room but Theo felt every nuance of it on him.

Theo felt weightless, as if his words had taken all his heft. "What do you think, Mr. Jamie Cooper?"

❧

THEO: I DON'T WANT TO **KISS** YOU. I WANT TO KISS YOU IN **front of everybody. All the time.**

❧

AS SOON AS THE LECTURE WAS OVER AND STUDENTS STREAMED DOWN the aisles to snag Jamie into conversation, Theo and Jamie held each other's gaze for one lingering, soul-tingling moment before Theo ducked out.

Now he relied on Sean and Leone to give Jamie directions to Theo's last gesture.

"Thanks so much for this, Alex," Theo said, handing him a stick of carefully preselected music.

He grabbed one set of skating gear off the counter. The other bundle waited for Jamie. "Turn on the music as soon as he hits the doors to the rink."

With butterflies partying in his stomach, Theo disappeared into the empty skating rink, dressed in his gear, and rolled out onto the polished floors. The neon lighting slashed blues and greens across the wood and Theo skated through them. Once, twice, three times he made rounds, pushing faster, propelled by this newly defined lightness that stretched through all his limbs.

He came to a cocky, swiveling stop in the center of the rink, right over their spot just as the doors to the skating rink thrusted open and Jamie strode inside, his hair slightly wind-whipped, cheeks flushed, eyes bright and trained intently on Theo.

Theo's breath caught as those butterflies amped up.

On the aisle coming toward the floors, Jamie strapped on his helmet, eyes glued to Theo. Music crackled over the speakers and "You Are the One That I Want" pumped into the room.

Theo flashed his dimples full-force and added a waggle of his brows.

Jamie's lips quirked and he stuffed his feet into his skates, yanked on the laces, knotted them, and rolled onto the rink toward Theo. Jamie moved with pose and purpose, and it sent a delicious shiver raking over him.

With a steady, tidy slide, Jamie swung right toward him and Theo quickly shifted. Jamie spun around. Tight and controlled. "You've been practicing," Theo said.

Jamie's grin grew. "I hoped it might come in handy sometime."

Again, Jamie lunged for him and Theo scooted out of the way.

"Why skating?" Jamie's eyes glinted as if he already knew why.

"I'm re-enacting our first date," Theo said, slowly skating backwards, beckoning him to follow.

"That was your date with Liz."

"But it wasn't, was it?" Theo lowered his voice. "I spent the entire evening skating with you and I never wanted to stop."

Jamie's throat jutted with a hard swallow and he picked up speed.

Theo skated backward, curving around the end of the rink, Jamie whisper-close to toppling into him. "This time though," Theo cleared the butterflies trying to rise out of his throat. "This time I want to make it clear. You are the one that I want."

Jamie surged forward and Theo almost let him catch him that time. Almost. Jamie's growl went straight to Theo's cock and he clenched, shortening his glide. Their song "One Way or Another" played next and Jamie gave him a devilish grin. "I'm gonna getcha by the end of this song, Theo. Make no mistake."

Theo sucked in his bottom lip. "Is that a promise?"

Jamie's eyes narrowed on his mouth. "It is, and when I do, we are leaving immediately."

Theo shook his head and laughed. "But I have a whole hour of songs for you. Songs to tell you everything about how I feel. How blind I've been, and—"

"I don't need to listen to them," Jamie said. "Just like you didn't need to ask me your stock date questions. I already know."

Jamie rolled faster, as if he had purposely been holding back. It caught Theo off guard, giving Jamie an advantage. Theo still could have darted neatly out of his reach but Jamie's next words surrendered him. "All I want is to hold you, Theo. I want to hold you and kiss you. And then I want to take you home and—"

Jamie reached out and clasped Theo's arms and they spun to a dizzying stop. Jamie's leg shifted between Theo's, flush against his hardening groin. Jamie ran his hands up and down his JLM shirt. He hadn't worn his wrist guards and Theo felt Jamie's warmth sink through the thin material. Their helmets bumped as Theo angled his chin up a half inch. Jamie's gaze stroked his face and Theo trembled with how much he needed Jamie to kiss him. How much he needed to kiss Jamie.

Their lips met halfway in a bruising, needy kiss that Theo felt echoing in his fingers, his toes, the tips of his ears, the base of his spine, his cock—definitely his cock, the weakening of his knees, the tops of his ankles where the skates rubbed.

Theo gasped into the kiss as he yanked off his wrist guards and tossed them aside. He ran his freed palms over Jamie's shoulders to the back of his neck, massaging a moan out of him. Jamie's erection pressed hard against Theo's thigh and he cocked his hips into it. Pleasure rolled through him and he lost his footing and rolled sharply back. Jamie steadied him at the elbows and Theo felt Jamie's grin mix into their kiss.

They parted an inch, breath hot and heavy between them. "Let's get home, Jamie. Or we're going to sully this skating rink."

～

THEO: TOGETHER WE COULD TAKE ON THE WORLD AND TWO eventual rugrats.

∽

THEO HAD BORROWED SEAN'S CAR, WHICH MEANT he and JAMIE had to drive separately. It felt like forever until Theo was parking, Jamie squeezing in behind him.

Theo bounced out of the car and into the empty apartment a few steps ahead of Jamie. Then he was stripping off his clothes on the stairs as he raced to Jamie's room. He shrugged out of his leather jacket, peeled off his left sock, then his right. He paused mid-way to shimmy out of his jeans and stepped on them to pull his feet free. With a warm laugh, Jamie followed swiftly behind picking up Theo's trail of abandon.

Theo flung open Jamie's door and leaped onto the bed, rolling onto his back, arms flung out, legs slightly spread.

Jamie paused at the door as he took in Theo on his bed wearing only the tighty whities he had worn at Jamie's roommate interview and the JLM T-shirt. They stared at each other, the tension between them taut and sparking. Theo drew up his heel and let his leg fall to the side. A hard-on punched at his underwear.

Jamie was far too overdressed.

He followed Theo's thought, because he stepped inside his room, dropped Theo's collected clothes on the floor and kicked his door shut. Carefully, he undid his watch and set it on his bookshelf. He worked the buttons of his shirt and shrugged out of it.

"Four," he said, gray eyes steeling Theo. Jamie tossed the shirt over his shoulder and it caught on the doorknob.

"Four what?" Theo palmed his aching dick.

Jamie's undershirt hit the armchair. "Four rugrats."

Pants pooled at the floor by the bottom of the bed, and Theo dimpled.

"Three."

Jamie whipped off his boxer-briefs and the mattress dipped as Jamie made even quicker work of climbing on the bed and stretching over Theo.

"Perfect," Jamie said, their noses bumping lightly.

Theo admired Jamie's thick cock straining against his own. He arched up into Jamie's grinding weight.

"But I think," Theo said, lifting his chin, "first comes some kissing?"

Their mouths met in a hot, desperate kiss that robbed Theo of all thoughts except one: closer. He needed closer. His hand jammed between their hot thrusting bodies as he shoved his underwear enough to free his dick, then gasped as Jamie spat on his palm and took both of them in a slick grip.

Their frenzy slowed with some massive will on both their parts.

They nestled together, still hard, still rubbing, but their focus had shifted.

Jamie spoke first after the softest brush of his lips to the bridge of Theo's nose. "The stupidest thing I ever said was that I only wanted in your pants. That I didn't care for falling in love. It was a lie, Theo. I already loved you the first time I kissed you, and I love you more now."

Theo soaked it in and rubbed his cheek over Jamie's just-prickling stubble. A giddy slam of nerves made him fluster and he resorted to his go-to response. "You should know this stroking of... my ego is very pleasant."

That earned him a light tug to his balls.

Theo rocked gently and pinched the nape of Jamie's neck. His sigh warmed the air between them. "I guess, in my own way, I was lying too. To myself. I've had these feelings for a while." Theo carded his fingers through Jamie's hair, studying the beautiful elation on his face. "I only understood them the night we... after Charlie. I didn't know what to do with the feelings and then I saw the Roommate Wanted posters."

"I started looking around for rooms because I thought my heart might break if you didn't want me back. I would have needed to leave."

Theo swallowed. "Just the idea of you leaving still makes me mad." He balled a hand and thumped it against Jamie's shoulder blade.

This only made Jamie smile.

Theo asked, "When did you know you were falling for me?"

"Early."

"What's with the twitch of your lips?"

"The first time we had Thursday coffee. The day you drank air."

Theo felt the heat rise up his neck and cheeks. "I don't know why I did that. You made me nervous even then, I guess. I didn't know what do to with myself. Looking back, it's clear that I liked you. I was so afraid of losing our friendship that it blocked me from letting myself see this. Us. This us."

They kissed again. Theo moaned and thrust against Jamie, wanting to feel more. Sadness, happiness, hope, and desire balled together between their stomachs.

Theo glanced at the side table, at the supplies he'd bought and placed earlier that day. "I need you to make love with me now."

"I thought you didn't believe in making love?"

"With you, I believe in anything."

A swivel of hips and a rush of excited shivers. Jamie stripped Theo's underwear off him. "You're keeping the shirt on."

Jamie gathered the shirt up to Theo's chin and kissed Theo's chest, lavishing attention to his sensitive nipples and making him buck.

Lube entered the equation, and the cool liquid met fingers that gently probed his ass. They had played like this before. But tonight, Theo would have Jamie filling him up and the thought had him fucking Jamie's fingers in anticipation. When Jamie swallowed his straining dick to the base, Theo thanked his lucky fucking stars.

Jamie sucked as he prepared him, then he torturously pulled off Theo and came up to kiss him on the lips. "I like how I make you squirm."

A small laugh slipped out of him as Theo fleetingly reminisced about the last two days. "Same here. You were so close to jumping me yesterday, weren't you?"

The condom came out of its package and Jamie rolled it on. A lot of lube slathered him next. He hooked Theo's leg up—wet fingers gripping his thigh. "I took a lot of cold showers."

Theo dimpled and lifted for one more kiss. "You can jump me now."

Jamie positioned himself, nudging his cock at Theo's entrance. For a moment, Theo clenched and stiffened despite yearning for this to finally happen.

Jamie must have felt it, because he stopped and kissed the inside of Theo's knee. His mouth parted and Theo cut off the *We can slow this down* that he was sure Jamie would offer.

Theo stroked himself. "Keep going, Jamie."

Jamie held his gaze as he inched inside, his expression focused, intense, and then slackening the more he filled Theo up.

Watching Jamie's face made the burn and discomfort worth it. He'd take any pain to make Jamie feverishly groan.

Jamie rocked slowly, his balls lightly slapping Theo's ass. Theo's grip loosened on the sheets as he relaxed.

Jamie shifted his angle and when he pushed in, Theo gasped. "More of that," he said and met Jamie's next thrust in a desperate need to feel that pleasurable pressure again. Every time Jamie entered him, Theo felt a need for more, harder, faster. He said as much, and Jamie gave it to him.

The pressure wave grew and he groaned loudly when Jamie gripped his dick and stroked in time to the thrusts. It sent him over the edge. Theo whimpered as pleasure slammed into him and his orgasm hit in thick, fast waves and he came in Jamie's hand.

Jamie pumped a few more times, thrust all the way in to the hilt and stiffened as he climaxed, cock pulsing inside Theo, making him clench.

Jamie let out a strangled moan, and his weight was warm and welcome when he collapsed onto Theo and pressed their mouths together.

Every part of Theo felt sensitive. Even Jamie's breath trickling down his throat made him shiver.

"We are definitely going to have to do that again. A lot."

Jamie laughed as he slipped out of him and dealt with the condom and getting a warm washcloth to clean up the bit of come that had seeped out of Jamie's hand.

With half-lidded eyes and a rather satisfied smile, Jamie lay next to Theo and smoothed his T-shirt down. "It's official. You are amazing in every way possible. Here," he touched Theo's head. "Here." Theo's heart. "And here." He swatted Theo's ass. "And I am very much on board with doing that again. A lot."

Jamie skimmed his fingertips up over Theo's arm and shoulder to his chin. Their lips brushed together. Theo closed his eyes and savored the sensation. The gentleness, the slip of tongue across his bottom lip, the electricity zinging when the tips of their tongues touched.

His heartbeat rammed in his chest and he was breathless.

This whole….*them* made him quiver inside, made him laugh.

Jamie pulled back, watching with a softly amused expression that made Theo vow to take all the risks and break all the laws so long as he could cause that again. And again and again and again.

THEO KNEW JAMIE HAD TO TEACH IN THE LATE MORNING, BUT JAMIE shrugged it away. He'd live off two hours sleep or less if they still had more to say.

Theo still had more to say.

"I told my mom about us." Theo happily tucked himself against Jamie's side. "I rendered her speechless. *My* mom!"

"I wish I'd heard. Or not heard as was the case."

"When she found her voice, she said she was happy for us and it was in the stars from the beginning." Theo pressed his palm to Jamie's raspy cheek. "I laughed so fucking hard, Jamie, because she was right. The proof is there, in our chat history, when I said—"

"You said it was destiny."

Theo swallowed, throat dry. "Yeah." He started blinking rapidly, heat creeping up his chest and neck.

Theo kissed Jamie again, before breaking off. "Minneapolis in July!"

Jamie pulled that thread of thought into something more coherent. "How about we go up to your mom's then mine together?"

"She'd like that. I'd like that. They'd like that. Fuck. We all would like that."

Jamie twined their fingers together. "When we get back—and take your time to consider the emotional and economic components —what if we shared a room?"

"And rent out the other?"

"That would be the economic part of it, yes. Could help to fund your master's year."

Theo tapped Jamie's temple. "Not just a handsome face. Let's do it."

Jamie slapped his ass and then dipped down to kiss it better. "Give it the summer."

"I will. Irrespective of the economic part, I like the idea."

"You look quite at home there."

Jamie upon finding Theo curled up in his bed.

Chapter Twenty-Three

The outdoor pavilion featured exposed beams, antlered chandeliers, and about a million fairy lights. Lights that reflected in the lake that edged the reception venue.

Far away from that end of the pavilion, Theo sat at one of the blue-clothed tables at the edge of the dance floor. He leaned an elbow on the lip of the table and bit the end of an ink pen he'd swiped from the guest book. Borrowed. He'd put it back soon.

Over the hundred-odd wedding guests sitting or dancing, Theo searched for Jamie, who'd taken Leone for a waltz while Sean left to check how many rowboats were available.

Kyle and Ben were stuffing mint chocolates in each other's mouths and kissing off stray smudges of chocolate.

"He's over there," Ben called to Theo, pointing toward the deck.

Theo's stomach flipped, like it did every time he saw Jamie. He leaned in his perfectly fitting suit against a wooden railing next to Leone, one hand on her shoulder as they spoke. She said something that made Jamie light up and glance over to find Theo.

"You've got it so bad," Kyle said. "You can say whatever friends with benefits bullshit you like, but I don't believe it for a second."

Theo dragged the end of the pen over his jaw and set the tip to the cream origami fan, careful not to blot the ink. He wrote a quote of the day, capped the pen, and refolded one end of the paper fan.

He slipped it into his breast pocket and looked over at Ben and Kyle.

"You're right," he tossed out there. "You shouldn't believe it."

At the same time, Ben and Kyle said, "I knew it!"

Ben leaned forward, playing his fingers over the plume of candlelight. "When did you figure out it was more?"

Warm hands curved over his shoulders and squeezed. Jamie answered, "I had hoped for a long time, but I knew the feelings had to be requited the moment I found him in the kitchen cooking for me on his own free will." They laughed, but Theo strongly felt there was truth to that.

Jamie spoke in Theo's ear. Tingles scuttled down his back and legs. "Dance with me?"

He let Jamie slide their fingers together and pull him out of his chair. "Dance me to the guest book? I have a pen to return."

The funnel-neck entrance to the pavilion holding the guestbook was empty of guests.

Once Theo dropped the pen in its place, Jamie pulled him close. The music was slow, meant for a moment of intimacy, and a fresh lake breeze added to Theo's shiver.

Theo spread his hands over the shirt under Jamie's coat, drawing in the warmth, smirking when Jamie flexed.

Sean surprised them by emerging from the night.

He blinked just once and then winked at them. "Where's Leone?"

"She's giving her congratulations to the bride and groom."

Sean bristled. He didn't like Leone's history with the groom. It was almost the same intense glare that Jamie had given Sam when Theo'd led her for a waltz. It had felt great. The glare, for sure, but even more the dancing with her and not caring. And then dancing with Leone afterward, laughing so deeply, because just as they had promised at the start of the year, they had moved on.

Sean narrowed his eyes toward the groom and Leone on the dance floor. "There are row boats, Hotstuff," he said to Jamie. "I've hooked two up for us."

Jamie rubbed his arm in response to the way Theo clutched him.

Theo relaxed. Before Sean took off to snag his girlfriend back, Theo said to Jamie, "You once asked me if Sean calling you Hotstuff bothered me."

Sean hesitated in Theo's peripheral vision.

Theo continued. "The answer is the same as it was then: hell yeah." Theo leaned in and lightly bit Jamie's ear, relishing Jamie's tremble against him. "You're *my* Aries. *My* Hotstuff."

Sean snorted and hoofed it to Leone. "Meet you on the lake, Hotstuffs."

Jamie didn't waste a moment. He backed Theo against a wide beam until they were flush. Their kiss started out possessive, needy. Theo gripped Jamie hard against him as if they could sink into one another. Jamie's groan whispering over his lips brought them back to reality.

"I suppose this level of passion has to wait," Jamie said.

"At least until more people are drunk," Theo said and flashed his dimples.

Jamie laughed and they kissed again. This kiss was soft and it sent Theo's heart racing. Theo drew out the fanned paper from his breast pocket. He was about to pass it to Jamie but a burst of upbeat jazz music interrupted. Theo threaded their hands together and led Jamie out of the pavilion.

Lanterns lit a path that forked, one path wound back to a parking lot, but it was the other Theo bravely took, leading to the lake. Tied to the piers under the pavilion were a couple of bobbing dinghies. The lake loomed large, dark save for ripples of reflected fairy lights and a shiver of moonlight.

Hairs lifted on Theo's nape and arms and he was sure Jamie could see his heart banging in his chest. As they drew close to the water, Theo's shoulders tightened and he licked his lips. Fear of water was only part of it.

Theo pressed the paper fan to Jamie's chest.

Jamie took it, arching a brow.

"Quote of the day," Theo said. "Read it."

Jamie opened the fan and read the words. Carefully, he tucked the fan into his breast pocket, and hooked a hand in in the lapels of Theo's jacket and gently tugged. Their foreheads met and Jamie's other hand cupped his neck, thumb brushing Theo's jaw. "That's what I said."

"Yes, and I said it, too. I'm saying it now."

Holding his breath and clutching Jamie's fingers, Theo stepped into one of the rowboats. Jamie's breath caught and he climbed in, sitting them down and scooping Theo in his arms.

The boat rocked gently and Theo shuffled into Jamie's warmth behind him.

Jamie tightened his hold on Theo's shaky body. "I'm going to need to hear you say it."

Theo looked at Jamie over his shoulder and grinned. "I love… that you're such a good swimmer."

Jamie pinched their lips together and stole the rest of Theo's words away. "Save the games for later."

Theo kissed him back. "I love you, Mr. Jamie Cooper. I *love* you."

THE END.

Signs of Love #1.5 - Leo Tops Aries

Overcoming your obstinacy is a tricky matter this week, Leo, but you won't rest unless you do. Look toward compromise and tackle your stubbornness into submission. If you don't, you're in for some sleepless nights.

Was it him, or were his horoscopes becoming unnervingly accurate?

Theo closed the mail his mom had sent and tossed his phone on the gray pleated comforter he'd pulled over his naked lap.

He rested against the cool headrest and took in Mr. Jamie Cooper's childhood bedroom: The rug Theo's palms and knees ached to become intimately familiar with; the dresser Theo imagined pressing Jamie against as he sank to his knees; the framed, smartass posters THE COMMA and THE APOSTROPHE Theo wanted to rattle...

He fished his hand under the blanket and palmed his arousal. Three days without sex with Jamie was killing him.

Why did he ever bet that a Leo could outwait an Aries?

Jamie walked into the bedroom, towel from his shower slung low over his hips. He hadn't bothered to dry himself and water dripped from his sandy hair and trailed over the planes of his chest.

Jamie stretched and his gently muscled stomach flexed. He dropped a hand to his treasure trail and played his fingers through it, dipping his fingertips under the towel into the fringe of his pubic hair. Theo's breath caught in his chest.

Jamie spoke, voice low, controlled. "Sure you can outlast me, Theo?"

Theo snapped his drooling mouth shut and looked up at Jamie's amused expression.

Plastering on his best bored smile, Theo shrugged. "You'll ask for it first, Mr. Jamie Cooper."

"We'll see," Jamie said nonchalantly. He unwrapped his towel and used it to scrub his hair and dry his chest. His cock swelled and stabbed the air toward Theo.

Theo's dick punched the comforter. Torturously, Theo ignored it and laced his fingers behind his head. "Say I win, Aries, and you can fuck me any way you want."

The heat in Jamie's gaze sent goosebumps racing over Theo's chest, perking his nipples; he clenched his fingers together to keep from tweaking them.

The towel slapped against the floor and Jamie climbed on top of him, a warm and satisfying weight. Leaning forward, Jamie bumped their noses. Amused gray eyes made Theo shiver.

The barest swivel of Theo's hips had Jamie pressing his thick length against his. They'd be touching it if weren't for the damn comforter! He swallowed a moan and grinned at Jamie.

Jamie's mouth curved and he whispered a kiss against the bow of Theo's mouth. "Tempting, Leo. But very little could top watching you squirm."

Jamie rolled off him onto his side of the bed, leaving Theo hot and bothered and hornier than hell. Overcome his obstinacy? With Jamie so blatantly pushing all his buttons? Never.

Theo punched his pillow, switched off the side lamp, and wriggled under the covers. Barely five minutes of glaring at the dark ceiling had passed when little bursts of air seeped under the blanket. The mattress quivered. Jamie's breathing came out strangled.

Jesus. This man would be the death of him.

Theo curled onto his side and pressed his nose against the nape of Jamie's neck, breathing in his old wood and dark vanilla scent. "Need a hand, Jamie?"

Jamie groaned and the quivering grew more violent. He rolled onto his back, stroking himself long and slow and then short and fast. Theo's dick throbbed. "I'm handling myself fine, Theo. But feel free to touch me if you can't resist."

"I can resist." Barely.

"Suit yourself." Jamie quickened his pace and groaned as he shot over his lower belly. He lay there, boneless, breathing a little choked. He winked at Theo and dragged himself to the bathroom.

Theo immediately shot his hand under the blankets and gripped his dick.

With a knowing grin, Jamie came back. He crawled over Theo and kissed the top of the arm that Theo had under the blanket. Theo stopped stroking.

"Don't stop. Clearly you need to jerk off."

Theo let go of his achingly hard dick and put both hands once more behind his head. "Nah, I'm good." *Whhhhhy?*

Jamie shook his head, lips twitching. "Change your mind any time."

"I can handle it." Shoot him. Shoot him now.

Looked like this stubborn Leo was in for a sleepless night.

"Coffee," Theo murmured to Jamie's mom as he schlepped into the kitchen. "Please. *Coffee.*"

He jumped as fresh-faced Jamie appeared from behind the open fridge, chuckling. "Morning, kitten."

Theo scowled at him. This bone-weary, aching tiredness was all Jamie's fault. Damn him for being nigh irresistible.

Jamie hummed to the song trickling out the radio and spooned natural yoghurt into bowls.

"Coffee," Theo pleaded.

"Out of coffee, I'm afraid," Mrs. Cooper said, drying her hands on her apron. "All we have is tea."

Theo rubbed his eyes and rested his forehead against the cupboard. In his peripheral vision, Jamie plucked a banana from the fruit bowl and peeled it slowly, smirking.

Theo slammed his eyes shut.

"You seem tense today, Theo," Mrs. Cooper said.

"That he is," Jamie said flatly. "Really pent up."

The cheek! Theo composed himself and calmly opened the cupboard for a mug. Just for that, he'd hear Jamie beg before the day was out. "Tea sounds perfect."

The phone rang and Mrs. Cooper left the kitchen to answer it. Theo flicked on the kettle and planted a tea bag into a mug on the bench.

Opposite him, Jamie sliced banana into the bowls, running a languid gaze over Theo's rumpled hair and favorite red JLM shirt. He took in the jeans Theo had slipped into. "Couldn't find pants of your own?"

Theo hooked a thumb into a belt loop, casually pulling it enough to reveal what little else he wore. Banana half cut, Jamie paused and murmured heavenward, baring the smooth column of his throat.

Theo wanted to leap over the island, shove him against the wall of family photos and suck his neck until debauched moans tickled his ear.

He spun for the kettle and poured water into his mug.

"Sean rang this morning," Jamie said. "We're meeting him and Leone around ten."

"Meeting for what?" In the snippets of sleep Theo got last night, he'd pictured spending the day rolling around with Jamie in bed.

"Cherry picking."

"The whole day?" Theo smoothed out his whine, and shrugged. "Super."

Jamie finished cutting the banana, a knowing twinkle in his eye. "Don't worry, Theo. When mom leaves, we have the house to ourselves for an hour beforehand." He lifted his brows. "Was there anything... particular you wanted to do?"

Theo dunked his tea bag into the water. Jamie's eye followed the motion; the dart of his tongue over his lower lip had Theo pausing.

He dazzled Jamie with his dimples and slowly, ever so slowly, dunked the teabag again. "I can think of something."

"What's that?"

"Crack open my laptop and touch up some web design work."

Theo couldn't be sure, but he thought he heard Jamie growl. Actually growl. His dimples deepened as he dunked that tea bag again.

Jamie reached over and grabbed a couple of apricots from the fruit bowl. He rolled them in the palm of his hand, eyes trained on Theo's mug. "Excellent. I've got work to plough through as well."

Theo gently squeezed the teabag. "We can do it side by side. What do you think?"

Jamie's gray eyes darkened. He pressed his fingers into the apricots, lips pressed in a tight line.

With a smirk, Theo lifted the teabag to his lips and sucked out the remaining tea.

"That was your sister, Jamie dear," Mrs. Cooper said.

Theo slapped a hand over the teabag he was debasing. The knee-jerk reaction shoved the teabag into his mouth just as Jamie's mom re-entered the room. Heat washed up his neck and bitter fruit grains seeped onto his tongue.

"She'll be home tonight. Would you and Theo make dinner while I pick her up?"

"We'd love to. Isn't that right?"

Theo's eyes watered. But that might have been the thought of cooking dinner.

Shaking his head, Jamie took pity on Theo, setting his apricots down and sidling around the kitchen island. "Doorbell rang, Mom. Might want to check."

"That bell is far too quiet from here…" Mrs. Cooper left again.

"Oh, Theo," Jamie said as he pinched the edge of the paper tab stuck on Theo's bottom lip. He tugged out the teabag and set it on the banana peel. Bracing a hand on Theo's hip under the edge of the T-shirt, he leaned in. His breath fanned warmly over Theo's nose before he sucked the beads of raspberry tea off his lips. "You have no idea."

"No idea?" Theo asked. "Of how much you want to jump me?"

Jamie's gray eyes smoldered and Theo's insides plummeted to his toes. Jamie fisted the JLM letters on Theo's shirt and pushed him against the hard lip of the island counter. Their thighs and lower stomachs pressed together. Theo grabbed Jamie's ass, fingers skating over the soft slacks he wore, dipping into his crease. Jamie was as hard as he was.

He grinned.

A hard squeeze came to the back of Theo's neck and Jamie dropped a single, feather-light kiss on his lips. "Let's eat." At Theo's last-ditch effort at turning that dirty, Jamie rolled his eyes and added, "*Breakfast*."

Slouched in an armchair with his feet propped up on the coffee table, Theo pretended to work. Halfway across the room, Jamie sat at the round dining table, fingers flying over his laptop.

Theo admired. *Nothing* phased Jamie when he was in the zone. All his concentration laser-beamed to the work at hand. He was so in control. So God-damned beautiful.

Theo opened a chat in his inbox and pinged Jamie.

Theo: That fruit salad tasted amazing, by the way. Particularly the apricots…

Jamie: Give in, Leo, and I'll give you another helping.

Theo: Give in? Have you met me?

Jamie: Go jerk off then.

Theo: I can hold out until you crack.

Jamie: We'll see.

Theo shifted his laptop, brushing over his hard on. A small groan wheezed out of him. Jamie plugged away at whatever the hell he was working on without a single glance Theo's way.

Jesus, it itched under Theo's skin to ruffle a few feathers.

To: Jamie Cooper

From: Theo Wallace

Subject: Give in and...

Straddle my face. Shove your hard dick into my hot, wet mouth and pound into my throat. When you're close, pull out and slide your throbbing head through my right dimple. Feel my hammering pulse in your balls as they rub my throat.

Groan my name and I'll smirk for you, Jamie. That dimple will deepen and you can fuck my smile until you come over my face.

Jamie's phone dinged with the incoming mail, and Theo surreptitiously watched as his guy stopped typing and clicked the touchpad.

Jamie's eyes scanned his screen. He blinked, hands pausing over the keyboard. Then he went back to typing.

What the hell was his guy made of?

Theo was one wrong twitch away from creaming his pants and Jamie had the clarity to keep working?

A new mail popped into his inbox.

To: Theo Wallace

From: Jamie Cooper

Subject: Give in and...

Wrap your hands in my hair as I kneel in front of you. I'll suck your balls into my mouth while I finger you until your legs are shaking. Then I'll massage your prostate until you've forgotten your name, and I swallow you down as you helplessly shoot your load.

Holy shit! Theo thought he was hard when Jamie resisted his efforts. Jamie joining the fight? Blue balls had never been so blue.

Ding!

Jamie: Top that, Theo.

Theo: How about I top you!

Jamie didn't reply, and his expression gave nothing away.

Theo wished he could crawl into cyberspace and retract the message. Sure he'd wondered what it might be like to sink into Jamie, how tight he'd feel; what sounds he would make as Theo plunged into him over and over. But Jamie had, quite matter of fact, said he only topped.

Theo *loved* Jamie breaching him and fucking his ass; loved the sweet, pleasurable burn and rub of his prostate; loved the intensity of the orgasm it gave him.

He also wanted to bury himself as deep into Jamie as he could. Wanted him to unravel on every level possible.

Theo sank back into the armchair and looked up at Jamie just in time to see the guy averting his eyes.

Jamie: You look good when you blush like that.

Theo: I'm sure I look better when I come.

Jamie: You are hands down the most stubborn person I know.

Theo: Is that you giving in, Aries?

Jamie shut his laptop and crossed the rug separating them. It was Theo's turn to keep his gaze rooted to his screen. Theo threw out a yawn for the hell of it.

A deep chuckle. Jamie rounded the back of his armchair and slipped his hands to Theo's shoulders. He squeezed and snaked his fingers over Theo's chest, then down over his stomach. Theo exploded in goosebumps; it took all his self-control not to curse with pleasure. He tilted his head back and looked at his lip-twitching Jamie.

Jamie dipped his head and pressed a kiss to Theo's forehead. He skimmed his mouth to the top of Theo's ear.

Theo shivered. His voice came out husky. "Something you want to say to me, Jamie?"

"Yes."

Theo's balls tightened.

Jamie reached for the laptop and shut it. "Time to pluck some cherries."

The cherry orchard was a twenty-minute drive — or a five-minute row — across the lake. A few months ago, crossing the deep body of water in a dingy would have been impossible for Theo. After a few swimming lessons with Jamie, he knew he was in confident hands. Still, a rush of nerves swept through him as he clutched Jamie's hand and climbed into the rocking dingy.

Jamie tugged him onto his lap, cocooning him. "I've got you, gorgeous."

Teeth softly scraped the curve of his shoulder, sending butterflies to fight his nerves. Theo wriggled closer, reveling in Jamie's responding hiss.

"If this is your way of distracting me, Mr. Jamie Cooper, it's working."

Jamie dragged his lips up Theo's neck and kissed him under the ear. "Good."

Stomach muscles shifted against Theo's back as Jamie dipped the oars into the water and pulled. Rowing was awkward and slow with Theo nestled between his legs.

"Should I sit on the other bench?" Theo said, cursing himself for the shake of his voice.

Jamie squeezed his thighs around Theo's. "You feel very good right where you are."

Theo looked over his shoulder into Jamie's steady gray eyes. Surrounded by his worst fear, water rippling with breezes, Theo had never felt so safe. The warmth of that feeling almost stopped his breath.

He couldn't give in first. Couldn't. Not after making such a fuss. Not after Jamie had upped the ante.

Theo winked. "If you get off rubbing that impressively hard length against my ass—it counts as a win for Leo."

Jamie snorted. "You forget, I've had much practice being patient around you."

Theo hid a sheepish grin and shifted on the bench.

Jamie lost the rhythm of his rowing, his breath hitching softly. The left oar dragged against the surface of the water, pulling the dingy to one side.

Theo pressed this sudden advantage. "What if I bend over that bench and let you take me in the middle of the lake? You can pump into me and I'll spoil the bottom of your boat."

"You'll do anything to get a rise out of me, won't you?"

"I'm thinking of one rise in particular."

"Fuck, Theo."

"That's the idea, Jamie."

Jamie's laugh rumbled through him making Theo's heart stutter. Jesus. He wanted to touch. Wanted to be touched so damn much.

They rowed the last couple of minutes across the lake and Jamie helped him onto solid ground. After knotting the dingy to a tree, Jamie led Theo into the cherry orchard. They grabbed a tin bucket and ventured deep into the trees. Hand in hand, they plodded through thick grass, passing old step stools, forgotten buckets, and trod-on cherries.

At the end of a narrow aisle, Jamie pulled Theo up against a tree trunk. His back hit the rough bark and Jamie pressed himself tight, one leg cozying at Theo's crotch. Their fingers untangled and Theo lifted his hands to either side of Jamie's face, greedily taking the kiss slanting over his lips.

A surge of sensation had Theo spinning them around, shoving Jamie up against the tree. He cocked his hips and swallowed Jamie's low moan.

He slipped his hands into the top of Jamie's pants and dropped to his knees on the carpet of overripe cherries. He pressed his nose against Jamie's hard dick and breathed heavily through the cotton. "Gonna say it, Jamie?"

Theo rubbed his chin against Jamie's shaft and watched the man's gray eyes darken, pupils widening in heady lust.

Theo popped open Jamie's buttons—

"Whoa!" came a startled male voice to their side.

Sean, leading Leone by the hand, had rounded into their narrow aisle of cherry trees. Theo scrambled to his feet while Jamie thumped his head back against the trunk and did up his pants.

Sean bounced his gaze between them, amusement and mortification warring for dominance. He began to step forward as if to curtain Leone from the sight and rocked back again. "I've never been so glad your sister's blind."

Leone arched an eyebrow. "Oh dear God. Thank you, Sean, for that wonderful imagery."

"Imagery? I didn't give you any. For good reason!"

"What *else* am I supposed to picture when you get all high-pitched like that? When I know your best friend and my brother are involved?"

Theo shoved his hands in his pockets and grinned. "Sorry, sis," he said. "Sean caught Aries finally giving in to Leo."

A light smack hit Theo's ass as Jamie passed him and moved to Leone's side.

"Looked like Leo was about to do the giving if you ask me," Sean said, and then cursed himself.

Leone laughed, and Jamie spun her into a hug, looking over her shoulder at Theo with an amused glint in his eye. "Let's get on with it."

~

After hours picking and eating cherries, Sean and Leone left to help prepare dinner at Sean's.

Theo and Jamie sent the cherries they'd collected with them and made a slow round through the orchard, passing families and couples. Theo rounded a sprawling-limbed cherry tree and almost smacked into someone. "Sorry—"

Theo looked up and froze. It felt like the wind had been punched out of him. Seriously? Of all the people to bang into, it had to be Jamie's ex?

Charlie stood in a shaft of late afternoon sunlight that made the copper in his hair pop and his eyes sparkle. He hugged a small bucket of cherries, took Jamie in from head to toe, and smiled.

Theo's stomach clenched tightly.

Charlie gave Theo a cursory glance, and focused on Jamie. "Home for the summer, then."

"Until next week," Jamie said.

Theo almost jumped when Jamie's thumb brushed the back of his hand. He glanced down, surprised to see he was white-knuckling Jamie's fingers.

"You should come to my party this weekend." Charlie glanced between them. "Both of you, of course."

A small growl slipped out of Theo's throat and Jamie's lip quirked.

"We might pass, Charlie. Thank you."

How *on earth* did Jamie stay so level-headed around this fuckwit?

Jamie gently tugged Theo closer, thumb moving in calming circles against the side of his hand.

Charlie's eyes dipped to their linked hands and settled on Theo. "So you were head over heels for him?"

Jesus. Theo had never wanted so badly to punch the grin off someone's face. He hated, *hated* the thought that Jamie had once laughed with this guy; kissed this guy; held him tight and maybe rubbed soothing circles on the back of his hand…

When Theo choked on an answer, Charlie continued, addressing Jamie. "Did you climb to the tops of the trees for the sweetest cherries?"

Theo blurted, "We haven't finished picking yet." They had. "I'll definitely get the top-most, sweetest cherry."

"Excuse us." Jamie swiftly shuttled Theo towards the boat.

Halfway across the water, Jamie sighed against Theo's hair. "The top-most, sweetest cherry, Theo?"

Theo palmed his head and groaned.

At home, Mrs. Cooper waylaid Jamie in the kitchen, and Theo trudged upstairs.

He flung himself somewhat dramatically onto Jamie's bed and evil-eyed the ceiling, picturing stupid Charlie's face.

Barely a minute later, Theo heard Jamie's familiar, steady gait along the hall. The door opened and clicked shut with a whoosh of air. Jamie rested against his dresser, studying him quietly.

Theo groaned, grabbed a pillow and tossed it at Jamie's amused, frustrated face. "Stop it."

Jamie sidestepped the puffy missile. "Stop what?"

"Looking at me like I need tutoring."

"You do."

Theo snatched the pillow from under his head and sent that flying too.

Jamie caught it and chuckled gently. "You wear your emotions on your sleeve."

"And you wear yours in your boxers!" At Jamie's raised eyebrow, Theo palmed his forehead. "Because, you know, under all the layers?"

"I should do something about that then." Jamie unstrapped his watch and set it on the dresser.

Theo watched, transfixed, as Jamie stripped. He pulled his boxers off his semi-hard dick and draped them on his other clothes. Neatly, of course. Then he crawled onto the bed and straddled his hot, naked weight over Theo.

"Talk to me," Jamie said, slipping the pillow back under Theo's head, "and I'll make it clear how I feel."

"Fine. I don't like that everything we're doing, you did with Charlie too. It makes me see various shades of green. None of them pretty."

Jamie crooked a finger under Theo's chin, held him with a sincere gaze, and then kissed him. "You *really* have no idea."

Theo's brows furrowed. "No idea?"

Their next kiss felt a lot like their very first. Surprising and impassioned and like Jamie was trying to make a point. Jamie drew back and the tickle of his breath had every inch of Theo burning with goosebumps.

"Oh."

Jamie's eyes crinkled. "There we go."

Theo crushed their lips together and rolled them over, Jamie warm and solid under him. Theo's hard dick ached to be freed, but he focused on Jamie, wrapping a hand around his cock and stroking him slowly.

"*Say* it, Jamie."

"You're clueless."

"The other thing."

"You really don't give up, do you?" Jamie said softly. Fondly. He drew in a deep breath. This was the moment Jamie would fold and give in.

Theo grappled with a thin tendril of triumph but it slipped out of his reach, leaving behind an uneasy prickle.

"Aries——"

Theo covered Jamie's lips in a deep, silencing kiss. No sooner their mouths connected the prickle disappeared and butterflies took its place. He drew back, yanked his shirt over his head, and dipped down for another kiss, teasing Jamie's lower lip between his teeth.

"*Leo* can't wait." Their bare chests met with a warm smack as they both lunged into another tongue-knotting kiss. "Leo has been on the cusp of folding all day."

A happy growl rumbled through Jamie and Theo felt it to his toes.

"I need you so badly it aches, Aries."

A whimper this time.

Theo rolled off Jamie and tugged off his pants and socks, flinging them on the floor, "If you fuck me right now, it still won't be soon enough."

Jamie reached to the drawer at the side of the bed and pulled out lube and condoms. "I want to do *everything* with you."

Ha! That email had worked some magic, then. "You wanna fuck my smile?"

"I'm going to have at that tongue-'n-cheek, all right."

Jamie pulled Theo back against him. His arms wrapped around Theo's chest and his cock nestled between Theo's thighs, rubbing his balls. Theo dropped his head back, cheek grazing Jamie's.

Jamie lightly nibbled his throat, rocking gently. "But right now? I want something else."

Theo clenched his thighs around Jamie's shaft. "Anything."

The request brushed the shell of his ear. "I want you inside me."

With quick-fire speed, Theo rolled onto the bedspread, cock sliding against the cool comforter. He pushed up on his elbows and grinned. "You sure, Mr. Jamie Cooper?"

Jamie stroked himself. "I haven't stopped thinking about it all day."

"Why didn't you reply then?"

Jamie lifted off the pillow, kissed Theo's cheek and licked his dimple. "Any more talk of you being inside me, and I'd have bent over the table and begged you for it."

"Damn. You've quite the poker face."

"How about you poker me right now," Jamie said wryly, and twisted onto his stomach.

Theo snickered. "You make me all warm inside, Jamie." He settled himself against Jamie's warm back and tucked his chin over

Jamie's shoulder. He breathed in, darting his tongue over Jamie's jaw. He tasted of cherry. "I love you."

The creases at Jamie's eye deepened, his cheek bunched and his lips curled. "I know."

Theo lightly bit Jamie's shoulder and down his arm as he slid down. The slide of his dick over Jamie's crack made them both moan. Settled between Jamie's thighs, Theo massaged the back of his knees and nipped the delicious curve of his ass.

Jamie's cheeks lifted toward those kisses and Theo reached for the supplies.

Lube trickled over his finger and Theo pressed it slowly into Jamie, drawing a pleasured moan. "It feels amazing when you're inside me. I want that for you too."

Theo licked the dimple of Jamie's ass as he curled his finger, searching for the button to make his man tremble. When Jamie rolled his face into his pillow and groaned, Theo tasted the second dimple and added another finger.

Jamie writhed under his ministrations and Theo tugged on his balls to stop from coming. Theo added more lube and continued playing.

"My patience only goes so far, Theo," Jamie ground out.

With a smirk, Theo rolled on a condom and lubed that up too. He positioned himself and slowly pushed in. Jamie hissed as Theo's head moved past his rim.

Theo stilled: a feat of epic proportions since his entire body screamed to sink into Jamie. But he was a Leo. He could handle it.

"Keep going," Jamie instructed in the same tone he used when tutoring. A little less dry and a little more pinched.

Theo pushed forward, and stopped again, giving Jamie time to adjust. Jesus, he was tight. It took all his effort not to immediately draw back and plunge in again. A thought came to him and he bent forward and kissed the spot between Jamie's shoulder blades.

"Think I found the top-most, sweetest cherry, after all."

Jamie laughed, relaxing under him.

Smiling smugly, Theo rocked gently. The intense grip of Jamie's ass on his dick was close to overwhelming. "How do you feel?"

"Stunningly full. Now make love to me."

Theo groaned and increased his thrusts, sliding a hand over the planes of Jamie's back and squeezing his nape. Jamie gave a surprised groan, and Theo reveled in a surge of triumph, pumping against that sweet spot.

Theo pulled out and urged Jamie onto his back. The guy was flushed, eyes dark with lust, and Theo couldn't enter him again fast enough. Their gazes hooked as Jamie grabbed his dick and began stroking in time to Theo's thrusts.

Theo dropped down and kissed him, a small whimper escaping from their lips as he thrust deep. Jamie felt so good. Theo grabbed the back of Jamie's knees and doubled his speed. The headboard banged against the wall and the posters above them rattled.

Jamie pumped himself faster, grunting, raw with passion. Seeing him made Theo's balls tighten. Jamie bowed off the bed, chin thrown back, Adam's apple jutting. He came over Theo's chest, his hole pulsing around Theo's dick. Theo thrust forward, suddenly coming hard too.

Jamie lay spent under him, eyes sated slits, lips wet from their kisses, chest rising and falling as he caught his breath.

Theo pulled out, making quick work of the condom, and dived on Jamie for another breathless kiss.

Jamie wrapped his arms tightly around Theo, his laugh sending goosebumps all over his sensitive skin. "You felt good in me."

"You felt amazing around me." Theo rolled off onto his back. "So spent. I'm going to sleep like a log."

"Now that you've overcome your obstinacy?"

At Jamie's follow-up snort, Theo twisted onto his elbow. "You read the horoscope Mom sent?"

"Particularly apt, that one."

Theo huffed, playing his fingers through the come trickling down his sides. "If Mom's sending you my horoscopes, I'm getting her to send me yours."

Jamie leaped off the bed and ducked out of the room. He came back with a warm washcloth.

Hands tucked under his head, Theo waggled his brows. Jamie wiped his stomach, then set the cloth on the side table. A small smile played at his lips.

"What's that smile for?" Theo asked.

The smile widened. "For how clueless you are."

"I am not clueless." He totally was.

"You totally are."

"What didn't I realize this time, then?"

Jamie lay down and tucked Theo into his side. "You held out four days. Four painful days—"

"You have steel balls, to resist all this."

A loud smack of Jamie's lips hit Theo's cheek. "If you'd refused to kiss me. I'd have given up in ten seconds flat."

Theo turned his head and looked into Jamie's deep gray eyes. "I might thank you for the leverage. But without kissing I'd have caved in five."

Jamie's chest filled out as he breathed in sharply. "God, I love you."

Theo flashed his dimples and stole the last word. "I know."

Acknowledgments

As always, thank you first to my wonderful husband for being supportive and not hesitating to entertain both our sons when I was riveted to writing a scene—or three.

Cheers to Natasha Snow for the cover art! Seriously, it's like you pulled Theo out of my head—you caught him and the mood of the story perfectly!

For beautiful chapter graphics of Leo and Aries, thanks go out to Maria Gandolfo.

Teresa Crawford, thanks for helping me to structure this story, especially during those first developmental stages.

Thanks to HJS Editing for copyediting. Your edits were simply brilliant, as always! Thank you so much!

Another thanks to Vicki for reading and offering valuable feedback, and to Sunne for reading while on holiday and catching those inconsistencies. And finally, big smiles to Wolfgang Eulenberg for test reading and catching final slip-ups.

Anyta Sunday

HEART-STOPPING SLOW BURN

A bit about me: I'm a big, BIG fan of slow-burn romances. I love to read and write stories with characters who slowly fall in love.

Some of my favorite tropes to read and write are: Enemies to Lovers, Friends to Lovers, Clueless Guys, Bisexual, Pansexual, Demisexual, Oblivious MCs, Everyone (Else) Can See It, Slow Burn, Love Has No Boundaries.

I write a variety of stories, Contemporary MM Romances with a good dollop of angst, Contemporary lighthearted MM Romances, and even a splash of fantasy.
My books have been translated into German, Italian, French, Spanish, and Thai.

Contact: http://www.anytasunday.com/about-anyta/
Sign up for Anyta's newsletter and receive a free e-book: http://www.anytasunday.com/newsletter-free-e-book/

Printed in Great Britain
by Amazon

45230273R00158